THE ANATALIAN COUNTESS

REBECCA MIKKELSON

AUTHORS 4 AUTHORS PUBLISHING
Marysville, WA, USA

Published by Authors 4 Authors Publishing
1214 6th St
Marysville, WA 98270
www.authors4authorspublishing.com

Library of Congress Control Number: 2022935472

E-book ISBN: 978-1-64477-150-1
Hardcover ISBN: 978-1-64477-152-5
Paperback ISBN: 978-1-64477-151-8
Audiobook ISBN: 978-1-64477-153-2

Edited by Renee Frey
Copyedited by Brandi Spencer

Cover design ©2022 Brandi Spencer. All rights reserved.
Interior design and map of Aratia by Brandi Spencer.

Authors 4 Authors Publishing branding is set in Bavire. Titles and headings are set in Beguns and Goudy Twenty. All other text is set in Garamond.

THE ANATALIAN COUNTESS

REBECCA MIKKELSON

Authors 4 Authors Content Rating

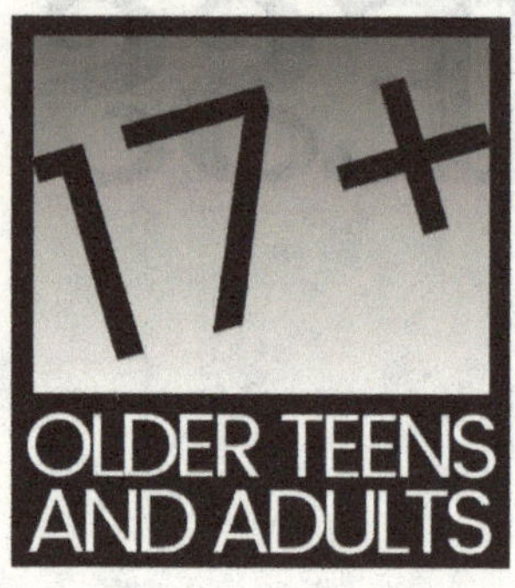

This title has been rated 17+, appropriate for older teens and adults, and contains:

- intense violence
- strong language
- brief sex
- moderate alcohol use
- sexual assault

Please, keep the following in mind when using our rating system:

1. A content rating is not a measure of quality.

Great stories can be found for every audience. One book with many content warnings and another with none at all may be of equal depth and sophistication. Our ratings can work both ways: to avoid content or to find it.

2. Ratings are merely a tool.

For our young adult (YA) and children's titles, age ratings are generalized suggestions. For parents, our descriptive ratings can help you make informed decisions, but at the end of the day, only you know what kinds of content are appropriate for your individual child. This is why we provide details in addition to the general age rating.

For more information on our rating system, please, visit our Content Guide at: www.authors4authorspublishing.com/books/ratings

DEDICATION

For Mr. M, for whom my heart beats.

I love you as far as the East is from the West.

Thank you for believing in me more than I believe in myself.

WORKS BY REBECCA MIKKELSON

"The Measure of a Princess"

The Anatalian Series:
The Anatalian Soldier
The Anatalian Countess
The Anatalian Throne
The Anatalian King
The Anatalian Queen
The Anatalian Heir

AZORAL BAY
RADOVAN
Zavonian Lake
FRASISCA
REPHAIM MOUNTAINS
ARIPALA
ARGLEU
SALATIA
MEKHOR
ARATIA
JALMAR
Bohack
CASSEN
TOLLAK
Rivack
Dorcia
Chenalieu
ANATALIA
Numetra
Silvica
Marbon
GLESSIC
Hamuel
Fradure
Hook of
Hamuel
Manolt
Zuev
REIS
Galiatic Lake
BRAGASSO OCEAN
SEA OF VICOSS
VICOSS
BOQUIDOR OCEAN
TYRADRICA
N
E
S
W

TABLE OF CONTENTS

1

Elbow-deep in dirt, Margaret Doremis harvested herbs from her garden, her pale face reddened by the heat of the afternoon sun. She'd bring them to the local healers of Silvica—they could always use extra for their stores, and she could not use them all herself.

Margaret struggled to find what was left after another morning of frost on the ground. It was earlier than usual, still being the beginning of Omonat, and she wanted to get as much as she could from her garden before a full frost settled. Letting out an irritated growl, Margaret cut yet another wilted sprig and threw it to the side.

The healers had come to rely on her patronage since Margaret and her father had made the small town of Silvica their permanent residence six years ago. She spared no expense when it came to her father's treatments; the healers had come daily, even sometimes twice a day to treat him when they first arrived. Now they only came when Margaret noticed tiny changes in her father's condition, no longer able to do anything for him. Even with their reduced service, she still paid a monthly retainer to have them on call for anything her father might need.

While Margaret dug, she thought about the life she could have been living had her father not grown so ill. She could have been flirting her way through court, playing wicked little games with her noble companions. She would have gone to the markets to spend her father's money or gossiped in the halls of the palace with anyone who wanted to exchange the juiciest secrets. Margaret didn't know if she actually missed her old life or just the constant chatter.

The countryside was quiet. Always quiet. Those who had come to call with any frequency had been married off and moved away with their own lives and husbands to tend. Now the only sounds were the farmers working in the fields and the children chasing the chickens, and even those rarely reached their ears. Many times the silence nearly drove Margaret mad, but the quiet was good for her father.

And she would endure anything for his sake.

Margaret drove the spade into the hard earth, sitting back on her heels. There were no more herbs in the ground—at least none healthy enough to harvest. She piled the medicinals into her basket, pulling the spade from the ground once she stood.

Wiping dirt from her gardening apron, Margaret went inside. She hung her gardening gear by the door, bringing her basket into the kitchen. Putting it aside, Margaret washed her hands free of dirt before she set to her task. She poured mineral water from the springs of Bomack into a kettle and placed it on the hearth. She only ever made her father's drinks with spring water in her efforts to keep him healthy.

Margaret fanned the flames back into existence to heat the water before she went in search of her father. His condition had not made him entirely helpless, but he still needed aid. She would help him in and out of his special chair when he needed the privy or to get in bed. But the rest of the time, he was able to push himself around, if a little clumsily, through the home and sometimes outside.

"Papa?" Margaret called before she scolded herself. He wouldn't be able to answer her, not really. He could make noise—not very loudly, though—but he could no longer form words as he once had before his stroke.

She found him outside in the back, his chair facing the open fields to the west, where farmers tilled the soil behind their horses. Her heart ached when she saw the longing in his eyes. He watched them so intently, he didn't even turn at her approach.

Kneeling next to him, Margaret placed her hand on one of his, startling him out of his trance. "Papa, I've some water on the hearth for your afternoon tea if you'd like to come inside?"

He looked back at the farmers for a long moment before wilting against the back of his chair. His mouth quivered as he tried to speak. When it would not cooperate, he let out a frustrated noise and nodded with a shaky head. One eye squinted as though to sneer at himself, but his mouth remained still.

Quickly, Margaret moved behind his wheeled chair to hide her wet eyes. She cleared the lump in her throat before speaking. "Where would you like to take your tea today, Papa? The garden?"

He shook his head.

"The parlor?"

Another shake.

"How about your bedroom? I'll find a book to read, and you can rest before I make supper?" Margaret began to push her father toward the house.

He nodded with a sigh, leaning further back into his chair.

Margaret wheeled him to his room. "I'll get you settled first, and then I'll get your tea."

She set to the task of undressing him. Margaret wasn't sure if he even enjoyed being dressed for the day, or if he let her do it to make her happy. Margaret hoped it made him feel more like his old self. He certainly looked healthier when he had pants and a waistcoat on. Once she'd stripped him to his nightshirt, she hooked her arms under his to lift him. With a grunt, Margaret turned to sit him on the bed. She looked him over. He seemed feeble now that he wore only sleeping clothes, like an old man on his way to having all of his meals served to him in bed because he was too frail to move. Silently, Margaret piled pillows behind her father before she moved his legs onto the bed and helped him lean back.

"I'll be back in a moment with your tea, Papa."

The kettle whistled as she walked toward the kitchen. Margaret gathered some of her skirts to pull the kettle away from the fire, letting it cool on the counter while she put dried tea leaves into a pouch for steeping. She poured the water before she went in search of a book to read to her father. Her fingers ran along the spines, finally settling on a book about the kings of Anatalia, *A Collective History of Anatalian Monarchs*. She smiled slightly. Her father seemed to enjoy this the most, though they never seemed to get all the way through it. They continually skipped around to her father's favorites.

Returning to the kitchen with the book under her arm, she found a tray for the tea. Margaret fixed the drink the way he liked before carrying the tray to his room. "Who shall we read about today, Papa? Perhaps the Amendola kings?"

He gave a weak nod.

"All right, then." Margaret smiled, settling in the chair next to the bed. She put the cup to her father's mouth and tipped it for him to drink. Margaret set it down to pick up the book and began reading about the Amendola kings.

By the time she read a page, her father's eyes were drooping. Putting down the book, she said, "Let's pull you down, hm?"

He looked at her sleepily, trying to sit up. Margaret moved her arm under his legs, pulling him down until his head rested on the pillows. She covered him with sheets before sitting back in the chair, reading softly until he fell asleep. It did not take long—only four pages. She gathered all she had brought in, taking them to the kitchen to be cleaned, but first, she would bundle the herbs for drying.

Even as sparse as it had been, Margaret was lucky that morning. The healers were in need of everything she had planted that season. Margaret tried to ensure she would always have what they needed on hand in case of emergencies, and that she could make her own draughts for her father. Margaret separated the herbs by breed before tying the ends with twine. Some she would hang to dry, and others she would put in oil to use later.

Margaret tore the herbs from their stems, placing several kinds in the same jar before pouring oil over them. When a knock sounded on the door, she jumped, spilling oil on the counter.

It echoed with an eerie quality, sounding out of place. Worry crawled down her skin until it overtook her senses, leaving a trail of goosebumps in its wake. Almost no one came to their home uninvited, much less at this time of day. The only people who liked to visit them anymore were halfway between Silvica and

Fradure, the nearest towns to them. It would have been too far for them to travel on a whim to see her and her father as they were a couple late in their years, having sent seven children into the world to marry. Margaret tried to wipe her hands free of the stains the green plants deposited and went to the door.

When she looked through the small window, the man's back was to her, giving her no clue as to who he could be. Cautiously, Margaret opened the door, peeking out just enough to see him in his entirety. He was tall—much taller than she. He stood over six feet tall by at least a few inches. The man looked as if he had not eaten anything of substance in at least three months. His clothes hung from his shoulders in tatters, and she could see from the gathered dirt that he had not bathed for some time. Her nose wrinkled when the wind blew from his direction. The man on her doorstep had dark hair tousled in the windstorm breathing its last breath.

He must have sensed her critical gaze, turning to look at her. Margaret almost reeled back when she saw him from the front.

She knew this man.

He was Liam Fulton, the criminal who had escaped from the king's dungeons before her father had fallen severely ill. The last time she had seen him, he looked much healthier. She could still hear him screaming his innocence while he was dragged away to await his execution.

Now, he looked much like he had when he was first dragged through the street by the king's soldiers to be imprisoned—the image of him being beaten by people on the street was one that would not easily leave her mind. She sometimes dreamed about the crowds jeering at him, her friends tittering that they'd been able to see it.

Margaret snapped away from the memory and realized he was staring at her expectantly, waiting for an answer. "I'm sorry, what did you say?"

"I asked if I could beg some food from you," Liam repeated slowly for her as if she were daft.

In the years that had passed, Margaret had forgotten how rich his voice was. She relished the sound of it; there was not much conversation to be had as of late. Being away from the capital by fifty leagues, she assumed he thought she would not have known who he was. She knew he wouldn't recognize her either. She had seen the changes in the mirror. Her face now looked world-weary after the years she had taken care of her father. At the young age of twenty-four, she was no longer vibrant in her expressions or quick to laugh cheerfully. She regretted she had not tried harder to hold on to the child-like joy she had experienced before her father's illness.

"We don't have much," —Margaret looked back in the direction of the kitchen— "but I suppose we have some we can spare."

Liam gave her a charming smile. "My thanks, kind lady."

Margaret opened the door wider, apprehensive, thinking of what could happen if she were caught even conversing with him. If she were taken back to the palace, she would surely be imprisoned, if not executed, for assisting him. Liam stepped past her to come inside, and Margaret caught another whiff of him as he walked by. She rubbed her nose to cover her grimace.

"Before I let you anywhere near my kitchen, I'll draw you a bath. You'll spoil your food before you get to eat it with the way you smell." She let out a small gasp, covering her mouth with her hand. Margaret did not realize how rude her words were until they had already passed her lips. Had she said something like that around her noble friends, she would have died of embarrassment. It had certainly been a long time since she had been forced into using her lady-like civility.

Liam chuckled, much to her relief, and gave her a courtly bow. "Lead the way, my lady."

Margaret knew it was meant to charm her, to make her feel important for helping him. He would have had no way of knowing she had been called that on a daily basis when she was around others.

She felt a small bit of privilege, leading him toward the bathhouse. It was not a common sight in the country, but her mother had proclaimed she could not live without her warm baths when they had first built the home nearly two decades ago. It was quite the indulgence, but it was worth every gold tal it had taken to add to the cottage. Margaret had been a small child then and had marveled over the construction of the building. It was a luxury Margaret took advantage of as often as she could, soaking for hours at a time while her father napped. She lit the fire that would warm the water and pumped it into the extravagantly large tub.

"Leave your clothes outside the door," Margaret commanded before leaving Liam to disrobe.

She went to her father's chest of drawers. Margaret looked over her shoulder at the bed, relieved to see her father was still sleeping. She did not want to explain why she was taking clothes from his drawers. Margaret would not have been able to keep this secret from him. She wasn't even sure why she was helping Liam in the first place. Perhaps it was because she remembered his testimony that day in court and could not reconcile the patriot with the guilty verdict of treason. His passion had struck a chord with her—she could not fathom him turning on his country after his tale.

Margaret laid the replacement clothing outside the door and went to find something she could give him and send him on his way. She got out a loaf of bread along with some cheese. It would last him a few days if he was careful. She grabbed a satchel he could put the food in. Margaret came across some dried meat in her search and looked for anything else she could send him away with. As she searched, she realized he probably had not had something hot in his stomach for some time.

She felt a pang of guilt at the thought of sending him away without a hot meal. She would not feel right about it; all of her lessons in etiquette her governess had so diligently instructed her in came flooding back.

Margaret fanned the flames in the hearth back to life as she thought of a quick meal. It made her laugh, thinking that now she would even cook for him. Six years ago, when they had moved out to the country, Margaret had no idea what a pot even looked like, much less how to use one, and now she was proficient at making her father's meals, sometimes with only what she had around her in the garden. She had grown to love the ease she experienced while cooking for her father. It brought her great pleasure to know she could provide this for him without having to rely on anyone else.

 **2** 

The bathhouse was lined with cedar panels, growing fragrant as steam rose from the tub. Liam rubbed his hands together, a grin spreading across his face. He had not truly had a warm bath since at least three years before the war started, but that would be nothing compared to the luxurious privacy provided here.

He left his clothes outside the door as requested before sinking in the hot water. It stung his skin, but he didn't care. It was better than bathing with water from the frigid streams. Liam grabbed the bathing oil on the table next to the tub and sniffed—mint filled his nose, and he poured heavily into the water. He'd need it.

Liam breathed in deeply as his muscles relaxed, sinking into the tub until only his head was above the water. This was the life. If he'd had the choice, he'd never leave. Closing his eyes, Liam sank even further into the water until he was fully submerged.

In the dark behind his lids, Lieutenant Alton Bryant stood over him. Liam shot from the water, gasping. When he wiped his eyes, Alton was no longer there.

Breathing heavily, Liam sank back against the tub. He hadn't thought of his old lieutenant in years. He didn't want to think about him. It was another moment that darkened his soul before judgment.

Liam pressed the heels of his hands against his eyes and saw Alton again. How Alton had nearly killed him. How Liam had attacked him from behind once he regained consciousness. How he'd held Alton in the Frasisca River until he no longer moved.

Shaking his head clear of the memories, Liam splashed water on his face. He couldn't let the past haunt him. If he did, he'd turn himself in before he was ever exonerated. Not that he had much chance of that with Alton dead and the evidence lost to the river. By now, it would have floated all the way to Tyradrica, if it survived at all.

Liam took in a deep breath and let the mint swirl in his head, his shoulders slowly relaxing. He was going to enjoy what remained of his hot water while he could—there was no telling how many years it would be before he could have another bath like this.

Liam watched from the doorway as the woman chopped vegetables and busied herself around the kitchen. He shouldn't stay long, but the smell of seared meat was too enticing. He could barely remember the last time he had eaten something generously cooked. Liam had lazed in the warm waters of the bathhouse as long as he thought he could get away with. He'd never seen one with its own pump and heating system in a home before. The young woman who'd let him in looked so humble, her dress plain and her hair undone. How could she have afforded something so expensive?

He wondered briefly if she was a mistress to some nobleman who had spawned a bastard child on her and this home was compensation. It did not look like a house with a child, however, and he quickly banished the thought from his mind. She was not exactly a prize a nobleman had to have—her face was pale, and he could see dark circles starting to form under her eyes. She was certainly not the most beautiful woman he had seen in his days.

Liam lifted himself from the doorway, straightening his new clothes. He could not stay long; he did not want someone put in a prison cell for showing such kindness to him. He knew she would go to prison rather than the alternative—she would have had no idea who he was, living so far from the capital, and would be able to use that as her testimony. He knew for a fact the king was hesitant to execute women. It would not make him popular with his people if they saw a woman on the chopping block. Most women who were put to death were executed behind closed doors, and the public was later informed. Liam wished he could stay and bask in her kindness, but that would be impossible.

He couldn't remember the last time someone had been this kind to him since he had left the Gollacks, a sweet couple in the town of Marbon. He was accustomed to being treated as a dirty vagabond, never allowed further than the doorway. Many times, he'd have bread shoved at him through a nearly shut doorway, then told to be about his way quickly.

Liam cleared his throat and chuckled when she jumped. "Thank you for the clothes." He was rewarded by her smile and a gentle assurance that it was no trouble at all.

"Dinner will be ready in a moment. It's not much, but it will be warm in your stomach," she told him.

Liam threw her a charming grin. "Warm is good." He sat and waited for her to join him. "I truly appreciate all you've done for me."

She smiled as she sat across from him, her own bowl of food in front of her. "You're welcome."

Liam took a tentative bite of the steaming food, closing his eyes to savor the taste when he found it was more than palatable. "This is amazing…"

"Margaret," she answered before he asked her the question of what to call her. "My name is Margaret."

"It's a pleasure." He shoveled more food into his mouth. "I am Liam."

Margaret watched him with subtly raised brows, eating much more delicately than he. "It's been a very long time since someone has enjoyed my cooking so…thoroughly."

Liam's cheeks colored as he slowed. "It has been a very long time since I had anything cooked for me, much less something cooked well."

Margaret fell silent as she ate, lost in her own thoughts.

As she set another bowl of food in front of him, there was a knock at the door. Liam felt the blood drain from his face as she got up. He couldn't help but stand in the doorway of the kitchen to see who it was when she opened the door. He already suspected who would be there. He had brought this upon her by coming here. Standing there was one of the king's soldiers—his blue uniform was speckled with mud.

"Can I help you?" she asked him.

"We're looking for the traitor Liam Fulton?" the soldier demanded. "My scouts reported seeing him within a day's walk of the area, and all homes must be inspected."

Liam's chest tightened. He hadn't seen any soldiers for weeks, and even then, he had been able to hide from them easily by moving into the woods. He had to get out of any line of sight. He couldn't risk her getting caught—he should have insisted on easy food and been on his way instead of treating himself to the luxury she offered.

Liam went into the only open room. He found a man lying in the bed, staring at him with wide, fearful eyes. Liam put his finger to his lips and slid behind a modesty screen in the corner of the room. It must have been purely for decoration. The man had clearly not been able to walk by himself for quite some time—there was a high-backed chair with wheels in the other corner.

Liam felt cowardly, hiding in the room of an invalid, shame weighing heavily on his shoulders. If he could not be found, the kind young woman could not be convicted of helping a known criminal. He would not be able to live with himself if she were harmed because of him.

3

Margaret glared at the soldier. She knew him better than she wished but recognized none of the men at the end of the property.

Lord Nicholas Oliphant looked Margaret over slowly, taking note of her lack of face paint and fancy dress. "My, how you've changed, Lady Margaret."

Margaret hated the condescending tone he tried to level her with. She knew he would be more than happy to deliver her to the king for punishment after she had humiliated him. "We all change," she sharply replied. "You certainly did, much to your father's disappointment."

Oliphant's mouth hardened to a thin line. "Where is he, Lady Margaret? I know you had sympathy for him when he first escaped."

"I don't know who you're talking about, Lord Nicholas." She looked away from him to hide her disgust. The sinking feeling in her stomach told her things would end very badly for her. He had hunted Liam with a sickening glee when Liam first escaped the dungeon years ago—it seemed now he'd made it his life's mission to find Liam. "I don't believe you're welcome here."

Nicholas shoved past her, looking into the kitchen. "Why are there two bowls here?" He looked back at her as if he had been the sole reason Anatalia had won the war against Salatia. "You would have no need for two bowls unless someone else was here with you."

Margaret placed her hands on her hips, her cheeks coloring with irritation. "If you remember, *my lord*," she spat out his title with disgust, "I care for my father."

She could see dark clouds brewing on his face before he turned away to examine the rest of the room. Nicholas walked out of the kitchen and looked about with careful eyes. Margaret followed him, making sure he didn't break anything in his anger toward her.

"Don't go in there!" Margaret yelled as he approached her father's room.

Nicholas sneered at her, stopping at the door. "Is he in here, then?" The lordling walked in, looking around. His eyes settled on her father lying helplessly in the bed, who looked at him with angered recognition. Nicholas picked up a vase, throwing it against the wall. "Where is he, Margaret?"

Margaret knew his anger had been piqued by the sight of her father. He was the reason she ended her courtship with Nicholas in front of all of her friends when he had proposed marriage.

"I don't know who you're talking about. There's no one here but my father and me." Margaret scanned the room, wiping her sweating palms on her skirts.

Was he even still in the house, or had the guards outside apprehended him on his way out? She wondered where Liam had gone, but she supposed it didn't really matter. She didn't know where he was, so she couldn't give Nicholas the satisfaction of capturing him. That gave her some measure of relief. A satisfied smirk settled on her face as she thought about how furious Nicholas would be at his failure.

The slap that came caught her off guard. Margaret looked up at Nicholas in shock.

"Where are you hiding him?" Nicholas put his face in hers, bearing down on her until she reached the wall behind her, his hot breath fanning her face. "Where is he, Margaret?"

She touched her cheek where it burned painfully. "I have no clue who you're talking about, Nicholas."

When the second slap came, Liam flew out from behind the screen in the corner, slamming Nicholas into the wall behind him. Margaret wiped the unbidden tears from her eyes. So that's where he'd gone—she supposed it was lucky for her Nicholas couldn't hurt her worse than he had.

But now they were both in trouble. Margaret could have lied her way out of having helped Liam; now she would have to beg the king's mercy for his love of her father.

"I see your education is still lacking in how to treat people, Oliphant. I suppose you were too distracted ordering your servants around to learn." Liam slammed him into the wall again with enough force that all the breath in Nicholas was knocked out of him.

Nicholas doubled, his face reddening, and the tendons in his neck became visible. He let out a cough before he was able to breathe again. The lordling gulped down a ragged breath as he glared at Liam.

Liam pulled Nicholas up, reeling back to hit him again.

Margaret gasped when Nicholas shoved Liam away, drawing his sword. "You shouldn't have lied to me, dearest Margaret." He shot a glare in her direction. "You're going to go straight to the block."

Liam kept himself between her and the sword, spreading his arms to the side. "She's not going anywhere. She's done nothing but give food to a stranger."

Nicholas laughed harshly at him. "You're no stranger to her—she knew exactly what she was doing." He came at Liam with fervor.

Liam pulled Margaret out of the way. Margaret watched as Nicholas came toward her bed-ridden father with a momentum he couldn't stop. The angry lord would have had to break his wrist in order to avoid hitting her father.

No, no, no—Margaret's breath barreled in her ears as she tried to pull away from Liam and move toward her father. Time seemed to slow as Liam pulled her out of the room. What was he doing? She had to get to her father. She could hear nothing now but her ragged breathing.

Margaret pulled against Liam's ever-tightening grip, her hair obscuring her face as she struggled. "Let me go!"

Bile threatened to escape her throat when she heard her father's strangled cry. For a moment, her breath stopped and her knees weakened. Liam grabbed her other arm and hauled her up to his chest before she could fall.

Coming into full contact with his body snapped her back to herself. "Papa!" she wailed. Margaret fought against Liam furiously. She tried to rip her arm from his grasp to no avail. "Let go of me! I have to get to my Papa!"

"You can't go back in there." Liam gripped her arms tighter, shaking her until she looked at him. "He'll only take you to the king, with or without me, and I know what those soldiers do to young women like you." He half carried, half dragged her back to the kitchen, standing in the doorway to keep Nicholas from reaching her. "Grab anything you think we can use. It's going to be a long journey."

Margaret shoved past him and ran back to her father's room, collapsing against the jamb upon seeing his bloody sleeping shirt. She let out a cry, rended from the very depths of her. She pushed herself from the door, stumbling to her father's side.

Nicholas looked satisfied with himself. "Not so powerful now, are you, Lord Dorcia?"

Margaret put her hands to the crimson stain blossoming on her father's sleeping shirt. Tears gathered in her eyes as she tried to put pressure on his side to staunch the bleeding, her fingers slipping on the blood-slicked shirt. In her desperation, she called to the man who had wounded her father. "Help me!" she begged Nicholas.

She did not want to condemn herself to execution by staying, but she could not leave her father like this. Nicholas Oliphant would weave a web of lies to the king to make sure she would be publicly humiliated and sent immediately to her execution, even with the love the king bore her father. She could hear Nicholas chuckle at her desperate attempts. It must have given him great pleasure to know after she had rejected him so thoroughly that he would soon be getting his revenge on her, starting with the death of the man who had caused his humiliation.

"Give up, Margaret. I'm taking you and the traitor to feel the king's justice firsthand." Nicholas sounded pleased with himself.

Margaret didn't know where Liam had gone at that point. He hadn't followed her back in. She hoped she never had to see him again and he would be caught by the rest of the soldiers. Her father never would have been in this position if Liam hadn't shown up at her door. She saw the resigned look on her father's face, and her breath hitched. Margaret screamed at him to not leave her to this.

4

Liam was aghast at the sight before him. He turned his disbelief on Oliphant—Liam saw the enjoyment on the other man's face as he watched Margaret despair over her father's mortal wound. Hearing her beg her father not to leave her battered against his heart with each cry. Liam tightened his grip on the knife he took from the kitchen, grabbing Oliphant by the scruff of his neck before shoving the blade into his torso. One more dark mark for his soul—this one he would not regret.

The wound would not kill him quickly. If he was lucky, his men would get him to the town before he bled out. Oliphant collapsed to the ground, curling in on his stomach from the pain. He looked to Liam with wide, shocked eyes, his arrogance draining from him as fast as the color did from his cheeks. Liam always knew Oliphant's hubris would be his downfall, but Liam didn't realize he'd be the one to bring it about.

"You should have paid more attention to your training," Liam remarked coldly before leaving the room.

Liam opened doors until he found Margaret's room. He looked around, not knowing where to start. Liam grabbed whatever he could find to keep them going for an extended period. Liam stormed her room as quickly as he could, not wanting to leave Margaret alone with her dying father. He grabbed any sort of bag he could find, stuffing it full of flannel petticoats to keep her warm in their coming trip, and other skirts, dresses, and underclothes she could change into on their journey—he threw everything he thought she could need into a bag. A glint from the vanity caught his eye. Several jewels sat in the open, and he swiped them into the bag. They could use those as currency if it came to it.

He could not allow her to stay here, where she could be taken to the king and punished for her kindness. Liam took one last look around the room before snagging a cloak hanging on the wall. He needed to return to Margaret—he could still hear her begging her father not to leave her in the other room.

Liam went next to the kitchen and stuffed as much food as he could into a satchel sitting against the wall. It already had some food in there—she must have intended to send him away with this before Oliphant and his soldiers showed up. They'd need supplies for a few days to allow him time to hunt the sparse game. He would keep her with him until he could find a suitable town to deposit her in so she could live a life away from worry. He did not want the other soldiers to find her and bring her back to the king.

Going back to her father's room, Liam grabbed Margaret by the waist. She gasped, grabbing onto her father's hand, hers slipping off easily. He dragged her into the stables, depositing her in one of the empty stalls to weep on the hay. They had to go, and they couldn't dally until she stopped crying.

He saddled her horse as quickly as he could, knowing he only had a short amount of time before the other soldiers came looking for Oliphant. He was thankful the stables were at the back of the cottage, where Oliphant's compatriots wouldn't see them leaving. He strapped the bag of her clothes behind the saddle on her mare.

Liam turned to the other horse in the stable. Oliphant must have circled the house first to ensure no one was outside before knocking on the door. The horse was nose-deep in haphazardly poured grain when Liam approached. He snorted. Of course, Oliphant would have a gelding—he was too milquetoast to handle a stallion. Luckily for Liam, Oliphant was still too lazy to take care of his horse and had left him saddled and laden with supplies. Liam looked up sharply when hooves thudded against the ground in the distance.

It was time for them to leave.

Liam lifted Margaret easily, put her on her mare, and climbed atop the wounded soldier's horse. Grabbing the reins of Margaret's horse, he led them away from the house at a trot. Margaret still wailed in her grief over her father's impending death. The knot in Liam's chest tightened as he led her away from her home.

They hadn't made it far before Liam heard the shouts of the soldiers when they found Oliphant on the floor. He hoped Margaret's father was still alive. He dared hope the soldiers would help him. Glancing behind him, Liam saw some of the men pursuing them on their mounts, galloping toward their trotting horses. Glancing at Margaret, Liam noticed her eyes were still filled with tears. If they went to a gallop, she would surely fall off her horse.

"Pay attention!" he snapped.

Margaret glared at him indignantly.

"They're catching up to us!" he yelled at her.

Margaret snatched the reins from Liam. He saw the sickened look on her face when her hands slipped, slick with her father's still-wet blood. He spotted a new ring on her middle finger he had seen on her father—she must have swiped it as he pulled her away. She shook her shoulders before squaring them and clucked her mare into a gallop, flying past Liam on his stolen horse.

Liam urged his horse into a gallop as well, moving in front of her to guide her to an open deer path. If the forest floor was filled with leaves, they might be able to get away undetected. The surrounding area was thick with trees, and they slowed their mounts to a walk to avoid an unnecessary fall breaking one of the horses' legs or, worse, one of theirs. It would do them no good to have no other option but to walk on foot when they were being followed. Liam held his hand up for them to stop, listening for any signs of pursuit. It was getting late in the afternoon, and the sun would set soon. He could see his breath in the air. It was colder in the shade of the trees.

Relief relaxed Liam's face when he could no longer hear the soldiers behind them. "We'll go a little further on foot and find somewhere we can camp for the night."

Her breath came fast, surrounding her with a thick cloud of condensation. "What if they find us?" Margaret looked around her, panic edging into her voice.

"They're too far behind now. It would be pure luck if they came anywhere near this path. They would have no way of knowing where we entered the forest or which way we were going." Liam looked her over, noting blood covering the front of her dress. If they came across someone, the stain would only raise suspicions. "We need to find a stream of some kind so you can wash that blood off, but first you need to change."

Margaret immediately looked down at her front, and a fresh river of tears poured down her cheeks. Liam regretted even bringing it up, but he knew she would feel better once she could no longer see her father's blood on her dress and hands.

He dismounted, offering a hand to help her down. "I went through your bureau for some of your things." His eyes softened as he checked her for any visible signs of injury. "It's going to be very cold tonight."

She nodded dumbly at him, searching for the bag he had packed. Liam turned his back to give her some privacy. He heard her gasp, and he almost turned around—she must have been shocked when the cold air hit the rest of her.

She cleared her throat to get Liam's attention. "I'm finished."

Liam looked at her with the gown in her hands. He saw the pained look on her face, opening his hands to her as he came to where she stood.

"Give me the dress." When she hesitated he went on, "If those soldiers happen to come across it here on the ground, they're going to know we went this way." When he had it carefully rolled up, he placed it in the saddlebags on his mount. "We need to move." He grabbed the reins of his horse and headed east.

"Where are we going?" she asked, panic bleeding into her voice. "There's no trail here."

"We're going to find one," was all he said before silence settled between them.

Looking at the sky, Liam saw it was almost dark. He glanced back at Margaret—the cold bit at her ears and cheeks, turning them red. Liam thought she blushed prettily, though this was certainly not the time to think of it. He canvassed the area, leading them in a new direction. "We'll need to find a camp soon."

A large snap sounded behind them.

Margaret gasped. "What was that?"

They had been leading the horses to give them a rest while they were searching for a trail. Margaret moved closer to her horse. The mare whickered and nudged the girl's shoulder with her nose, sensing her fear at the noise. Margaret smiled tenderly at the horse.

Liam watched the exchange with a small smile. Margaret seemed to soften when she was near her mount. He, too, had heard the noise but was unconcerned. The soldiers would not have been able to follow their exact route. He had been taking them in random directions in hopes of throwing their pursuers off their trail.

"I don't think it's anything we should worry over." He tried to reassure her with a smile.

He saw the doubt in her eyes. He couldn't blame her—nothing would feel safe to her for a very long time. She had lost her whole world only hours ago. Her father was more than likely dead by now. And now he had made her a fugitive right along with him.

Margaret jumped at every noise the forest made. She climbed atop her horse, her knuckles white as she gripped the reigns.

Liam's chest tightened—she must be terrified. "Mar—"

"Liam!" Margaret cried out before they were rushed.

Liam quickly mounted his horse and commanded Margaret to follow him. He took off at a gallop, holding up his hand to keep stray branches from hitting his face. Liam looked back when he heard her frightened cry. The soldiers were gaining ground on them.

Damn it.

Liam looked to the front, searching for any open trail. The wind picked up, swirling the coniferous trees this way and that.

There!

Further up the trail, he caught sight of a small bend beyond the branches. Without the wind, he never would have seen it. He looked back again and saw Margaret lagging behind, her horse's eyes wide as branches brushed against her. Hopefully, that meant the soldiers' were having the same problem.

He slowed, sliding off the saddle next to the hidden trail. Liam pulled the branches back, urging his stolen horse forward. "Margaret, this way!" he yelled when she got close.

She looked around, squinting to find him. Margaret was nearly stopped now. He didn't have time for this—the soldiers could show up at any moment. He ducked into the main trail, grabbing the mare's reins.

Margaret's mare started to rear, her eyes rolling as she panicked. Liam yanked the reins down hard to stop her. Margaret was about to scream—Liam held up a finger to his mouth. He quickly mounted his horse, leading her down a trail. They had to get out of any eyeline before they could stop and rest the horses. The trees were so thick here, Liam feared they couldn't squeeze between the firs without breaking the branches.

Liam heard the soldiers ride past the hidden trail with shouts to one another that they were falling too far behind. Margaret leaned against her horse's neck and let out a shaky breath.

"Stay close to me," Liam whispered.

He prompted Margaret to dismount and follow slowly on foot to avoid any unnecessary noise that could bring back the soldiers. They followed the trail for what seemed like hours—the sun had been down for more than two hours by the time Liam stopped and looked at their surroundings. He could hear Margaret's teeth chattering as she shivered. Looking back at her, he could see she walked against her horse to get whatever warmth she could provide.

"We'll stop here for the night."

Margaret looked around warily. "Is it safe?"

"As safe as we're going to be. We won't be able to light a fire." Liam saw the dismay on her face as he spoke the words. The look she gave him brought a stab of guilt to his stomach. "Maybe a very small one. The soldiers will be looking for light or smoke from a fire to locate us."

In the end, Margaret's pleading look won out, and Liam dug a deep hole in an attempt to hide the light from any wandering eyes in the forest. He scowled as he saw the triumphant look on her face. He could tell she was used to getting what she wanted. He supposed this was the least he could do for her in the scheme of things. He was the reason she was out here with her teeth chattering and her fingers numb with the cold, after all.

"We'll need to find water for the horses." Margaret looked at him pointedly, running her fingers through her mare's tangled mane.

"Once the camp is set up, I'll go in search of water." Liam resisted the urge to roll his eyes. As if he didn't know that.

It didn't take long for him to set it up—they didn't have any tents to protect them from the elements, so all he had to do was find wood for the fire and light it.

"Will you be all right to stay here with them?" He saw the flash of fear in her eyes.

"I'll be fine," Margaret told him. She gently stroked her horse's nose, who rewarded her with a pleased snort. "Duchess will warn me if anyone is coming."

He nodded. "I'll be back shortly." He disappeared he said before disappearing into the woods.

Liam sucked in the fresh air with relief. He was glad they were no longer being followed for the moment. He knew the soldiers could come up at any moment and searched quickly for any water source. After a few tense minutes, he heard the light trickling of a stream. It would suffice for their needs, he supposed. He would lead the horses to the stream when he returned, and they would be able to rest for the night. Liam squatted and splashed water onto his face.

He needed to figure out a plan for what he was going to do with Margaret, and quickly. He couldn't keep her with him for too long; he needed to get her far away from where anyone would recognize her. He had to operate under the assumption that Oliphant would have uttered Margaret's name to the other soldiers in order to ensure she would be punished along with him. Kidnapping would be the fastest way to convince people to look for the young woman and, in turn, him.

When he returned, Liam found Margaret once again in tears. He could not blame her. He imagined she would be like this for quite some time. She would have no time to mourn other than when they were resting. Liam watched as Duchess drew closer to her mistress to add a comforting presence.

Liam looked at Margaret over the fire, watching the light dance across her face. He remembered what the lordly soldier had said to him in Margaret's home. He was trying to figure out how she would have known who he was. She did not look familiar to him. He studied her features as he tried to remember her. He thought she had a rather pretty face when softened by the light, but he would not consider her to be one of Aratia's greatest beauties. She had a pointed chin and high cheekbones colored from the warmth of the fire and soft full lips. He could not place her face anywhere.

"What did Oliphant mean when he said you knew exactly what you were doing?" Liam asked.

Margaret's eyes snapped to his face when he spoke. "I was at your trial."

"You were what?" Liam's stomach dropped as her words sank in. He watched Margaret turn her face away from him. It made his stomach grip even tighter.

Why would she risk herself in such a manner for him? He ran a hand over his face, a range of emotions running through him. He should have been more careful. It was quite by chance the soldiers had even seen him.

The Anatalian soldiers went on routine patrols, even in the midlands, to make sure Salatian rebels were not harassing the Anatalian people. The war had been over for seven years, but every so often, there were skirmishes in the border towns. The treaty in place did little to curb the enthusiasm of the Salatian soldiers with a taste for war. When the issue was brought up to the Salatian monarch, he denied sanctioning any such actions.

"I attended your trial with the other courtiers. It was quite the event, if I remember correctly." Margaret did not look at him as she spoke. Guilt washed over him like a tidal wave. "With all that's happened, I should go to Jalmar to settle things before it's too late."

Liam's mind raced. He realized what the arrogant lordling had been touting was true: Margaret would have been executed if Oliphant had succeeded in bringing them both in. She still might if the pompous lord lived to tell his tale. Liam studied her carefully as he thought. Why had she helped him if she knew who he was? Margaret knew what the consequences were for her, and even her father, for letting him into their home.

"Why would you do something so stupid?" he demanded, livid she would put herself in such danger.

"Why are you yelling at me?" Margaret asked, her eyes wide with surprise.

"Answer my question!" He shot up from where he sat on the ground, guilt gnawing at his gut.

He was angry at her for letting him into her home, and he was guilty for taking advantage of her feigned ignorance. Even angrier at himself for thinking he could get away with accepting her generosity without repercussions. He thought he had learned his lesson the last time.

Liam paced in front of the stolen cloak he had used to keep the earth from dirtying his new clothes. It escaped him why she would put herself in such a situation. It was possible she did not recognize him in his diminished state; he was a shadow of his former self. After going hungry more nights than he cared to remember, he looked more like a street beggar than a broad soldier who proudly served his king.

Margaret glanced away from him, a stubborn set to her jaw. Liam could tell it was not going to be easy to get any information from her. He couldn't blame her; he was the reason she was out here in the cold and dark, sitting on the ground. She should be sitting in front of a large fire, nursing a cup of tea in her home while her father rested.

"Margaret, I'm sorry," Liam tried to apologize.

Margaret remained quiet, her jaw set, refusing to look at Liam.

5

Margaret stared at the fire as it hissed and seethed at her, a glow dancing upon her pale face as the heat writhed endlessly inside its wooden prison. Her eyes narrowed as she recounted the day's events. Her father was gone—she could feel it in the pit of her stomach. She had seen the light already fading from him as Liam pulled her away. If only she hadn't let Liam in—if only she hadn't been desperate for someone's company—she wouldn't have gotten her father killed.

The fire popped its disapproval at her glower. What had she done that was so terrible in her life that the universe felt the need to punish her in this way? Life, acting as a scorned lover, dug up her past and threw it at her as if to tell her their chapter had not yet been finished and would not be for some time. Of all the doors Liam—and Nicholas—could have knocked on in her humble town, it had to be hers. She could see in her mind's eye the wicked grin of life taunting her in her torment. She wished she could return to that morning when she had been blissfully unaware of how her day would end.

As her lids drooped, Margaret tried to make herself comfortable. The ground was solid beneath her, refusing to give way as her bed had at the cottage. Even the spongy layer of leaves did not help her comfort. The night was cold, and Margaret knew the small fire would not be able to keep her warm through the night. She tried to close her eyes and settle down, but the silence of the night was oppressive. Margaret scooted closer to the fire for warmth, her cloak and flannel petticoats unable to keep her warm enough.

"Your skirts will catch fire in the middle of the night if you stay that close." Liam looked at her with soft eyes, a slight frown pulling at his lips, as her teeth chattered.

"Then how am I to keep warm?" Margaret demanded. She was irritable from the cold and did not want him to start telling her what to do.

"Would you like me to sleep next to you?" Liam asked.

"No!" Margaret snapped.

She pulled her cloak tighter around her, trying to ward off the cold. Margaret did not want to have Liam near her while she was still angry. Besides that, it would not be proper to have him so close to her while she was sleeping.

"Then tuck your feet under your skirts, and try not to think about the cold." Liam sounded offended she had not taken his offer to keep her warm. "I have no plans of molesting you during the night, if that's what you are thinking."

Margaret lay awake until she was sure the sun would rise any moment. She had little experience with the wildlife inevitably lurking near their campsite, attracted by the light of the fire. She felt eyes on her and shifted every which way to dispel the feeling of being watched. Margaret heard every tiny noise made near her. First, a shuffle in the leaves, most likely a tree-climbing rodent making its way to shelter for the night. Soon came more rustling in the fallen foliage. She figured they had to be larger animals, based on the amount of noise they made. It could not have been one of their pursuers, the crunching of dead leaves being more delicate than what blind footfalls would have afforded.

A howl erupted from deep in the forest, shooting a bolt of terror through Margaret. The hairs on her neck stood tall. Her heart raced. Margaret wished she could hide away under the covers still adorning her bed. She didn't know if the animals making the noises would come any closer to them. The possibility that they would petrified her.

"Liam?" Her voice sounded small and high.

"What is it?" he asked groggily, his eyes cracking open.

"I'm scared."

She heard him sigh before he moved behind her, wrapping an arm around her waist.

Margaret shied away from him. "What about something for modesty?"

Liam sighed again. "Is your own cloak not enough?"

Margaret looked back at him over her shoulder pleadingly.

Liam let out an irritable noise, putting his stolen cloak between them, partially covering her with the rest of it. He once again wrapped his arm around her, placing his other arm beneath his head. "Better?"

Margaret nodded silently. She felt safer with him at her back. She fell asleep quickly, pressing herself closer to Liam. She felt his arm tighten around her before she drifted off to her dreams.

Margaret woke, her back cold. It was already bright outside, and she looked around, confused. "Liam?"

"I'm here," he called. He had cleared their campsite, letting her sleep as long as possible.

She stood slowly, stiff from a night on the cold earth. "Where are we?"

"I would say about five or six miles from Silvica," Liam told her with an off-hand tone, brushing Duchess down until her coat gleamed. "I would like to make at least another ten from here today."

Margaret went to Duchess. She was impressed to find her mare was being well taken care of. "Where are we going?"

"I'm not sure yet. I want to get as far away from here as possible." He looked as if he wanted to get as far away from her as possible instead.

"What's going to happen to me?" Margaret asked, her voice hitching as anxiety crawled up her chest.

Clearly, it was too early in the morning for to ask questions. He closed his eyes for a moment before saying, "You'll be put somewhere safe, where no one can find you. You can't risk being found for a little while—let things settle first."

"I'll be 'put somewhere'?" There was a finality to his tone she did not like. "And you're the one to decide where I'm going?"

"If you were to decide, you would go straight back to the capital and to your execution," Liam told her pointedly. "I can't allow you to do that."

"You can't allow me to?" How dare he! Margaret put her hands on her hips, an indignant cock to her head. She could easily go to her lands in Dorcia…but she would need to ask the king for her title of countess to ensure they weren't sold to the highest bidder first.

Liam mounted his stolen horse, looking pert. "You'll only get yourself killed without me."

"Oh, would I?" Margaret's eyes flashed dangerously, gripping Duchess's reins tightly in her hands until her knuckles were white. He was treating her like a child.

"Yes, you would. Now, do as I say, and get on your horse."

Margaret was outraged but got on her horse nonetheless.

It had been a week since Margaret was abruptly removed from her home. It had taken the majority of that time to stop weeping every time she wallowed in thoughts of her father and her people. She had no idea where they were going, and she was weary to the bone. She had never once had to spend the night on the road as the daughter of a count.

Margaret slowly grew accustomed to having Liam near her at all times. Eventually, she got used to the noises of the forest, though she could not shake the fearful tightening in her stomach whenever a twig snapped too close to her.

Margaret worried the soldiers would appear again. Liam had done all he could to help make her as comfortable as possible—although they could not light a large fire at night, he made sure she was always warm, even if that meant giving up his cloak and being miserable. His gentlemanly behavior made Margaret wonder where he had learned this inestimable quality.

After the trial, everyone had attempted to ascertain who he really was. Liam had been a mystery to all who had attended. No one had come to offer support for him. There was so little known, he might as well have been a ghost. Was he the son of a minor lord or the product of a poor family? Listening to the twaddle of court, he had grown up poor and joined the ranks to provide for his family. Perhaps his parents had sent him to live with the family of a lesser-known lord, possibly a baronet or knight for a small fee each year. Liam would have learned the art of chivalry, how to address the nobility, the proper bows to accompany those he addressed, and to read and write. Could he have been a bastard child? Margaret would have to ask him once they made camp for the night. There were many men like him who would not have been nearly as willing to make her comfortable.

Liam's face had dirtied in the week since he had come to her home—hers had too—but it did not take away from his features. The grit and grime brightened his blue eyes. She could see his cheekbones were high, a result of good breeding somewhere in his family line, and he had a strong jaw many ladies would swoon over. His nose was thin and straight, bulging slightly at the tip. Margaret thought it added to his charm rather than taking away from his looks. Her eyes moved to his hair—it was dark, a deep chestnut she found appealing. It had been too long, she felt, since either one of them had been able to wash. Liam refused to let her wash her hair in the cold water of the river, claiming she would get sick and they would be forced to go into a town too close to where they had fled.

Margaret had no idea how far they had gone since they left her home. To her, it seemed like they could reach the king's palace any day now. She was accustomed to traveling on well-marked roads, where she could see exactly where she was and how far of a journey remained. She refused to complain about the way her feet ached or how her thighs were developing saddle sores without proper riding clothes. She did not want to seem spoiled to Liam, a hardened vagabond. Margaret wondered why she even cared what he thought of her—he would be depositing her in some small town, never to see her again. The only time they were able to get along was during the night. He would automatically move behind her and wrap her in his cloak to keep her warm, and they would talk until she fell asleep in his arms.

Margaret looked over at her traveling companion, wondering how long they would be on the road together before they parted company. "How far away are you going to take me before we find a place?"

Liam looked thoughtful for a moment. "There's a small river town called Marbon I can take you to. I think you'll do well there. I've been to most of the towns and cities in Anatalia since my escape, and this one will most suit your needs."

"What if I don't do well there?" Margaret asked.

It was a worry that nagged at her stomach. She had been comfortable in her country home with her father. She knew the small town he spoke of would never hold the same comforts she had been accustomed to in her own home. Margaret did not think she would find anywhere as relaxed as it had been. She dreaded their arrival in the small town.

Liam looked at her sympathetically. "I highly doubt you will at first, but you'll learn to like it."

"How am I going to live on my own?" Margaret looked at him questioningly. She had not technically lived on her own, despite her father not running the house or being capable of making any decisions. She knew a woman of her age could not live on her own unless she was a widow, or she made her living in a bed.

She shook her head. Why was she even letting him take her anywhere? She had her own life, and he couldn't take more from her than he already had by depositing her in some backwater place for an undetermined amount of time. She was a noblewoman, for goodness' sake. "I want to go back home—take me back home."

"You can't, Margaret. There will be soldiers looking for you and me. Do you understand that you could die if you go back home?" Liam spoke very slowly and made hand gestures to better articulate his point. "There's a family I did work for who I know will take good care of you." The look he gave her said the discussion was over.

She deflated slightly. She didn't want to die—what would her people do without her and her father? Margaret looked over his face; it irritated her that he felt he could order her around in such a fashion. She was out here because of him, and she felt she should have some say in where she was going.

She did not want to stay anywhere he put her, but she could see the benefits of going somewhere else until things blew over and she could return to the capital unscathed. Margaret looked back at the bag with mismatched clothes strapped to Duchess—she would also need time to recuperate her losses if she was going to make an appearance at court. Though, if she showed up in this horrid state to Jalmar— No. It would not be easy to explain her way out of helping a criminal who almost turned the tide of war, and she needed to be seen as a countess before the king to plead for her title and forgiveness. She needed to ensure her people would not be taken from her.

Margaret's stomach tightened. She didn't know for certain if Nicholas had survived the encounter in her father's bedroom. If word reached court before she did, she would be seized immediately upon her arrival and put in a cell to live out her days, her people and lands sold off to the highest bidder. If that were to happen, she would have to make an appeal to King Sorren. She did not think the king would actually put her to death; he had loved her father, especially how he utterly devoted himself to the king after being granted a title. The thought of her father brought tears to her eyes. She could still see his face clearly.

She closed her eyes tightly. Margaret wanted to see him, and didn't want to see him. Her mind was all over the place, and she couldn't settle on a single thought or feeling. It was unsettling, and she suspected it was part of the reason she let Liam take her wherever he wanted. She had been so sure of herself with her father around, and now…? She didn't know.

What was she going to do without him? She could not live on her own, and she was not prepared to live with a guardian who would assume responsibility over her. Taking care of her father had given her a sense of independence; she didn't know if she could be under someone else's rule. Even Liam telling her what to do made her hackles rise.

Margaret looked at her surroundings with disdain. She would not have chosen to be surrounded by dirt and wildlife. She would have taken well-traveled roads and stayed at inns where she could take a long hot bath and wash her hair. Margaret picked the grime out from under her nails, scrunching her nose as the first was removed.

"Liam."

He looked at her. "What?"

"I want to stay somewhere in town."

"No."

Margaret looked at him with gelid eyes and spoke through clenched teeth. "Then let me take a bath in the river."

"It's too cold for that, and we can't make a large enough fire to warm you up. You'll end up killing yourself." Liam was clearly frustrated they were having this conversation again. "We're still too close to where you came from. People will have heard your description, and they will think that I've kidnapped you."

They had been traveling under the assumption that Nicholas Oliphant had survived the ordeal and passed on the incriminating information about Margaret. She could not help the panic that rose when she thought of her people under a cruel master. Liam was right: proclaiming kidnap would be the fastest way to get the local people to help find them.

Glaring at him, Margaret placed her hands on her hips, pouting. "I have dirt in places there should *not* be dirt. I want to bathe."

"Margaret, it's too dangerous for you to bathe in the river, and it's too dangerous for the both of us to go into a town near the one you lived in." His face reddened with frustration.

Margaret knew when to stop pushing. She knew he wouldn't lay a hand on her, no matter how much she pushed, but she didn't want to take the chance. He had been out in the world, with no laws but his own, for seven years. Margaret would keep quiet for now. If only she had the skills to make it on her own, she could escape on a main road and find a town to have a nice dress or two made in and take a carriage to the capital. Then she would not have to wait to make an appeal to the king and take over her father's lands and business.

Charles came to mind. He loved her father like his own and would certainly help her in her time of need. If she could only find a way to escape her captivity with Liam and a way to Charles, she would be saved. He would find a way to get her out of the trouble she had gotten herself into, and he could even become her new guardian until she could arrange a marriage. Margaret briefly wondered if he was still married to that woman who had stolen him from her grasp. If Charles were her guardian, it would only be a matter of time before he realized his error and cast his eye on her and divorced his wife. Margaret smiled at the thought. That was her new plan: Escape Liam, find Charles, then marry him. It wasn't often she didn't get what she put her mind to.

"Something on your mind?" Liam asked.

Her smile dropped as she turned to scowl at him. "I was thinking about an old friend," came her reply, irritation radiating off her.

"Who would that be?" Liam dug.

Margaret hesitated, her lips pursed. "If you must know, I was thinking of a friend of my father's who would be adequate as my guardian."

"I see…and how would you get to this friend?" Liam's eyebrows rose.

Margaret glared at him.

6

Liam let the conversation drop. He would just end up yelling at her in his frustration. If he had learned anything in the last week, it was how easily she provoked anger in him. He wondered where that sweet woman who opened her home to him had gone. Liam hoped once they reached the Gollacks' her attitude would change. He would not wish to inflict her sour mood swings on a sweet couple such as them. Liam would stay at least a few days to make sure she was settled and behaving properly toward the two of them.

He would have to keep a close eye on her throughout their time together traveling. It would not be safe for her to be out on the road by herself if she tried to leave his care—and after the look he had just seen, he suspected she might try. There were plenty of men who would be happy to cause her harm if she were caught alone on the road. He looked her over as she rode next to him. Liam had never met a woman so stubborn and determined in his life. If something didn't go her way, she argued until he gave in to her. He wondered what she would do if he kept refusing to let her bathe.

Liam slowed his horse—whom he had decided to name Ashka after the fabled horse lord who had traveled the world with nothing but his horse and the clothes on his back—to a stop, looking around the clearing they had come across. They had been on a hunting trail in the forest. "Are you tired?"

"I can keep going," Margaret told him stubbornly, though her eyes were starting to droop.

He knew she had not slept well since they started their journey the week prior. Liam had gone at a remarkably slow pace in the forests between Silvica and Marbon so he wouldn't exhaust her or the horses. It was a difficult journey with her at his side—he was accustomed to traveling with little to no baggage, and very rarely with a horse. They had to stop more often now to water and rest the beasts carrying them. Liam was unable to drag Margaret and mounts through the thicker parts of the forests he was accustomed to traveling in for his own protection. Even so, she could barely handle that pace. Though, Liam was surprised she had not complained, even when he had seen her stiffly walking after a long day's ride.

"Why don't we stop for a day or two so I can hunt? The supplies we have are starting to run low," Liam told her as he dismounted.

He put his hands on her waist, helping her down from Duchess. She looked around the clearing, her face twisting into a dubious expression. He glanced around to see what caused it—there were only a few scattered branches in the tall grass. It would be one of the nicer places they had stopped at. He would never be able to understand her.

"How far are we from Marbon?"

"A little over halfway," Liam answered. "We'll take another week to get there if we stop to spend a few days here."

"Aren't we risking being found here?" Margaret looked warily at the trail behind them.

"The soldiers will have stopped looking by now, and not nearly this far east. They'll rely on the people to report appearances of us instead of wasting their manpower searching." Liam started to sharpen a stake to hunt with. "You have nothing to worry about, Margaret."

Margaret watched the horses free feed as she sat against a large tree. "Are there hunters on this trail?"

"Not at this time of year. The big game have not migrated yet." Liam had seen the migratory patterns of several different species in his wanderings and knew their routes well. "I'll start a fire before I leave—I don't know how long it will take me to find food."

Margaret simply nodded. "Be careful."

Liam finally returned hours later, a small doe resting on his shoulders, his brow glistening in the dying light of the evening. Liam was pleased to have even found her—not many deer were in the area at this time of year. "We should have food for the rest of our journey with this!"

"How are we going to cook it?" Margaret looked at the deer skeptically.

"I'll build a spit while you gather more firewood," Liam informed her with a smile. "We'll be warm for the first time."

Margaret's face erupted into a bright smile. She more than happily rose to the menial task. It took her several trips to gather an adequate amount of wood to continually feed the fire. She watched as Liam constructed the spit and placed the impaled deer atop its braces. Soon they could hear the fire sizzling with the grease dropping from their dinner.

"Why won't you tell me who you are?" Liam asked Margaret. "Did I know you from the capital?"

"No," Margaret said quietly. "You didn't know me."

"Then why so secretive?"

"Because I don't want to talk about it." Margaret looked away from him, that stubborn set in her jaw returning.

"You're putting us both in more danger by not telling me who you are," Liam tried to explain.

"I am putting you in no more danger than you are putting me in, Liam," Margaret pointed out before turning quiet again.

Liam let the subject drop, knowing once she had the stubborn look on her face, there would be no talking to her. It annoyed him that she would not tell him anything. Liam had no idea how much danger the both of them could be in. For all he knew, he could be traveling with the daughter of a duke and could immediately be taken into custody for her supposed kidnap. He would be happy when they arrived at Marbon and he could leave her safely.

Liam lay back against one of the trees, starting to cough until his throat was sore. He usually developed a small cough when he traveled in the cold. Liam hoped having the large fire to sleep near would dispel the rattling in his chest before it worsened. He caught the concerned look Margaret gave him but turned to ignore her. Liam was frustrated enough with her and did not want to engage in another conversation.

Had Liam been alone, he would have already been in Marbon, a small town that thrived on an offshoot of the Frasisca River. Liam had encountered an older couple who took pity on him when he had first escaped his imprisonment. They had never been anywhere near the capital and had no idea he was a convicted traitor. Aram and Elizabeth Gollack had welcomed him with excitement, glad to have a visitor of any kind. They had clothed him and fed him with what little they had. Liam had offered work in payment for their kindness and what they sacrificed for him. He had worked for them on several occasions as he traveled to and from Salatia.

Liam smiled at the memory and the prospect of seeing Aram and Elizabeth again. Margaret would feel at home quickly with those kind people. They had made him feel like part of their family within days. It had been the first time in years he had felt at ease on Anatalian soil. They didn't care he was a convict. When Liam had asked why they had never condemned him like the rest of Anatalia, they told him it was because he had reminded them of their late son.

Liam woke late, his arm still wrapped around Margaret. Even with the bigger fire, they elected to sleep as they had their entire journey thus far. She felt safer that way, according to her. He caught a fragrant scent wafting off of her—it had a soft quality to it that smelled of a garden filled with roses and hydrangea, with a hint of spicy sharpness. It must have been one of the things he grabbed when he was raiding her items. As much as she complained about not bathing, at least she didn't smell bad.

Raising himself on to his forearm, he looked at her face. Softened by sleep, he found her features more attractive. Her full lashes swept against her cheeks, giving her the appearance of a sleeping doll young children carried.

He should get up, but it was comfortable to be in a woman's presence again—it had been some time. Women had not been terribly hard to come by during his travels, especially when he crossed the borders of the other countries and could stay at an inn rather than making camp in the woods. He would have to work hard for his stay, but at least it was warm. Somehow, he always managed to make his way back into Anatalia and was reduced to traveling far off trails and begging for food. He knew he could live the rest of his life elsewhere and not worry about capture, but Anatalia had a special hold on him he couldn't describe. Perhaps it was because he was unwilling to give up on his search for evidence to exonerate him, or perhaps it was because his parents were laid to rest there.

Margaret stirred, and he pulled away from her. Definitely time to get up. There were things to be done, starting with watering the horses and letting them graze. He stood and started coughing as the wind picked up. Liam hoped that would have gone away in the night next to the fire, but they could stay an extra day to try to get rid of it.

Liam went to the horses and they sniffed at him, Duchess shoving her nose into his chest. He laughed, running the back of his fingers down her cheek.

"She likes you," Margaret said behind him.

"She's a good horse." He untied them and led them to the stream not too far away from their camp.

A thin layer of ice, already melting in the sun, covered the edges of the stream. Whenever they left the clearing, they would have to push themselves a little harder before it got too cold for them to be able to sleep outside.

When he returned to the clearing, he let the horses loose to graze. They'd be fine on their own—all military horses were trained to stay where the people were, and based on how attached Duchess was to Margaret, she wouldn't wander far. On his way back to the fire, Liam grabbed thin branches that had fallen on the ground. He could smoke the rest of the venison so it wouldn't spoil before they could finish it. He could never waste so much food.

Liam sat in front of the fire and brought out his knife, debarking the branches to keep the meat cleaner.

"Is there something I can help you with?" Margaret asked.

Liam looked up at her. She looked more cheerful than the night before. "If you wouldn't mind gathering some of the longer grass so I can tie these to the spit, that would be really helpful."

To his surprise, Margaret returned promptly with far more than he needed.

Margaret shrugged. "In case you break some." She sat across from him, watching him work.

Liam pulled out another knife, handing it to Margaret hilt-first. "You could start cutting the venison if you'd like. They shouldn't be wider than an inch."

They spent the rest of the day preparing and smoking meat. He didn't feel much like talking, and it seemed neither did Margaret. They stayed mostly silent until it started to get dark and they settled in for the night.

It was time to leave the clearing. His cough had not gone away as he had hoped with the larger fires. Perhaps he would stay for a week or two to rest and catch up with the Gollacks. The rest at the couple's home would rejuvenate his health and spirits. It had been close to two years since he had last had the chance to see them. It would be a nice change of scenery for him.

Liam looked back over at Margaret; she was still smiling with self-satisfaction, and that worried him. If the last week had been an example of the way things were going, she would not keep behaving like that.

7

Now only two days from Marbon, they decided to make camp in the late afternoon to rest the horses. They had come to an agreement that Margaret would brush the horses once they stopped for the night, and he would water them and build the fires. In the last two days, he had been making the fire larger due to the growing cold. The early winter was almost upon them—there had been frost on the ground when they awoke. Margaret would be happy when the fire was lit and she could warm her numbed fingers on it. She looked up when Liam returned with wood in his arms.

"What would you say to having a fresh dinner tonight?" Liam asked her. "There's a stream teeming with fish back in the woods."

"Even in this cold?" Margaret was hopeful at the mention of a stream. "If you catch them, I'm almost certain I can cook them."

"Good." Liam smiled at her, a charming smile Margaret could not help but return.

"Now about this stream." Margaret dragged out the last word, her eyebrows raised suggestively.

The smile immediately dropped from Liam's face. "No, Margaret."

"Listen to me, Liam." Margaret waited for his face to change to a compliant look before continuing. "What if you let me wash just my face? I can't stand all the dirt on it."

Liam examined her face closely. He didn't seem like he was going to budge. She looked at him hopefully, resting a hand on his arm.

"Just your face." He was unprepared for Margaret to fling herself at him with a happy squeal, stumbling back a few steps.

"Where is it?" Margaret grinned up at him, her arms still wrapped around his waist. "While I'm gone, you can make a spit to put the fish on."

Sighing, Liam pointed in a direction. "It's about a quarter-mile that way."

Without saying anything, Margaret headed that direction.

"Margaret."

She turned around, her mouth pursed and arms crossed.

"Promise me you'll only wash your face. I don't want you to get sick from a full bath."

She glared at him but said nothing. She was reluctant to make a promise she didn't know she could keep.

"Promise me, or I'll make you stay here," Liam told her seriously, a stern look donning his face.

"Fine, I promise," she clipped before she was gone. She was furious he was still treating her like a child.

Margaret inhaled deeply, enjoying the quiet. Enjoying being alone—that was almost laughable considering she had been so desperate for company mere weeks ago. It was the first time Liam had given her such allowances. Margaret sighed contentedly, her excitement growing when she heard the stream gurgling.

Margaret knelt beside the flowing water and stuck her hands in. She gasped and immediately pulled them out. Her skin turned bright red, fingers burning from the icy cold. She had planned to take her time scrubbing her hands and face clean of the building grime, but now she realized she could only stand having her hands in the water for short bursts. Margaret was reluctant to admit Liam was right. She almost let out a scream when she splashed the frigid water on her face.

Margaret's face still burned and was surely as bright pink as her hands were when she returned to the camp. She glared at Liam when she saw him.

"Something wrong, Margaret?" He could barely hide his smirk as he knelt next to a pile of broken sticks, preparing to light their fire for the night.

"Oh, be quiet." That would be the end of the conversation until she had warmed herself by the fire.

Liam hissed suddenly as his spindle slipped, pulling his hand quickly to his chest.

"What happened?" Margaret asked him anxiously, moving to his side as her anger melted. "Are you all right?" She immediately snatched his hand into hers. A gash crossed the center of his palm where the spindle had ripped the rough flesh.

"I'm all right, Margaret," Liam told her, trying to pull his hand away from her.

Margaret pulled it back to her with a petulant pucker of her lips. She poured a portion of their water over his wound. She went to the saddlebags and grabbed her bloodied dress Liam had hidden. Margaret hesitated, her stomach curling at the memory of her father. She looked back to Liam and sighed, finding a clean section for his hand. She ripped a wide strip of fabric spanning the circumference of her dress to wrap his wound tightly.

"There," Margaret said with a proud smile.

Liam curled his fingers around the bandaging. "Thank you," he said quietly.

Margaret looked up at him, unprepared for the tender gaze in his eyes. She looked away, her embarrassment unnoticeable on her already colored cheeks. "Perhaps now the fire can be lit to warm my frozen fingers?"

Liam chuckled and went to do as he was subtly commanded.

After their stomachs were full and their bodies warmed by the fire, Margaret turned her eyes on her traveling companion. "Liam?"

"Yes?"

"Tell me about your past."

Liam looked at her surprised. "My past?"

Margaret nodded. "No one was ever able to ascertain who you were when you were put on trial."

"Only if you tell me who you are."

Margaret hesitated. Liam was using her curiosity against her. He was more than likely just as curious about her as she was about him. She liked her anonymity; people would expect less of her if they did not know she was the daughter of a count. Even in Silvica, only a few people knew who she and her father were. Any time she went into the town, she introduced herself as Margaret, and requested the people who knew only call her Lady Margaret in private.

"Well?" Liam asked her.

Her curiosity won out.

"My name is Margaret Doremis, daughter of Jerone Doremis, Count of Dorcia." Her shoulders slumped. "I suppose that means I'm now the acting Countess of Dorcia." Margaret didn't know if she could actually take over the title, but she was her parents' only child.

Liam raised his eyebrows. "Why didn't you have any servants in Silvica?" He did not remember seeing any there.

"They left to start their own lives, but honestly—I was never any good at being their mistress," she admitted. "I don't particularly enjoy ordering people around."

Liam laughed outright at her confession. "You've been trying to order me around ever since we left."

Margaret looked at him sheepishly, a blush creeping up her face. "Fair is fair—tell me about you."

Liam mockingly bowed at the waist. "As my lady commands." He chuckled again when she glared at him. "You already know about my trial and escape."

Margaret watched him expectantly. Her curiosity would finally be sated seven years after his trial had ended. She leaned forward to hear him better.

"There isn't much to tell," Liam started, throwing grass at the fire he'd built. "I grew up near Jalmar in a small village with my parents. My mother always told me I was destined for greater things because of my lineage, but we were a very poor family." He furrowed his brow. "She had been a little overzealous about the idea. She taught me how to read and write, and my father instructed me in swordplay and the courtesies deserved to the members of court. I always thought it was strange that they were so well-versed in court life."

Margaret was surprised also. "What are their names?"

"Zachariah and Marie Triburn. My mother made me take her maiden name, Fulton, though. They typically went by Fulton out in town but with us, it was always Triburn. I tried to learn about the family name, but there was nothing to be found." Liam looked as if the decision still confused him.

It did not confuse her, however. Thanks to her night in the Triburn Room with Prince Gareth, Margaret knew Liam would only have to go to Glessic or Mekhor and say he was the last of the Triburn family and was ready to take back his throne. He would have hordes of men at his side.

Margaret was taken away from her thoughts when Liam coughed wetly and said, "Fulton was a good enough name for me."

"Are you all right?" Her brows furrowed when she looked at him. It was hard to tell against the warm firelight if he was pale or feverish. Everything took on an orange glow.

"Fine," Liam snapped, letting out another round of coughs.

She let it drop, but her concern for him still grew. "And you don't know why she wanted you to have her maiden name?" Margaret wanted to gently probe what he knew.

"I had been forbidden to talk about it at a very young age, and both of my parents died of pestilence before I escaped from prison."

That answered her question as to why no one from Liam's family showed up to support him. "So you have no idea what she was talking about when she said you were destined for greater things?"

"Every time she brought it up, my father would command her to be silent. I would be beaten with a switch until I stopped asking." Liam didn't look as though he was curious about why his parents had reacted so.

Margaret looked him over. She was traveling in nobler company than he was. "Do you ever wonder what she was talking about?"

Liam shrugged. "It doesn't really matter now, does it?" His face sank into a melancholy expression.

"I'm sorry for your loss," she said quietly. "Don't you think you should try and find out what she was talking about?"

"Margaret, she's dead now. There is no finding out."

Margaret chewed on her bottom lip. "What if someone else knew?"

"My parents were very private people. They wouldn't have told anyone," Liam said, starting to get irritated.

"They might have if it were really import—"

"Leave it, Margaret," Liam said. "It doesn't matter anymore."

Margaret pursed her lips. "I'm sorry, Liam, but this is important for you."

"Drop it," Liam commanded. "I'm going to sleep."

The night was the coldest of their journey. Even with Liam to her back, she shivered and her teeth chattered. He tried to hold her close, but he was just as cold.

"Will you allow the both of us to be covered by your cloak?" Liam snapped.

Margaret eventually complied, unable to stand the cold. She turned toward him to make it easier to envelop the both of them in two layers of their cloaks, her face pressed tightly against his chest. Liam rubbed her back in an attempt to warm her further when her teeth still chattered. They had only two more days until they would reach Marbon. "Can't we just stay at an inn along the road?"

Liam looked at her, frustrated. "Do you want to get the both of us killed, Margaret?"

"I'm trying to keep the both of us from being killed by the cold," Margaret snapped. She was angry that she was so cold because the fire was never big enough to keep the both of them warm. "You need somewhere warm to help you rid yourself of this cough."

"No," he told her stubbornly. "Now go to sleep."

Margaret gave him the hardest glare she could muster. She was uncomfortable being so close to him without something between them but tried to sleep nonetheless.

Margaret let her eyes wander as they entered the river town of Marbon. She had never heard of the town before Liam told her about it. As she looked around, she inhaled deeply and smelled the sweet fragrance of freshly baked bread. Margaret would bide her time there while she made arrangements to go back to the capital. Liam had kept too close an eye on her for Margaret to find a main road.

Marbon was a metropolis compared to her little Silvica—there were several shops lining the main street. Margaret could identify a bakery, a seamstress' shop, and an apothecary just in her first glance. She wondered if there was a banker's bench in this town where she could remove a large chunk of her money to commission gowns for herself and hire a few servants to make a proper appearance in the capital. She needed to ensure Nicholas had not reached the capital himself to inform the king of her actions. Margaret could feed the economy of this town for a month or two while she waited.

Margaret saw Liam immediately relax as he entered the town. The weight he had been carrying rolled off his shoulders as they straightened. He even seemed to cough less. Margaret was amazed at the change in him. He looked years younger, a jubilant smile on his face.

"We're almost there," Liam said, an excitement in his voice she had never heard before.

"Will they care we're dirty?" Margaret asked, rubbing her cheek in an attempt to banish any grime that had built since she was allowed to wash her face in the stream.

Liam smiled. "They will not care."

Margaret was only slightly comforted by the answer. She had never once been this dirty in her life and did not plan on ever letting it happen again. "Could we find an inn to wash at first?"

"Margaret, I can almost see their home." Liam scowled at her. "Aram and Elizabeth won't care that we aren't at our best."

Margaret wrinkled her nose in consternation. "What if we—"

"No, Margaret." Liam gave her a hard look. "It's right there." Liam pointed to a house nearly half the size of what she and her father had in Silvica. He dismounted, giving his horse an affectionate slap on his neck before grabbing the reins and leading him to the back of the building.

Margaret followed him, trying once more to wipe her face clean of whatever dirt had settled on it. There was only a rail to tie the reins to. Margaret frowned. With as cold as it was, she'd have to find stables.

She watched as Liam knocked on the door, waiting impatiently for one part of the couple to answer. Margaret saw a small woman with white hair answer the door, looking up at Liam with a perplexed look on her face quickly changed to excitement. Liam was suddenly embraced by the small woman in front of him. She had wrinkles all over her face, particularly around her mouth and eyes, showing Margaret the woman frequently smiled and laughed. Margaret awkwardly swiveled on the balls of her feet, looking away from them. She did not want to intrude on a private moment.

Her brown eyes were on Margaret after the reunion was over, still bright from her excitement of seeing Liam. "Liam, who is this?" the woman asked. "Is she someone special?"

Liam smiled, a blush dusting his cheeks. "No, Elizabeth, she's no one special." He wrapped his arm around the older woman's shoulders. "I've stumbled into a bit more trouble, and I need you to look after her for a while."

"Liam!" Elizabeth looked alarmed.

"She's not with child, Beth," Liam assured her. "There's no need to look at me that way."

Margaret's mouth parted slightly, her eyebrows raised high. She crossed her arms tightly in front of her. Margaret was rather offended the old woman immediately jumped to the conclusion she was some trollop Liam had taken up with. He had ruined her life, and now, in this woman's mind, she was his whore.

Liam spotted the look on Margaret's face. "Perhaps we could talk about this inside while Margaret takes a bath?" He certainly knew a bath would raise Margaret's spirits.

Elizabeth looked Margaret over. "Of course, come in." The older woman disappeared into the home. They could hear her voice carry as they followed. "I'm afraid it will take a while to get a bath ready for you, my dear."

Margaret smiled at her with the most charming smile she could muster. "I'll be happy so long as I can wash off this dirt."

Margaret let out a contented sigh as she stepped out of the hip bath. By the time she was done, the water had turned a murky gray that made her wrinkle her nose. She vowed she would never get that dirty again. She went to the room she would be staying in for the remainder of her time there. As Margaret looked around the space, she wrinkled her nose again. She would make do with the accommodations she was given. Margaret was determined she would enjoy the temporary stop in her journey, rather than making all of them miserable. Margaret went to where she heard talking, taking in everything.

Elizabeth and an older man were sitting at a table with Liam, each with a cup in their hands filled with what Margaret assumed was tea. She knew by the pitying looks on the faces of the older couple Liam had told them about the circumstances that brought the both of them to Marbon. Margaret suddenly felt uncomfortable with their stares.

"Hello…"

The older man and Liam stood when she spoke. The old man was tall, with a wide girth and blue eyes that looked at her kindly. He held his hand out toward the remaining chair. "My dear girl, sit down."

Those simple words made Margaret feel like a small child as she sat in the proffered chair. She looked between the Gollacks, and her shoulders drooped as she realized the full weight of the situation she was in. The previous confidence she had in herself to make all these plans and changes was gone. She felt the prickling of tears behind her eyes. The old man was by her side in an instant.

"My dear, it's all right." He gently patted her hand with his age-spotted one, kneeling next to her chair with a look of concern. His crow's feet wrinkled deeply. "You can stay here as long as you need." The older man looked over at Liam. "Liam wouldn't have brought you here if he didn't know we would take care of you."

Margaret nodded, unable to speak.

Liam rose from his chair. "Margaret, why don't we go for a walk, and you can take some time to calm down?" He offered his hand to her.

Margaret looked at his hand, unsure. Liam saw Aram and Elizabeth nodding at her encouragingly. Margaret took Liam's hand, and he pulled her up from the chair. He led them out to a branch of the formidable Frasisca River, not far from the Gollacks' home. The rushing water visibly helped relax her—her shoulders dropped into a more comfortable position. She deeply inhaled the fresh river air that often brought Liam comfort.

Liam had not let go of her hand yet and was surprised she had not tried to pull away from him. It brought him comfort to know she would be with a caring family like the Gollacks while she adjusted to the loss of her father. They would treat her as if she were a relation of theirs.

Liam watched her closely as she began to relax even further. "This river has helped me sort out a few things for myself too." He smiled at her. "Sometimes it's nice to have somewhere you can escape when you're feeling unsettled."

"Thank you for getting me out of there." Margaret's cheeks flushed, wiping the last remnants of her tears away. "I don't like to cry in front of people."

Liam squinted at her dubiously. "You cried in front of me for almost an entire week."

Margaret looked at him sheepishly. "I didn't think you were paying much attention to what I was doing."

"I was paying very close attention to you, Margaret." Liam raised his brows at her. "I thought you were going to run off and do something foolish again." He continued lightly, "Like help another criminal."

Margaret had the decency to look chagrined. "It was pretty reckless, wasn't it?"

Liam smiled briefly before turning serious. "Why did you help me, Margaret?"

Margaret's smile slowly fell from her face. "I didn't think you were guilty. Listening to you and watching your face, I knew you couldn't have done the things they said you did. You're too loyal." Her brow creased with her frown. "I never understood how His Majesty could have declared you guilty just because it was Lord General Crompton laying the claims against you."

Shocked, Liam stopped walking. He looked at the woman in front of him in a new light. It was courageous of her to have a different opinion than the king and help him so willingly when it meant she could be put to death alongside him.

"What?" he asked.

"I listened to your testimony the same as everyone else, and I didn't think you did it." Margaret looked down at her feet. "After you had accused the king of being blind to the traitors in his own house, it seemed he unilaterally made the decision you were guilty instead of giving you a fair judgment."

The Gollacks had not thought him a traitor either, but they had not been at his trial and seen the evidence presented against him. They believed him innocent based on his character. She was the first to know the whole story and still not think him guilty.

Liam pulled her into his arms and held her close. "Thank you," he whispered.

"You're welcome." Margaret leaned her head against his chest.

Liam held her for a while, jubilant he was not condemned by all Anatalia. He couldn't remember the last time he had felt this happy. "We should go back to Aram and Elizabeth now that you've composed yourself."

Margaret broke their embrace, straightening her dress. "Of course."

"Are you quite recovered, my dear?" Elizabeth asked when Margaret and Liam entered the home again.

"Yes, I believe so," Margaret told her. "Thank you."

"Very good." Elizabeth smiled. "Do you have any clothes other than these?"

"Yes," Margaret told her, "but I would very much like to start commissioning some new dresses as soon as possible."

Elizabeth smiled at the young woman in front of her. "Tomorrow I will take you into town and show you the seamstress shop."

Margaret smiled at her. "That would be wonderful, Elizabeth."

Liam looked over Margaret carefully. He had a feeling she would try to leave too soon, and would only get herself into trouble. He only wanted to keep her safe from the damage he had caused.

"Liam?"

Margaret stood in the doorway. She fidgeted with her pointer finger, her brow furrowed. He had never seen her behave that way before. "What's wrong?"

"I asked Elizabeth about stables for the horses, and she said there aren't any public ones." Margret seemed to realize she was playing with her finger and clenched her fists briefly before dropping her hands to her side. "I can't stay here if Duchess can't be taken care of."

Liam pulled in his bottom lip as he thought. She couldn't leave Duchess out in the elements, especially with it getting colder by the day. It'd be unlivable without shelter sooner rather than later. "I can build her a stable with Aram."

Her eyes widened. "You would do that?"

Liam nodded, standing. With the weather getting colder, he would need to get started as soon as possible. If he was lucky, there would be enough supplies. "She needs somewhere just as much as you do—so does Ashka."

"Thank you." She smiled tentatively. "Is there anything I can do to help?"

"Let Aram know we'll be building, and he'll gather some of the other men to help. We'll have it done in a few days."

"That soon?" Margaret furrowed her brow. "Will it be suitable?"

"These country men know how to build, and how to build fast." He tried to smile reassuringly, coming to stand in front of her. "Don't worry, I won't let Duchess suffer."

She grabbed his forearm, squeezing it gently. "Thank you, Liam."

 **9** 

Crompton wasn't happy to be back. The king had pulled him from the Salatian border for an update on their progress. Once his horse was unsaddled, Crompton made his way to the palace's chapel, his footsteps echoing in the empty hall. He inhaled deeply. There should be more people. Many had fallen further from the faith the longer his cousin was the king—Sorren often felt himself above Theotes's plans.

Crompton stopped when found the chapel dark. Where were the priests? He furrowed his brow. Why were the candles not lit?

Crompton's stomach curled as he scanned the room. Why was the altar dark? The altar should never be shrouded in shadow.

Grabbing a matchstick from the back of the chapel, he swiped it against his boot and lit the candle at the back door. He would have words with the prelate and his lack of commitment to his church.

Once the chapel was lit, Crompton approached the altar and knelt, covering his face in deference.

He sighed heavily, running his hands down his face. The past few weeks weighed on him—the past few *years* weighed on him. All the lying. All the scheming.

All the deaths.

He didn't know how much longer he could do this.

"Lord, help me," he whispered, lowering his head, "guide my steps—"

"Your Grace?"

Crompton's eyes shot open. "What is it?" He glared over his shoulder with enough vitriol that the page stepped backward.

"His Majesty requests your presence."

"Tell him I am in prayer," Crompton snapped.

The page shifted uncomfortably. "He already knows, Your Grace. Someone saw you come here instead of reporting to His Majesty. He commands you come immediately."

"Theotes give me strength," Crompton growled under his breath before he stood. "Where is he?"

"In his chambers, Your Grace."

Crompton wetted his lips, rubbing them together. He didn't want to see his cousin right now. But there was no choice. Sorren was king, and Crompton was his servant. "Let His Majesty know I'll be there in a moment."

Once the page left, Crompton looked up to the portrait of Theotes and the six-pointed sun hovering over his hand. "All in service of you," he said with a sigh before he stood and went to Sorren's chambers.

"Has there been any resolution for our borderlands?" King Sorren looked away from the scroll in his hand.

"We were working on one," Crompton almost growled, "until you summoned me." Just looking at the king made him sick.

Sorren fingered his livery collar before waving his hand in dismissal. "Return to where you were then. You're of no use to me yet."

Crompton bowed deeply to the king, his nose flaring and mouth set to a hard line. He could not wait to kill the bastard—there had been several attempts before he threw his hat in the ring, making it more difficult to get to Sorren. It needed to happen, and it needed to happen soon. The glint of gold at Sorren's neck unwillingly brought the memory of when his hate for the monarch had truly started.

Tobias Crompton had gone to his cousin, Sorren Platiri, the soon to be King of Anatalia. He had never spent much time with his older relative, but he knew Sorren was not the most pleasant of people to be around. His father, King Reuben III, doted on him more than he should have; but then, the prince was an only child. Tobias dreaded when he would be required to participate in the prince's coronation. All he wanted to do was return to Rivack and rule over his people in peace.

Crompton lightly knocked on the door of Sorren's study, entering without waiting for an answer. He had an appointment and did not want to wait in the hallway like a servant. He stopped short at what he saw.

Sorren was behind a young maid who had her skirts thrown haphazardly around her hips and the golden livery collar Sorren would wear as king around her neck, pulling her toward him roughly.

Tobias stopped short as the maid clawed at her neck, her face growing redder by the second. He could barely hear her choked out plea to stop.

He felt like vomiting. He had defended his cousin when rumors flew of the future ruler's mistreatment—the *rapes*, Crompton corrected himself—of several women in and out of court. This was who their king, chosen by Theotes himself, was supposed to be? Chosen by Theotes the Gentle?

No.

He couldn't be.

Theotes would never choose someone so vile. So cruel. So *disgusting*.

The crown prince growled obscenities at the maid that made Crompton's stomach reel. Crompton cleared his throat and politely turned his head to the side.

"What do you want, cousin?" Sorren asked between grunts.

Bile curled up Crompton's throat. Sorren didn't even have the decency to stop. There was no hint of shame in his face.

"We have a meeting, Your Highness."

"Your Majesty," Sorren corrected.

"As your coronation has yet to happen, it is still Your Highness," Crompton told him pertly.

Sorren pulled the maid roughly, causing her to cry out. "I am the king's only son and heir, and my father finally had the decency to die so I could ascend the throne. So, *Your Grace*, you will address me as 'Your Majesty,' coronation or not."

"As you wish, Your Majesty," he conceded reluctantly.

The future king let out a disgusted growl and shoved the maid away. "You've ruined her for me now." He curled his lip. "Let's get this over with so I can get back to my business."

"Yes, Your Majesty." Crompton tried to keep the disgust out of his voice.

"Get out!" Sorren yelled at the crying maid, causing her to jump and scurry from the room.

Crompton watched the young woman flee before turning his attention back to Sorren. He had no respect left for his royal cousin—there was no way he would allow Sorren to stay king for the rest of his life. He would shame Anatalia in Theotes's name, making a mockery of all their god stood for. He would destroy this country.

Crompton fingered the six-pointed sun sewn into the bottom of his vest. Theotes help him, he wouldn't allow it.

When Crompton, face pale, returned to his chambers, he sent his valet to the servant's quarters to retrieve the maid from the incident earlier. He stood when the door opened.

The maid curtsied to him, a pained look on her face. The crosses of Sorren's livery collar were bruised onto her neck, her eyes rimmed with red. "You called for me, Your Grace?"

"Please, sit." He went to her side, gently leading her to an overplush chair. Once she was settled, he handed her a goblet of wine from his own province.

The maid readily drank from the goblet.

"What is your name?" Crompton asked, sitting across from the servant.

"Nicolette, Your Grace."

He leaned back in his chair. "Nicolette, were you a willing participant in today's event?" He asked bluntly.

Her hands shook, and she looked at him with wide eyes. She remained silent as she watched him.

"You don't have to be afraid—there is no trickery here," he urged her gently. "Please tell me."

Tears flooded her eyes as she rubbed her throat. "No."

"And was this the first time?"

The held tears slipped down her cheeks. "No."

It was as he feared. Rumors were circling the court that Sorren had a predilection for the female staff, sometimes venturing out to the ladies in the court. Crompton looked at Nicolette sympathetically as he poured her another glass of wine.

"If there were a way for you to leave, would you take it?" Crompton asked.

"In a heartbeat if it meant being away from His Majesty, Your Grace," the maid admitted freely after taking another large gulp of wine.

Crompton pulled the bell to summon his valet to the room. "See that this young lady's personal items are moved to my home in Rivack, where she will join my household. Make sure it is done today, and if anyone raises any questions, I will be happy to dispel any issues they may have."

Nicolette looked at him in disbelief. "His Majesty—"

"Let me worry about His Majesty, Nicolette," Crompton cut her off. "You will be safe from him, I promise."

Nicolette had relaxed in her seat, looking like a heavy weight had been lifted from her shoulders.

The door slammed behind him, pulling him from his memory. He couldn't wait for Sorren to be out of the picture. Crompton rubbed his face with a sigh as he walked back to his chambers. She had only been the first Crompton helped escape from under Sorren's thumb, but she had not been the last. He couldn't even remember how many it had been now.

He needed to act, and swiftly.

10

It was easy to settle in with the Gollacks. Their lives had an ebb and flow that, at first, made Margaret uncomfortable. There was no order to how things were done, nor were they done in the timely fashion she was accustomed to. Their philosophy was that things would happen when they happened and there was no need to worry about it. Margaret had learned at court the only way to get things done was with haste and assertiveness. She found after the week she'd been there, their lackadaisical lifestyle seeped into her usually rigid schedule and slowed it to a more delicate pace.

The Gollacks were the perfect hosts for her needs. She could feel their silent support without the feeling she was being pitied. Elizabeth took her to the heart of the town to the banker's bench.

"I need five thousand gold tals, sir," Margaret told the bench man, setting her father's signet ring in front of her.

Elizabeth blanched at the amount Margaret requested, telling her it was unseemly to have that much money on hand. Margaret smiled at her patiently. While living in Silvica, she and her father had accumulated upwards of eighty thousand gold tals. It was almost as much as the royal coffers held.

After examining her ring, the bench man told her, "My lady, I can't give you that much today. We don't carry that much here."

"Then get it," Margaret told him more harshly than she intended. She looked at him apologetically, knowing from experience that kindness got her further than anything else. "I'm sorry, I've lost all my possessions, and I'm anxious to rebuild and sustain myself on my journey."

The bench man looked over some papers strewn over the bench. "I will send notices to the surrounding towns and cities that you are in need of resources."

She smiled at him brightly. "You have my greatest thanks, good sir."

"It's a pleasure, my lady," he responded modestly.

"How much can you afford to give me now?" Margaret wanted to get started as soon as possible replenishing her wardrobe.

"We can only give you the equivalent of one thousand gold tals, broken up with tholar and drica to make it easier for you to spend it, of course, my lady." He looked her over curiously. "The other bench men will break up their installments similarly, I'm sure." He swallowed hard. "What brings so fine a lady to our humble town?"

"Family acquaintances." She smiled at him again before standing. She did not want people to know she was here running with a convicted traitor. "Be sure to call on me immediately when you've received the rest of the installments."

The man stood as well. "Of course, my lady." He bowed as she left.

Margaret left with a flabbergasted Elizabeth. "Five thousand gold tals, Margaret?" The older woman sputtered. "That's more than what all of the townspeople combined make in a year—in five years, even!"

Margaret smiled patiently at her. "This is going to have to last me almost a year, and I have many things to commission." Margaret looked around happily. "The seamstress is going to be a very rich woman by the time I'm done with her."

They walked to the seamstress's shop, not far from the banker's bench. "Mistress Laphar?" Margaret called out when she entered the shop.

Elizabeth and Margaret had been in the shop a few days prior to commission simple house dresses and allow Mistress Laphar to take her measurements with assurances she would pay upon completion and commission other dresses from her. Elizabeth had told her when the seamstress was younger, she had gone to the capital in hopes of working for the royal family.

"I'll be with y' in a moment," Mistress Laphar answered her.

Margaret ran her hand lightly over the fabrics as she waited. "She's going to have to send for fabrics from the capital," she said to Elizabeth.

"What can I do for y'?" The seamstress asked Margaret, setting down a bolt of cloth. She was short, with bright red hair pulled into a tight bun, her bangs curling on her forehead. She was a slightly rotund woman with a rather large bust accentuated with a waist apron.

"I need to commission fifty dresses made suitable for the king's court," Margaret said.

"Fifty courtly dresses!" Mistress Laphar crowed shrilly. "M'lady, that will take all year!"

"That is unacceptable, Mistress Laphar," Margaret told her firmly. "I need them by spring."

"I'll have to hire more girls, m'lady, to help with the sewin'," the seamstress told her.

Margaret raised her eyebrows. "Whatever it takes, madam. I'll pay you an extra seventy gold tals for your trouble."

Both Elizabeth and Mistress Laphar let out gasps. "M'lady, that would hire ten girls for a year!"

"I trust you'll make good use of it, then." Margaret smiled. "Now we need to discuss the cost of all the dresses."

Margaret and Elizabeth left the seamstress' shop, one in shock and the other satisfied. Mistress Laphar charged her one-hundred and twenty-five gold tals for the courtly dresses and the simple ones she had commissioned the previous visit—including her promised bonus, Margaret made it an even two-hundred for easier counting. The seamstress estimated all the dresses would be finished by springtime with the extra help. Margaret would enjoy spending the winter getting to know the Gollacks. She already knew they would be gracious hosts.

As Margaret walked, the glinting of metal from a small trinket shop caught her eye. "What's this?" she asked the shopkeeper.

The shopkeeper picked up the pocket watch she pointed to. It had a shiny golden surface with a 'T' topped with a crown etched into it, niello rubbed into the crevices to blacken the design. It shook in his frail, age-spotted hands.

"A pocket watch from the old line of kings," he said. "A man sold it to my father when King Reuben III came to the throne. Said he was one of the old king's family and wanted no evidence of it. No one here could afford a nobleman's favor, and I didn't have the heart to sell it cheaply."

Margaret looked over the shopkeeper's face. "Of the kings before the Platiris, truly?"

"Truly," the shopkeeper confirmed.

Margaret set down ten gold tals on his bench, well over the cost of what it would have been worth in gold alone. It would be much more precious once it was in the hands she intended it for. "I would like to have it, sir."

The shopkeeper happily handed over the pocket watch to Margaret. "It's yours, m'lady."

By the time Margaret had gotten back to the Gollacks, Liam was waiting for her with a disapproving look on his face. Margaret looked at him sheepishly. He must have heard of her adventuring in the town. Not many people could afford to withdraw over one thousand tholars after a lifetime of saving, much less one thousand gold tals in one sitting. News must have traveled through town there was a very rich woman somewhere in it.

"What do you think you're doing?" Liam demanded when she reached him.

"What do you mean?"

"You can't go flaunting your wealth around these people, Margaret. You'll end up getting their homes robbed, or, worse yet, attracting rebels with the news of a wealthy patron residing in Marbon." He gave her a hard look, his coughing taking away from the seriousness he tried to portray.

"I don't plan on staying here for very long, Liam."

Liam grabbed her arm. "I think we need to have another walk, Margaret."

He took her to the river for privacy. Liam kept his hand clasped around her upper arm. He walked at a fast pace, making Margaret take two quick steps for his one. He did not stop until she ripped her arm from his grip. He turned to face her, breathing hard, a whispering wheeze filling her ears.

"I don't see what there is to discuss." Margaret crossed her arms over her chest. "You've deposited me in this town for my own 'safety,' and now what I choose to do with my time here is none of your business!"

"You're planning something."

"How very astute of you. Tell me more."

"Tell me what it is." Liam's lips thinned and he slowly blew a breath from his nose.

"Once Mistress Laphar has finished a suitable wardrobe for court, I'm going to go back and prevail upon the king's mercy and find a husband." Margaret gave him a proud smile. "I've already got the whole thing planned out."

Liam looked at her expectantly, his brow raised.

"I'm going to go back to the capital and tell my dear friend Charles and the king about what has happened—leaving you out, of course—and then I'll get Charles to divorce his wife and marry me, and we'll have a wonderful life together."

Liam grabbed her by her shoulders roughly. "You can't just go around trying to marry other people's husbands, Margaret!" His voice held a mixture of anger and disappointment. "How are you going to get this Charles to divorce his wife? And better yet, how do you know the king will believe you?"

"Because the king has always loved my father and me; and Charles's wife hasn't given him any children, and I can; and I can use my father's lands and business to tempt him into a divorce." She had adopted an offhand tone, flippantly waving her hand at him.

"Grow up, Margaret." Liam looked disgusted by her plan. "Stay here where it's safe and not where you could be killed. Do you know how stupid you're being?"

Margaret stamped her foot with her conviction. "I'm going to the capital, Liam." She gave him a withering look. "You put me in this town, and now I'm not your concern."

Liam grabbed her by the shoulders once more, looking at her directly. "You'll always be my concern, because you don't have a father anymore and that's my fault."

Tears welled up in Margaret's eyes. While he was constantly on her mind, Margaret did not like for her father to be brought up. "If I had refused you entrance, my father would still be alive. I wouldn't have had to leave my father to die alone and scared." Margaret's jaw was tight, the tears she refused to let fall standing in her eyes. She looked away to avoid Liam's stricken gaze. "*I am the reason my father is dead.*"

"Margaret, I'm sorry—I shouldn't have brought it up." He gently cupped her cheek in his calloused hand. "I didn't mean to upset you."

Margaret brushed his hand and her tears aside, steeling herself. "I bought you something in town," she said, trying to change the subject.

"What is it?"

Margaret pulled the watch from her pocket. It was large in her small hands. "I found this pocket watch and thought of you." She looked at him, unsure of how he would react. "I hope that it isn't too much."

Liam took the watch in his hand, examining it. "It's very beautiful, Margaret, but I'm afraid that it is too much."

"I want you to keep it." Margaret knew Liam should have it as the last known Triburn in Anatalia, at least to her knowledge. "Think of it as a thank you from me."

Liam grabbed her hand and squeezed it gently. "It is a kingly gift, and I will cherish it."

Margaret smiled ironically. "Speaking of kings—"

"Margaret, Liam! Please come back to the house," Elizabeth called out from a bend in the river close to them.

When they entered the Gollacks' home, Margaret could hear Aram sputtering. "Fifty courtly dresses?" he asked Margaret in disbelief. "Five *thousand* gold tals?"

"Yes, Aram," Margaret said patiently. "I require all of those things to prepare for my journey to the capital."

"You *require* them?" Aram asked, indignant. "You're just a girl. How can you afford such things?"

"I'm the Countess of Dorcia," Margaret informed him. "Until His Majesty deems to tell me otherwise, I've inherited my father's lands and title."

Aram and Elizabeth immediately tried to bow and curtsy to her, shocked looks on their faces. "M'lady," they both murmured.

"Please don't," Margaret said. "I don't want you to treat me differently— bowing and calling me 'my lady' will make all of us feel uncomfortable."

"My dear, if you're the Countess of Dorcia, then why are you here?" Elizabeth asked Margaret.

"I had no idea who she was when I brought trouble to her home, and she refused to tell me until we were almost here," Liam answered for Margaret. "She is wanted for helping me, and Dorcia would not be a safe place for her at the moment."

Aram looked at Elizabeth, startled. "We will keep you safe here as long as you're willing to stay," Aram told Margaret.

"And you will be repaid tenfold for your kindness," Margaret told the couple passionately.

Liam entered the kitchen with sunken eyes. His phlegmy cough echoed through the small home.

"Are you feeling unwell, Liam?" Elizabeth asked, her voice slightly higher with concern.

Margaret set the tea she had been steeping on the table. "You look miserable," she told him, a playful smile on her face.

"I appreciate that, Margaret," Liam said flatly, though his tired eyes danced with mischief.

"You look like you've caught something worse than your cough." Elizabeth put a hand to his forehead. "You're on fire!"

"I feel fine," Liam said, "will you stop mothering me?"

Elizabeth rolled her eyes. "Go back to bed, Liam."

"Beth—"

"Now, Liam," Elizabeth commanded.

Margaret covered her mouth with the tips of her fingers to hide her smile as she watched him retreat to the small room the Gollacks had crafted for him. "I don't think he appreciated that either."

"What a shame," Elizabeth said sardonically.

Margaret checked on Liam several hours later and saw he was fitfully sleeping, his face drenched with sweat. He was violently tossing in his bed, as though he were fighting off a nightmare. She gently touched his forehead and found it even hotter than before.

"Elizabeth?" she called out anxiously.

"What is it?" Elizabeth asked, coming to the doorway.

Margaret's brow furrowed. "I think he needs a healer."

"Is he getting worse?" Elizabeth came into the room to touch Liam's head.

"Much worse," Margaret said gravely.

When the healer arrived with Aram, he immediately went into the room. "How long has he been like this?"

"He's been coughing for two weeks, but the fever started several hours ago. He got better for a few days before he built a stable in the back," Margaret answered. "We sent him to bed to rest, and when I came to check on him, he was like this."

The healer thoroughly examined Liam and stepped away quickly before saying, "I believe he has the winter fever."

Elizabeth gasped, covering her mouth. "Are you certain?"

"Very."

"What should we expect?" Margaret looked at Liam with her brows drawn together.

"At best, fever, chills, coughing, and difficulty breathing."

"And at worst?" Margaret asked hesitantly.

The healer looked at each woman in turn, unsure of who to settle on. He eventually settled on Margaret. "Death."

Margaret raised her chin defiantly, as if her stubborn strength would combat Liam's illness. "Thank you for your time."

The healer nodded, taking the hint he was no longer welcome. "I will return later with a regiment of draughts for him and instructions."

"Thank you, Healer Williamson," Elizabeth said as he left.

"We need cold cloths to try and bring down his fever," Margaret commanded, trying not to let her anxiety show. She sat next to Liam on the bed and wiped his sweaty brow clean.

Elizabeth retreated and returned quickly with as many cloths as she could find and a basin of frigid water from the well. She dumped the cloths in the water, wringing one out for Margaret.

"Thank you, Elizabeth," she said quietly. "You should leave. I don't want you to catch this sickness."

"What about you?" Elizabeth asked, worried.

"I'll be fine," Margaret said stubbornly. "Now go."

Elizabeth looked at her disapprovingly, but she left the room all the same.

Margaret rested a cold cloth on Liam's forehead. He flinched away from her but sighed at the comfort the cold brought him. She tried to strip away the extra clothing he was wearing to help release the heat. She saw his arms were covered with scars.

Margaret lifted him up against her to remove his shirt. She ran a cold cloth along his back, his weight resting heavily against her. She let him rest on his side so she could wipe the moisture off his back.

When she turned back around with the dry cloth, she gasped at the sight of the thin white scars coating his entire back. He would have to have been whipped on countless occasions to have the amount of scarring he did. Margaret gently patted down his back, feeling if she patted too hard, she would hurt the old wounds. She knew it wasn't possible, but she felt the need to be as gentle as she could be.

Margaret stayed with Liam until the healer arrived again with his draughts. Liam had calmed his tossing after Margaret bathed him with the cold water.

The healer looked at Liam critically when he came close. "He looks as though his fever has lessened," —he put his hand to Liam's forehead— "but not by much."

"It calmed him to be bathed with cold cloths."

"Not too cold, my lady," Healer Williamson instructed. "It will do him more harm than good."

"How long will he be ill?" Margaret asked.

"It's hard to say, my lady," he told her quietly. "Anywhere between two to four weeks of sickness, and as much or more to regain his strength."

Margaret nodded solemnly. She knew she could not allow Elizabeth to risk her health trying to care for Liam. Margaret had never had more than a small cough in her life. She was healthy enough to care for Liam without worry.

The healer handed Margaret a wide glass bottle. "There are more of these here, but he should take a spoonful every hour until his fever breaks and then six times a day until his cough stops."

"Thank you," she said as he left.

Elizabeth poked her pale face in the room. "Is there anything I can do?"

"Fresh water," Margaret commanded, giving Liam his first dose of the draught.

Liam coughed, fighting against the liquid slipping down his throat. It would be a very long night ahead of them both.

Margaret struggled to keep her eyes open as the dawn rose. She had barely left Liam's room since he had become bedridden two weeks ago. Liam was sleeping peacefully for the first time since he had fallen ill. She hated to wake him for his medicine and decided she could put it off for another hour. The sleep would do him as much good as the draught at this point.

Margaret left the room to change her clothes and give herself some fresh air. She stood outside in the cold, breathing deeply. The frigid air helped wake her. She was only able to sleep in short bursts between giving Liam his medicine, and she was worn out—she had gotten more rest on the ground during their travels than she had sitting at Liam's bedside.

iam tossed and turned in the hard bed, somewhere between waking and sleeping. He was back in his cell, awaiting his trial. He had just received the news the war had been won by the Anatalians. Liam furrowed his brow—this was wrong. He had already done this. He had been sentenced and escaped. Liam felt himself on double-time as he was grabbed by his arms and taken into the long hall to attend his trial.

He saw the gaggle of courtiers there to attend his trial, the only one in attendance standing out was the woman in a red dress. Her face was hard to make out, but the color of her dress stood out distinctly. Liam felt himself going through the motions of the trial, giving a testimony he could not remember saying. The king stood red-faced and condemned him to death immediately. The courtiers gathered around him, the woman in red standing directly in front of him.

"Hold his head," King Sorren commanded the woman, sliding the sword at his hip out of its scabbard.

There were gentle hands on his cheeks, holding his head firmly in her hands. Liam looked at the woman holding his face. He saw Margaret's heart-shaped face, her dark curls framing her face.

"Margaret," he breathed.

Tears slipped down her cheeks. "I'm sorry, Liam…but you've betrayed our king."

Liam felt the sword hit his neck, and he gasped, waking instantly. He looked at the familiar ceiling, relieved he was not being executed in the courtroom. He felt weak, barely able to turn his head to the side. Liam saw Margaret sitting next to his bed with a burgundy shawl wrapped around her shoulders, a book starting to fall from her hands.

"Margaret?" he asked weakly.

She inhaled deeply as she woke. "You're awake!" Margaret slid onto the bed next to him and felt his forehead.

Liam looked at her confused. "Of course, I'm awake. I only took a nap."

"You've been in and out of consciousness for two weeks, Liam," Margaret told him.

Liam rubbed his face and felt the thick beard attesting to her statement. He tried to sit, struggling until Margaret helped him up. "Is there anything to eat?"

"You can have some broth Elizabeth made." Margaret moved some pillows behind him. "We've barely been able to get anything more than broth and milk with honey down your throat since you went to sleep."

He leaned back against the pillows as Margaret left the room to get his broth. He could hardly believe he had slept for all that time. Margaret sat next to Liam on the bed with a bowl of broth and spooned out a small amount, blowing to cool it. She slipped the spoon easily into his mouth. It was a well-practiced move Liam was sure brought back memories of her father.

"I can feed myself, Margaret," Liam said flatly, irritated he was seen as weak.

"Go right ahead," she said, unruffled, handing him the spoon.

He scooped out his broth and shakily brought it to his mouth. All the contents spilled over the edges before Liam could put the spoon in his mouth. Margaret said nothing and wiped off his chest with a cloth, taking the spoon back and feeding him until the broth was gone.

"I'll call in Aram to help you use the chamber pot, and I will start boiling water for a bath," Margaret said gently, wiping his mouth and chest once more before she left the room.

Aram soon took Margaret's place, helping Liam stand with a grunt. "You'll gain your strength back soon enough," he said when he caught Liam's frustrated look.

"You'll have to thank Beth for taking such good care of me," Liam said.

"It wasn't Beth." Aram helped Liam sit back on the bed. "Margaret refused to let us near you so we would not catch your winter fever."

Liam was amazed—he would have thought Margaret would have avoided him after their last chat. "Margaret took care of me?"

"She barely left this room before this morning when you woke up," Aram informed him.

Margaret returned to the room with a steaming pail of water and an apron tied around her waist. She laid a large cloth down on the floor. "Aram, if you would be so kind as to help Liam stand on the cloth?"

Aram did as he was bid and helped Liam to stand once more. Margaret pulled off everything save his underwear and began to scrub his skin with the hot soapy water. Liam didn't know how Margaret stood the heat. He was barely able to stand it on the small part of his body she was scrubbing. Her hands were cherry red, the suds spilling over her fingers and her exposed forearms.

"You'll burn yourself, Margaret," Liam told her weakly.

"Hush now," she chided, continuing to scrub his skin raw. "You'll feel much better once you're clean again."

Liam remained silent for the rest of her labors, happy to finally be sat back down on the bed. Just standing—assisted, at that—the length of his bath made his legs wobble and shake. It would be quite a long recovery if his strength was so easily taken from him. Liam felt himself drift off to sleep as Margaret patted him dry.

He woke in fresh clothes, and the linens on his bed had been changed while he slept. Margaret must have gotten help from Aram to change him. Liam weakly ran a hand over his face. He felt pathetic having Margaret take care of him so intimately. He saw his door open, and Margaret walked through with a book in hand.

"You're awake." She smiled. "How are you feeling?"

"Exhausted," Liam told her, trying to raise himself on trembling arms.

Margaret put her hand on the center of his chest, her fingers splayed out. She gently pushed him back down, sitting on the edge of the bed. "You need your rest."

"I need to move about," Liam bit back.

Margaret brushed away his attitude. She straightened his shirt before she spoke. "Would you like for me to help you take a stroll?"

Liam frowned at her, a small one that could be seen as pertness rather than anger. "If it is the only way for me to get out of this bed."

Margaret helped him dress in warm clothing, the weather having turned even colder since Liam's confinement. She picked up her shawl and wrapped it tightly around herself. Liam stared at her, seeing not the woman in front of him, but the Margaret from his dreams weeping and holding his face in her hands.

"Are you sure you're feeling well enough to take a turn?"

"Yes," Liam said quietly, still staring at her.

Margaret furrowed her brow at him, taking Liam's arm to help him out of the small home. They slowly made their way into the center of the town, people splitting to avoid their set path.

"I know who you are," Liam told her with a pointed look.

"Of course, you do." Margaret looked at him confused. "I told you who I was last month."

"No," Liam insisted, stopping in front of the bakery. "Who you were at my trial."

Margaret raised a single brow. "There was nothing of import about me at your trial."

"You were the only one in that entire room who didn't look at me with hate or disgust," Liam told her. "Even though your companions did—you were the one in red."

"You have a good memory," Margaret told him, "but I don't know why that was so important to you."

"Because you were the only one who didn't hate me at that moment, Margaret. That was important to me. Why wouldn't you just tell me who you were or how you recognized me?" he asked irritably, leaning against the bakery wall, smelling the warm aroma of freshly baked bread.

"I didn't want to speak to you at the moment," she retorted just as irritably. "My father had just been mortally wounded, I had to flee from my home with an escaped traitor, and you were yelling at me."

Liam scowled at her, pushing himself off the wooden panels. "Let's go back."

Margaret came back to his side and linked arms with him. Liam had caught another glimpse of the spoiled brat she had been on their travels. He didn't know which one was her true self, and which a front to protect herself. Liam liked the caregiver in her much better than the countess. His hackles rose whenever the smallest hint of the countess appeared.

Liam leaned heavily on Margaret as she led him back to the Gollacks' home. She walked slowly for him, idly chattering about the weather and what she thought they should expect. He knew from experience and the frosted smell in the air they would soon have a snowstorm. One he was happy to have a roof over his head for. Liam could feel his strength starting to wane, his eyes drooping.

Margaret led him to his room, starting to undo the strings on his shirt. Liam grabbed her hand firmly in his own. "I can undress myself, Margaret."

"Are you sure?" she asked.

Liam squeezed her hand. "I'm sure."

"I'll make you something to eat, then," she told him, not pulling her hand from his.

"Thank you," he said quietly before letting go of her. He peeled his clothes off after she left the room and sighed contentedly as he slid into the bed. He had barely put his head on the pillow before he fell asleep.

When Liam awoke, Margaret was not in her usual spot in the chair next to his bed. He dressed, rather slowly, and went into the common room of the house. Margaret was reading quietly in the corner chair while Elizabeth mended a few of Aram's shirts. It was a domestic scene if he had ever seen one. He cleared his throat to garner their attention.

Elizabeth looked at him with a delighted smile, standing to greet him. "Liam! It's wonderful to see you walking about on your own."

Liam gave her a halfhearted smile. He was ready to sit even after the short walk from his bedroom to the common room. "It is looking like a speedy recovery in no small thanks to Margaret."

Margaret only smiled, looking at him briefly before lowering her lashes.

Elizabeth led Liam to sit next to Margaret. "She has been a godsend to us."

Margaret blushed prettily. "Surely not, Elizabeth," Margaret said, brushing aside the praise. "I only did what any other person would do."

Elizabeth looked at her incredulously. "No one I know would go for days without sleep to watch over someone who was sick, especially one they barely knew."

Liam gently took Margaret's hand in his and kissed her knuckles. "I can't thank you enough for what you've done for me."

12

argaret left Liam's room after giving him his last dose of the draught Healer Williamson had given them. He had finally stopped coughing, but he was still incredibly weak. She would need to go to the apothecary to get him another draught to restore his energy, much like one she had given her father on the days he could barely lift his head off the pillow.

She found Elizabeth mending one of her day dresses in the common room. "Elizabeth?"

"Yes, dear?" She didn't take her eyes from her work.

"I am going into town to see Healer Williamson," Margaret told her. "I'll be gone for a few hours. Will you check on Liam while I'm out?"

"Of course. Would you like Aram to accompany you?"

"No, he should rest—he hasn't been feeling well. I'll be fine on my own," Margaret assured her, shrugging on her cloak.

"Be careful," Elizabeth called as Margaret walked out the door.

Margaret lifted her hood, looking at the blue-gray clouds obscuring the sun. The air was crisp, dryly pricking her nose, smelling of burning wood. She inhaled deeply, the smoky pine pleasantly caressing her senses. It was a smell she loved. Margaret let out a content sigh, her feet crunching the frosted grass as she walked. It took her less time than usual to reach the town. Margaret suspected it was the cold urging her quickened steps.

"My lady, what is it I can help you with?" one of the healers asked no sooner than Margaret walked in the door.

"Where is Healer Williamson?" Margaret asked, looking around the shop.

Healer Williamson came out from the backroom, setting down his mortar and pestle. "Lady Margaret, has the patient fallen ill again?" Concern wrinkled his forehead.

"No, your draughts have helped him immensely," Margaret said. "I am concerned about his lack of energy. Some days he can barely walk to the common room from his bed without assistance."

"I see." The healer started to rummage through cabinets.

"I would like for you to make a draught with ginseng, roseroot, and holy basil," she instructed.

Healer Williamson looked at her, surprised. "We do not have any ginseng or holy basil—they're too expensive for us to carry."

"Fine, then make one with nettles, roseroot, and peppermint," she commanded.

"As my lady wishes." Healer Williamson bowed his head. "Would you prefer to return home, and I will bring you the doses when I am finished?"

"I will make a visit to the seamstress and return when I am finished to retrieve his treatments," Margaret told him before she left the shop and was hit with the bitter cold. Even the few minutes she was in the apothecary, the temperature had dropped by nearly ten degrees.

Margaret could see a few fat snowflakes starting to lazily drift to the ground, making the sky look more gray than blue. She quickly walked to the other side of the town, politely nodding to the people she passed. Mistress Laphar was throwing a thick mat on the ground in front of her door to prevent any snow from being tracked onto her impeccably clean floor when Margaret approached.

"M'lady," Mistress Laphar's high voice whined. "I was not expectin' to see y' any time soon. Beth said y' were takin' care of a friend."

Margaret smiled pleasantly at her. "I'm waiting for Healer Williamson to finish a new batch of draughts for my friend, and I thought I would stop by and check on your progress."

The seamstress smoothed down her shirts. "Aye, as ye'd like m'lady." She opened the door for Margaret to go through. "We've managed only to finish the house dresses. I wanted to make sure the new girls I hired learned proper work before I set them on the courtly attire."

"I appreciate that, Mistress Laphar." Margaret let out a breath, relieved to be in the warmth of the dressmaker's shop.

"Please, m'lady, call me Susanna," the seamstress told her, pulling out her completed dresses.

Margaret looked at the stitching closely, seeing it was tightly done. "This looks perfect, Susanna," she told her before she moved on to the embroidery on another dress. "Who did the embroidery?"

"I did, m'lady," Susanna said proudly.

"You could see any woman at court wearing this," Margaret praised. "I'll be the envy of all there if all of my dresses are at this caliber."

A wide grin spread across Mistress Laphar's face, the rounded apples of her cheeks coloring red in their strain. "Thank you, m'lady."

"Have you received any of the fabrics yet?"

"Only one." Susanna rushed to the back room to grab the bolt of fabric. She brought it back, laying it on the counter in front of Margaret.

Margaret gasped excitedly when she saw the fabric; it was a midnight blue and silver floral brocade. "Susanna, this is beautiful!"

The dressmaker's eyes were alight with pleasure. "I'm very pleased that y' like it, m'lady."

"I love it," Margaret corrected. "I cannot wait until this one is ready to be fitted!"

"Shall I box up your dresses for you to take home?"

"Yes, if you would."

Margret waited patiently as other customers entered the shop to pick up their items, interrupting Susanna from her task. She didn't mind; she was sure Healer Williamson had not finished making Liam's medicines. She enjoyed watching the seamstress interacting with her other customers, listening to their idle chatter as Susanna retrieved items from the back room. When the last customer left, the seamstress placed a large box held closed by an oversized ribbon in front of Margaret.

"Thank you, Susanna," she said with a smile. "I look forward to seeing what you do next."

"Have a safe journey home," Mistress Laphar told her.

Margaret nodded and returned to the apothecary to check on Healer Williamson's progress. The snow was falling more purposefully now. A gust of wind picked up the flakes, twirling them to music Margaret could not hear. She slipped into the apothecary gratefully, brushing the snow off her shoulders.

"Lady Margaret," Healer Tromedlov, the other man in the building besides Healer Williamson, called out to her. "We are almost done with your order."

Margaret smiled at him. "That is wonderful to hear."

She sat as she waited, watching them work. They were bottling the medicine in glass bottles that could be carried easily in a satchel. Margaret could see from the window the snow was starting to fall harder, sticking to the cold ground.

Healer Williamson went to Margaret with a leather satchel. "Whenever Liam is feeling weak or you notice his energy is low, give him a small spoonful. He should not have more than three doses a week."

Margaret stood and put the bag over her shoulder. "Thank you, for this. I'll come back if we are in need again."

"Hurry home, my lady." Healer Williamson nodded toward the window. "It is starting to snow harder outside."

Margaret turned to look out the window. It was harder to see, but not impossible yet. "Thank you," she said as she pulled her hood up and left the shop.

The cold bit at her cheeks as she walked quickly, the cold air dryly running down her throat, making her cough. She covered her mouth and nose with her free hand in an attempt to keep herself from breathing in the cold, dry air. The snow started falling rapidly at an angle, obscuring whatever landmarks she could use to make her way back to the Gollacks' home.

Margaret looked down at the ground to try to see the beaten path, finding it had been snowed over. It had obviously been snowing longer here than it had been in the town. She looked around, the silence surrounding her deafening. She should have taken Duchess instead of going on foot to save her horse from the cold. Margaret walked forward, hoping that if she kept in a straight line, she would find her way home. The cold bit at her face viciously as the wind blew the snow at her face, making it impossible to see anything through her squinted eyes.

She pulled her hood as far forward as it would go to protect her face. Margaret felt her foot fall into a hole the snow hid. She let out a cry as she fell forward, splayed on the ground, her box of dresses a few feet from her. Margaret heard a crunch and rolled on her side to check the satchel for any damage. Two of the glass bottles had broken in her fall, leaving only six untouched for Liam.

Margaret tried to stand, letting out a curse when her ankle rolled under the pressure and she fell back to the ground.

"Is there anyone out there?" she yelled, the snow muting her bellow to a whisper.

She searched the white-gray void for any hint of another person, finding none. Her hands started to shake from the cold, and she pulled her cloak tightly around her. There was nothing she could do; no one was there to help her.

"Hello?" she yelled, her hope dwindling with the rising wind.

13

Rubbing his hands on his face, Liam lay in his small bed. Exhaustion already weighed on him, even having just woken from a nap. He was glad now he had decided to see Margaret settled before he left—had he been traveling still, he never would have been able to get the care the healer or Margaret gave him.

He still had trouble believing she had taken care of him for so long, even to the detriment of herself. Especially given the circumstances of her arrival here and the part he played in it.

Liam made his way into the common room, finding Aram and Elizabeth by the fire, mending clothes and whittling a walking stick respectively. The only one missing was Margaret. He furrowed his brow, an unfamiliar tightening pulling at his chest. "Where is Margaret?"

"She went into town to see Healer Williamson." Elizabeth looked up from the shirt she was mending. "Sit down—you need to conserve your energy."

"How long has she been gone?" Liam ignored her command to sit. Only yesterday, he'd smelled snow approaching—the last thing he wanted for Margaret to recklessly put herself in danger. He'd caused her enough turmoil on that front. Going to the door and opening it, he found a blizzard blowing full force outside. "You can't see anything out there."

Elizabeth joined him to look at the white out, her frown deepening the lines of her face. "She's been gone a few hours, but she told me she would be away for close to that time. She probably stayed in the town if this started while she was out."

Hesitating, he closed the door. "You're probably right."

"Are you hungry?" Elizabeth asked him as he sat.

"Extremely." He laid his hand on his stomach as it growled, protesting its lack of food.

Liam relaxed next to the fire after his stomach was full. The logs popped lazily, red-hot tendrils waving above the wood. Worry nagged at his stomach since Margaret had still not returned. She could have easily gotten caught in the storm if she had left before it started. Learning from his travels with her, he knew her stubbornness would have kept her going even if she had been caught in a blizzard. Liam looked at the door, expecting it to open any moment.

Elizabeth followed his gaze. "She's fine, Liam. Margaret's a tough girl."

"She should be back by now," Liam protested.

"Margaret more than likely stayed in the town because of the snow." Aram examined his whittled piece of wood to see what he would need to shave off next.

"I'm going to go look for her." Liam stood.

Elizabeth gasped. "You'll make yourself ill again!"

Liam ignored her, putting on winter clothes to search for Margaret. He knew she was out there. He could feel it. She had probably gotten lost and couldn't find her way back. Liam would need to find her before she froze.

"Margaret?" he yelled out, the snow dampening his cry.

The snow was deeper than Liam expected for the few hours it had been blizzardy. He grabbed one of the many walking sticks Aram had made, sweeping aside a small path that would not easily be filled by the time he returned. He slowly made his way toward the town, calling out to Margaret every few moments.

His lungs burned as he breathed heavily. This was too much for him, but he couldn't let her stay out there. He couldn't be the reason the Doremis line ended. He had to find her.

About halfway to the town, Liam saw a mound in the snow.

"Margaret?" he called, hoping it was only a small boulder along the road.

"Liam?" came her sleepy reply.

He went to the miniature hill, finding Margaret just past it. She was covered with a light layer of snow. "Margaret!"

Her lips were starting to chap in the cold, blued only slightly, her cheeks nearly as pale as the snow around her. Margaret barely opened her eyes to look at him. "Liam, you should be in bed resting," she protested.

Liam bent and pulled her up to him. "We need to get you back to the Gollacks'."

Margaret weightlessly crumbled against him, groaning. "I can't walk," she told him. "I fell."

He picked her up, stumbling slightly from the unfamiliar weight. His shoulders strained, his arms wanting to collapse. He was still too weak from his sickness for this—he should have insisted Aram come with him. Grunting, Liam straightened his back and pulled her tightly to him.

"My dresses!" Margaret tried to reach for them, nearly slipping from Liam's arms. "They'll be ruined if they're left!"

Liam grunted, pulling her closer to him so he wouldn't drop her when he set her down. "Where are they?"

She plunged her hand into the lump of snow, pulling out a box. Margaret held it to her protectively, her eyes drooping.

Liam gathered her in his arms once more, slowly trudging back toward the Gollacks' home. The path he had made was starting to fill with snow quicker than he anticipated. His back strained, unused to the weight. His energy was a mere wisp. If he didn't make it back soon, it would snuff out. Liam's lungs burned, his legs moving slower with each step. Margaret rested her head on his shoulder, burying her face in his neck.

Liam was happy when the house came back into sight. He burst through the door, almost dropping Margaret when he did so.

"Liam!" Aram jumped in surprise before he went to him.

"She needs blankets and hot tea," Liam told them, taking her in front of the fire.

Elizabeth took the box from Margaret's hands before she went to the kitchen.

Liam knelt in front of the fireplace. "More wood for the fire," he commanded, pulling Margaret's cloak off of her.

He rubbed her arms quickly to try to warm her as Aram left to get the logs. Margaret was still shivering in his arms, her teeth chattering. Liam found her skirts were cold and wet; he struggled with whether or not he should be the one to remove them. He waited impatiently for Elizabeth to reappear as she gathered as many blankets as she could find. It took longer than he would have liked, and he started to unlace her skirts and petticoats, shoving them off her shivering body.

"I'm s-so c-cold." Margaret shivered against him, too cold to protest his actions.

"Where are those blankets?" he yelled to Elizabeth, holding Margaret close to him to try and warm her.

Elizabeth came rushing into the room, stopping short when she saw Margaret only in her shift. "Liam!"

"Her clothes were soaking wet and freezing," he defended himself, wrapping Margaret tightly in the blankets.

Liam held her close to him, rubbing her blanketed form. He scooted as close to the fire as he could, hoping she would warm quickly. Margaret slowly stopped shivering as she cuddled against him. He brushed her hair back as she fell asleep on his lap.

Aram returned, raising his eyebrows at the scene in front of him. He said nothing as he added more wood to the fire, returning to where he had been whittling.

Elizabeth brought in the heated pot for tea. Seeing Margaret was already asleep, she put it next to the fire to keep it warm until she woke. Elizabeth sat close to Liam to keep her eye on him, looking at them disapprovingly.

He glared back. He didn't care as long as Margaret was safe.

14

argaret woke with arms tightly wrapped around her, much warmer than when she last remembered being conscious. She swallowed hard, grimacing—her throat was raw. She squinted against the light of the fire; she was no longer in the snow, and she was not sure when she had been moved. Margaret looked up to find Liam with his head lolled to the side, mouth agape as he slept.

She tried to move as delicately as she could. Liam inhaled deeply, his arms constricting around her in his drowsy state.

Her cheeks colored brightly. "Liam?"

Liam looked down at her sleepily. "You're finally awake." He loosened his grip on her.

"When did I get here?"

"A few hours ago." Liam adjusted the blankets that fell off her shoulder. "You were caught in the blizzard. Do you remember what happened?"

"I was walking back when the blizzard started getting worse, and I was too close to turn back," Margaret said hoarsely, looking around for Aram and Elizabeth. "Then I tripped in a hole and twisted my ankle and couldn't walk. I kept yelling for help, and no one would come…eventually I just lay down to wait."

Elizabeth came into the room, teacup in hand. "Margaret, how are you feeling?"

"Tired, but warm," she said with a smile.

"You're lucky our Liam insisted on going out to find you." Elizabeth pulled the tea off the fire. "We told him that you would have stayed in the town, but he insisted on searching for you."

Margaret turned on him with wide eyes. "You could have made yourself sick!"

"And you could have died," Liam countered, tucking hair behind her ear. "I'd much rather be sick than to see you buried."

Her heart fluttered briefly at the look he gave her. She hadn't had anyone gaze at her like that in a long time. Margaret turned her head to hide from his stare, but she could still feel it blanketing her.

"Why don't we get you dressed dear?" Elizabeth asked as she poured the tea to steep.

"Dressed?" Margaret asked, her eyes wide with surprise.

"I, um…" Liam's face reddened as he coughed. "I took off your wet clothes to warm you quickly."

Margaret's blush was not satisfied to stay on her cheeks, spreading down her neck to her chest. "You undressed me?"

"Beth was taking too long," Liam tried to defend himself. "And I did not want you to get any worse than you already were."

Margaret tensed. Even with the blankets between them, she felt uncomfortable so close to him with so little clothing. "I would like it if I could put dry clothes on."

Liam moved her from his lap and stood before picking her up again, taking her to her room. She automatically wrapped her arms around his neck for stability, the blanket falling from her shoulders. Margaret was amazed at the strength he had, even being weakened by his illness. She assumed it was the adrenaline fueling his ability to lift her like a child.

"Would you like me to stay to help you stand?" Liam asked, his cheeks still stained red.

"I think she will be fine without you," Elizabeth told him sternly.

"I will be fine," Margaret assured him. She smiled, placing a hand on his chest. She nearly snatched it away when he tightened his grip on her, his heart thudding against her palm.

Elizabeth put her hands on her hips. "You can put her down now, Liam."

Liam set Margaret down carefully, holding her at arm's length until she was settled firmly. He looked between the two women. "Call me if you need my help."

"Thank you, Liam," Margaret said quietly, pulling the blankets tightly around her, watching him carefully as he walked away. She shivered when he closed the door. It was as though he took the heat with him when he left.

Margaret sat with her foot wrapped in bandages propped on a pillow, an embroidery hoop in hand. Elizabeth had not allowed Margaret on her feet since Liam had rescued her from the blizzard. She looked down at her handiwork, a small frown on her face. It was sloppy work; embroidery was not a talent she possessed, no matter how hard her mother tried to correct her skill. The vines were lopsided, and her stitching was inconsistent in width and spacing. Margaret knew the end product would not turn out as well as she intended.

"My dear, would you like a cup of tea?" Elizabeth came into the room, a small smile on her face and two cups in her hands.

Margaret gratefully put down the hoop with the stretched fabric. "Yes, please." She took the offered cup.

"How is your ankle feeling?" Elizabeth sat across from her, sipping her tea.

Margaret tentatively stretched out her foot to test the sprain. "Better than before. How is Liam feeling? I've barely seen him the last few days."

Liam had been avoiding her since finding her in the blizzard three days prior. He had been overly protective of her, and once he had deposited her in her room, he had barely been able to look at her. Margaret wasn't sure what to make of his behavior. Perhaps he had felt the same heat she had and wanted to let it cool.

"He's feeling fine," Elizabeth assured her, taking another sip of her tea. "He and Aram took a trip into town to get more of the energy draught for himself and a salve for your ankle."

Margaret smiled. "That was kind of them."

"May I see what you're doing?" Elizabeth nodded toward the embroidery hoop.

Margaret handed over the work, embarrassment flaring in her cheeks.

Elizabeth forced a smile to her face. "It's nice, dear."

"It's horrible," Margaret corrected.

"It's horrible," Elizabeth agreed with a relieved laugh.

Margaret was no stranger to the fact she could not sew in a straight line, much less a pattern to look pretty enough for a pillow as many of the other noble ladies made. She certainly would not have fit in with the queen's ladies in waiting as she had once hoped. There was nothing the queen loved more than her embroidery and going to church services.

Margaret looked down at the nearly opaque liquid in her cup, her lips pursed in a frown. Her thoughts were just starting to wander toward the awkwardness setting between Liam and herself when the men returned. Liam looked to be breathing harder than he should be for a short walk.

Elizabeth stood to greet them, smiling. "Was your trip successful?"

Aram gently kissed Elizabeth on the cheek. "It was, my dear. We were able to procure both items without issue."

Margaret smiled at the shared tenderness, averting her eyes for their privacy. She caught Liam looking her over, her cheeks warming. Margaret dropped her eyes demurely with her chin dipped subtly to the left.

"Healer Williamson sends his regards, Margaret," Aram said as he emptied out the contents of their satchel.

Liam grabbed a jar from Aram, going to Margaret and lifting her foot into his lap.

Margaret quickly grabbed her stretched hoop, turning it over to hide her sloppy work. She would have been embarrassed for him to see it.

"What are you doing?" she asked when he unwrapped her foot.

He lifted the lid off the clay jar, revealing the white cream. Liam scooped a glob of the cream out with one of his fingers. "Putting the salve on your ankle, Margaret." He rubbed it into her skin with firm hands.

"That isn't necessary, Liam. I can do it." Margaret pulled her foot away.

He grabbed her ankle firmly, pulling her foot back into his lap. "You've taken care of me, Margaret. Let me take care of you."

She lowered her eyes, unable to look at him during his ministrations, allowing him to rub the salve into her skin. "How often is this to be done?"

"Whenever your ankle hurts." Liam moved from her ankle to her foot.

Margaret looked Liam over thoroughly. He was a fine-looking man, there was no doubt of that. She had seen the muscles he had hidden under his shirt when she bathed him in his sickness. There was a far leap from physical attraction to feelings, however. She smiled at him when he looked up at her, her heart fluttering when he returned it with his dimpled one.

In another life, Margaret could have easily let herself fall in love with someone such as Liam. Had she been the woman she pretended to be in the country, he would have made a perfect husband for her. Liam was a protector and a hard worker, someone suited toward that kind of woman. That woman would give him a brood of children and live far out in the country, knowing nothing of the treachery of court life. But she was not that kind of woman, not truly.

On the other hand, if the Triburns had not lost the throne, Liam would be the crown prince of Anatalia, and she would have been at court, fawning over him with the rest of the young noblewomen. Her mother would have tried to arrange a marriage, and Margaret would have happily supported the match between the two to become the Queen of Anatalia. Unfortunately for him—and for her—the Triburns had been culled to near extinction.

It was not as though she did not wish she could have those feelings in their current situation, but she knew it was impossible. They were not a match made for making.

"Liam?" She should try to tell him of his heritage now that he was in a better mood. "I—" She stopped when Aram and Elizabeth came into the room, sitting across from them. She didn't want them to muddle the information—she didn't know if Liam would believe her in the first place, but adding the older couple into the conversation might turn it into something entirely different.

"Yes?" Liam looked up at her, grabbing the bandage to wrap around her ankle.

"Thank you, Liam," she said quietly when his ministrations were finished. "This was very nice of you."

Liam nodded to her, his eyes starting to droop. There were dark circles under his eyes that had been there for weeks now.

"Why don't you lie down?" Margaret asked. "You look as though you could use the rest."

"I can wake you for dinner," Elizabeth assured him. "Get some rest."

15

Liam paced restlessly in the common room. He needed to leave.

He was putting them all in danger.

Liam could do nothing but bring ruin and destruction to their lives if he stayed much longer.

He had already been at the Gollacks' for over a month, much longer than he had anticipated staying.

Liam needed to leave. Immediately.

His mind raced in every direction as he started to gather his things in his satchel.

"What are you doing, Liam?"

Liam turned to find Margaret staring at him in confusion, a small plate of sweets in her hand.

"I need to leave," he told her anxiously.

Margaret immediately scrunched her face, looking at the closed-up windows letting in a sporadic flake of snow. "You can't leave. You'll get sick again, and I won't be there to nurse you back to health."

"I can't stay here," Liam protested, "I can't bring trouble to Aram and Elizabeth's door."

Liam didn't miss the slight hardening of Margaret's mouth. She set down the plate to stand in front of him. "The soldiers won't patrol in an active snowstorm, and it's been snowing for almost a week now. Stay for the winter to regain your health."

"I don't have the luxury of staying in one place for long, Margaret." He put the satchel over his shoulder, heading for the door.

"So you would leave without even saying goodbye to Aram and Elizabeth?" Margaret demanded. "To me? You would disappear without a word for us to worry over?"

"Well, no." Liam fumbled for an explanation. "That isn't what—"

"That's exactly what you were going to do," she interrupted irritably.

"Why are you so cross?"

"Because I don't want you to leave and kill yourself." Margaret's lips stretched to a flat line as her brow furrowed.

"You don't want me to leave?" Liam raised his brows.

"I don't want you to kill yourself by leaving while you're unhealthy," Margaret retorted, crossing her arms over her chest.

"You, along with Aram and Elizabeth, are in danger as long as I'm near you," Liam reminded her.

"We'll be safe through winter, Liam. The soldiers won't come for you here."

"Then I'll stay for you," Liam told her, removing his satchel.

"You shouldn't be staying just for me," Margaret said. "You should be staying for your own health and safety. You'd be staying for Aram and Elizabeth—they love having you here."

Liam sighed. He loved being there with them too, but it was always risky to stay too long. Despite the hard set of her mouth, when he looked at Margaret, her eyes held worry. His shoulders drooped, his resolve melting. "I'll stay."

Margaret's eyes lit, a small smile starting to form. "Through the winter?"

"Through the winter." He sighed again, but the smile she gave him made him hope it would be worth it.

Liam watched Margaret from the corner of his eye. It has been snowing on and off for another week—if it snowed for much longer, they wouldn't be able to get out of the house. Margaret sighed, picking at the thread on her embroidery. She tossed it to the side, crossing her arms.

Liam raised his browns at her, his mouth twisting.

She blushed when she realized he watched her. "I'm bored," she confessed. "There's only so much of this" —she waved her hand at the hoop— "you can do before you go mad."

"We could always do something together," Liam suggested.

Margaret looked at him expectantly.

He quelled now that the pressure was on him to name something. He hadn't thought it through before he offered to entertain her. "Have you ever had syrup taffy?"

She shook her head. "What is it?"

"You burrow out bits of snow and fill the hole with syrup and let it freeze, and then you eat it," Liam said.

Her expression looked more dubious than he'd seen it before. "And this is supposed to be…fun?"

Liam cleared his throat. Not when she said it like that. "You're supposed to do other things while you let them freeze."

She smirked as he squirmed under her gaze. "Such as?"

Now she was being deliberately obtuse. If she kept it up, he would make it as awkward for her as she was for him. "Anything you want—a meal, a snow fight, other things. I've heard plenty of things people do while they wait."

Her cheeks colored at the implication. Aram and Elizabeth were taking their afternoon nap—they could easily do *other things* if they wanted. He cleared his throat and pulled himself from that line of thinking by standing. "Come on—I know where Beth hides the good syrup."

"Will she be upset we've used it?" Margaret wet her lips as she stood, looking back toward the older couple's bedroom.

"She'd insist." He dug through the cupboard until he found it. "Grab your cloak—it'll be too cold without it."

She came into the kitchen with her cloak tied tightly around her, his cloak in hand. "Here," she said, holding her hand out for the syrup. "We don't want you to get sick again just as you've gotten better."

He put on his cloak without protest, watching her as he did. He liked watching her. She blushed, looking away from him. He couldn't understand her exactly—she liked having the attention on her most of the time, but in more intimate moments, she shied away from it.

"Let's go out this way—the snow has built up more in the front than the side and you won't have to step in it as much."

Liam led her through the kitchen door and to the snow drift near the front. His breath clouded around him in a white mist. He used the tip of his pinky finger to bore five small holes into the snow. "It shouldn't take more than fifteen minutes to freeze."

"Just enough time to feed Duchess and Ashka," Margaret commented.

"I fed them earlier," Liam said, "but I'm sure Duchess would like to see you."

Liam led her through the path of snow he'd shoveled out to get the horses that morning. He closed the door quickly behind them to keep the warm air in. He stoked the fire on the far end of the stable to bring it back to life—with only two beasts, they wouldn't stay warm enough alone.

Duchess whickered at Margaret, nosing her over her head and face. Ashka pawed at the floor, and he went to pat him on the neck. Liam was pleased he'd won him over.

"Margaret," he said quietly.

"Yes?" She turned to him, and Duchess pulled her back for scratches by hooking her head over Margaret's shoulder. She laughed, rubbing the horse's neck.

"Are you doing all right here?" It was something he had worried over, but had been too scared to ask.

Her face fell, and she inhaled deeply. "I think so. The Gollacks are lovely people, and I'm going to relish my time here, but I wish I had been able to go to my home and figure things out there." She stroked Duchess's neck as she paused. "The roads won't be passable until spring at least—especially not with what I'll need."

"I did the best I could," Liam said, "especially since you wouldn't tell me who you were."

Margaret nodded. "I know, and I've stopped being mad at you about it."

That was a relief.

"But I'll still be leaving in the spring" —she lifted her chin— "whether you like it or not."

Liam frowned. He didn't like it, that was for certain. He hoped she would change her mind before he had to leave—he knew without a doubt that if she left, something would happen to her he couldn't protect her from.

Margaret gave Duchess another pat. "Should we check the syrup taffy?"

"We should," Liam agreed. He rubbed Ashka's nose before opening the door for Margaret.

She smiled at him as she passed, and his chest warmed. Maybe he could convince her to come with him instead—it wouldn't be the life she deserved, but he could keep her safe. He was sure of it.

Upon inspection, the syrup had become tacky. He grabbed two out, handing one to Margaret. "You're going to love this." He popped his in his mouth and watched as she ate, her eyes lighting.

"It's so good!" She snatched the next two, handing one to Liam.

"I told you you'd love it," he said before eating the next.

"There's only one left," Margaret said as she eyed the treat.

"I'll fight you for it."

"You'll fight me for it?" Margaret laughed. "What's it going to come to, fisticuffs?"

Liam grabbed a fistful of snow. "Not quite." He threw it at her, missing her by a few inches.

She screamed, grabbing her own fistful of snow. She threw it, hitting him square in the chest. Margaret let out a whoop, lifting her hands in the air.

Grinning, he brushed the snow away. "You're going to get it now." He grabbed an overflowing handful of snow, throwing it at her.

She screamed again when the snow hit her, erupting into laughter soon after. Liam pulled her against him, one arm constricting around her middle. Her laughter died as she stared up at him with wide eyes, her lips parted.

He leaned toward her—would she let him?

Aram cleared his throat gruffly.

Liam pulled away while Margaret gasped, loosening his grip on her. He didn't let go of her entirely, looking to Aram.

The older man crossed his arms over his chest, raising his brows disapprovingly.

Liam looked back to Margaret. Her face flamed scarlet, and she avoided looking at Aram. He let out a slow breath and picked up her hand. Liam waited until she looked at him to kiss her knuckles.

"You can have the last one," he said, finally letting go of her.

16

ram stood close to Elizabeth, his eyes on Margaret and Liam in the common room. They were seated closely, Margaret quietly reading to Liam as had become their custom before everyone retired for the evening.

"I don't know if I like the way he behaves with our girl," Aram murmured quietly to his wife.

Elizabeth's eyebrows leaped up her forehead. "'Our girl'?"

Pink bloomed on Aram's cheeks. "Well," he stammered, "she's our responsibility at the moment."

Elizabeth gave him a knowing look, pouring water over the tea leaves to steep. She looked to the common room, where Liam leaned in closer to Margaret to examine a word on the page neither one of them could make out.

"He's smitten with her," Aram huffed. "Far more than she is with him."

"It's not our place to say anything, dear," Elizabeth reminded him.

Aram crossed his arms over his chest. "That boy is going to give her the wrong idea."

"And what idea would that be?" Elizabeth tried and failed not to look amused at Aram's indignant huffing.

"That they could get comfortable with each other without consequences," Aram whispered intently in her ear, his eyes still on Liam. "He's had his eyes all over her since he brought her here. I caught them almost kissing outside the other day—it won't be long before it becomes more than that."

Elizabeth poured milk into her tea and stirred silently.

"Well?" Aram demanded.

"What do you want me to say? That you should tell him to stop *looking* at her?" Elizabeth asked tersely. "They are young. They are attractive. We were that, once. Don't you remember what it was like?"

"Well, yes," —he could clearly remember catting around until he met his wife— "but it's inappropriate."

Elizabeth sighed heavily at him. "He never touches her without her permission. The only person he's making uncomfortable here is you."

Aram sputtered after her as Elizabeth joined Liam and Margaret in the common room.

17

argaret sat at the table across from Elizabeth. There was a pile of wheat grain next to her and a large mortar and pestle in front. Their hand-crank mill was broken, so their only choice was to grind flour by hand if they wanted bread. Elizabeth was threshing the grains, setting the stalks aside to stuff into a new pillow. They could not winnow the piles of wheat grain indoors in the winter, leaving Margaret to pick out the edible grains to add to her growing pile to be ground for flour.

Elizabeth brushed the chaff to the floor before she grabbed a new stalk to knock loose the grains to begin again.

Margaret hunched her shoulders forward to stretch her back. The work was tedious, but there was no getting around doing it. She started to pile some of the grains in the mortar, looking up when Elizabeth stopped her.

"We still need to put them through a sieve," the older woman told her.

Margaret looked confused. This was her first time making flour, having always bought flour from the locals of Silvica. "I don't understand."

"It's to get rid of any remaining chaff or debris we missed," Elizabeth told her, coming to her side of the table. She swept the piles on the table into a meshed box, small bits of debris already falling through the bottom of it.

Margaret dumped what she had put in the mortar atop the rest of the grains as Elizabeth began to beat the sides of the box, spraying more debris on the floor. The round, hard grains started to gather in the center as the older woman beat the sides of the sieve.

Elizabeth put some of the filtered grains into the mortar for Margaret, spreading them evenly around the pitted stone surface.

"When you start to grind the kernels down, don't try to pulverize it into oblivion. We'll run it through a finer sieve to get rid of the shell," the older woman instructed. "We can sell that as feed."

Margaret held the pestle firmly in hand and struck the grains roughly, breaking them open. She could see a small amount of white pooling out at the bottom. She found the harder she hit, the more the berries bounced out of the mortar. Frustration started to bubble as she had to continually try to keep them in the stone bowl, eventually covering half with her hand while the other smashed with the rounded stone club.

"Try and keep the bran as large as possible dear." Elizabeth brought over a finer sieve and a small bowl. "You can get rough with it later."

"Yes, Elizabeth." Margaret dumped her product into the container and scooped more of the wheat berries into the mortar.

Her hand was already aching and her flour, if one could even call it that, was crystalline and gritty, mixed with small flakes of the bran. It was nowhere close to the final product; there would be several more rounds of being ground before it could be used for baking. Margaret broke all the grains to Elizabeth's satisfaction, and the older woman collected the large flakes of bran into a sack.

Margaret ground the sand-like grains to a fine powder, finding if she circled the mortar with the pestle, it made her work easier. It made the meaty muscle under her thumb burn the longer she ground, her forearm tiring from the work. Margaret stood to put more force into her ministrations, her shoulders and back straining with the constant motion.

As rewarding as she was sure the end result would be, Margaret would be more than happy to pay another to do the work for her. It was a laborious task she did not enjoy performing.

"Why don't we take a break?" Margaret asked, noticing that one jar Elizabeth brought in while she had been working was filled to the brim with flour.

"I'll make us a bit of lunch." Elizabeth dug around in their provisions.

"Where are Aram and Liam?"

Margaret had barely noticed in their labors that the two men had not appeared once.

"They are chopping wood to store for the rest of winter," Elizabeth told her. "Aram did not store enough to last us as long as we thought, and Liam offered to help."

Margaret nodded as she put a small pot into the lit fire to boil the water. She took two mugs of beer and set them outside with a square of cloth over to the top to chill. She could hear the grunting and the quick thwack of the wood splitting as the men swung their axes. Margaret returned to Elizabeth, hearing the hiss of the water boiling over the side of the iron pot.

She grabbed it quickly with her bundled apron and let it cool a moment before pouring the steaming water into tea cups filled with tea leaves.

"I'll be back in a moment." Margaret spirited away to the mugs she had set outside.

She felt the outside of the cup and saw her fingers came away with condensation. Margaret slicked away the moisture on the sides of the cups before she brought them to the two men working behind the home. Despite the cold, neither one of them were wearing a coat, their foreheads beaded with sweat. Margaret smiled at them both with genuine happiness.

"Margaret, my dear." Aram looked surprised at her appearance. "What are you doing out here?"

She held up the beer. "I thought you and Liam could use some refreshment."

Liam hesitated, ax still in hand. Only a few logs were left in the split pile.

She could feel the indecision rolling off both men. Their task was much closer to completion than hers and Elizabeth's. Margaret raised her eyebrows with a smile, suggestively raising the mugs higher until both men took their beer.

Aram drank fully, letting out a sharp, growling breath of air when he was finished. "That's refreshing."

Liam drank his more slowly, watching Margaret over the rim of his cup. Her breath caught in her throat—she couldn't help but think back to when he had almost kissed her. Did she want him to? She wasn't sure.

She smiled at him, waiting patiently for them to finish so she could return to her work. Her cheeks were starting to pinken from the cold. Margaret, like Liam and Aram, had not worn a coat for such a short trip. The tiny, pebbling skin of gooseflesh began to rise on her arms.

"You should go back inside where it's warm," Liam told her.

"I can wait," Margaret protested.

"Go inside, dear." Aram handed her his cup and gently pushed her in the direction of the door.

Margaret hesitated a moment before she returned to Elizabeth.

Margaret leaned back in her chair, her shoulders tight. She rubbed the palm of her hand, the muscle under her thumb still burning with the effort of grinding the grain to powder. Her eyes were closed, Elizabeth clanging in the background.

"Not used to grinding, are you?" Elizabeth asked, amused.

"This is a first," Margaret told her.

Her arms would be tender tomorrow, unused to the exertion. At least, not for so long a period. She and Elizabeth alternated grinding the wheat for nearly seven hours. Margaret felt gentle, prodding fingers on her shoulders to help loosen the muscle.

"You're just as tired, you don't have to do that, Elizabeth," Margaret commented, her eyes still closed.

The fingers dug deeper into the sore flesh. Margaret to let out a contented sigh. It was relaxing after a day's work.

"She isn't," Liam said.

Margaret's eyes shot open, a small squeak escaping her lips. "What are you doing?"

Liam looked at her confused. "Rubbing your shoulders…?"

Margaret grabbed her shawl off a hook on the wall, wrapping it tightly around her. "How are you feeling after working? Regaining your strength well enough?"

"Well enough." Liam looked her over. "Though I think I should try to rest before supper."

Margaret nodded, still feeling the pressure from his massaging fingers on her shoulders.

Liam walked next to Margaret as they entered Marbon proper, occasionally glancing to the side to look at her. They had already spent part of Nomonat and almost all of Demonat with the Gollacks, the latter month producing more snow than the southern part of Anatalia was accustomed to. They would be celebrating the coming of the New Year and the start of Jamonat that evening, Margaret volunteering to cook the feast on her own.

Her eyes were bright with excitement as she looked at the vendors still selling wares for others preparing their dinners for Jamonat. Margaret began to fill her basket with carrots, peas, potatoes, and other produce. She paid, happily chatting away with one of the farmer's wives. Once all inquiries over family and health were made, they moved on to the next vendor.

"We need a chicken," Margaret said suddenly, as if she had just remembered.

Liam led her to a coop, raising an eyebrow when she stopped abruptly. "Is something the matter?"

"I've never picked a chicken before," she admitted quietly.

"It's not hard. You point at one, say you want it, then pay and you leave."

Margaret scrunched up her face, still hesitant.

"Where do you think your meat came from, Margaret?" Liam asked, his brows raised.

Her lips pouted out, an indignant look coming to her face. "It was always dead by the time it arrived for me to cook. I would pay one of the villagers to bring it to me in Silvica."

Liam sighed, leading her closer to the coop.

The chickens were clucking at each other, wings flapping wildly when one was snatched away for someone's supper. Margaret grew queasy at the distressed squawks of the hen that had been taken. She let out a small gasp when they heard the cleaver that took off the hen's head hit the wood with a resounding thump.

Margaret retreated from the chicken coop as another was taken away. "We can come back at the end of our errands to pick a hen."

"Would you like me to pick one for you?" Liam's brows were still raised, an amused smirk twisting his lips awry.

"I don't think I could consign one to death," Margaret admitted, avoiding looking at the coop. "The poor thing not knowing what is about to befall it."

"I'll be back in a moment."

"Liam?" Margaret called after his retreating form.

"Yes?" He turned only slightly.

She smiled as she held her hands wide. "A big, fat one."

By the time Liam and Margaret left the town, his arms were full of wares and Margaret held the chicken in the crook of her arm, cooing at the bird as if it were a child.

Margaret opened the door for Liam with her free hand, following after him. Elizabeth sat next to the fire, warming her fingers around a ceramic cup full of tea. There was a familiar crinkling of her eyes when she looked at Margaret and Liam, a happy smile coming to her face.

"Back so soon?"

"Yes," Margaret said, and then to Liam, "would you put those on the table?"

Liam nodded, doing as he was bid.

"What will be having, dear?" Elizabeth asked, taking a sip from her cup.

"Aram's favorite—chicken pie." Margaret pulled the chicken forward, much to the creature's dismay as it tried to flap its wings to flee.

"My goodness!" Elizabeth gasped, holding out her hands to examine the bird. "Look at how fat it is!"

Margaret smiled proudly, handing it to her. "Liam picked it out. I still need to kill—"

There was a squawk as Elizabeth grabbed its neck and twisted it, and then the chicken was dead.

Margaret let out a small gasp, looking at the dead bird in horror. "I…should get started on the pie."

She grabbed the bird and stiffly walked into the other room, trying to keep her pace set so she did not flee. Tears in her eyes, she nearly ran into Liam.

"What's wrong?" He grabbed her by her arms.

"The chicken is dead," she said thickly.

Liam let out a small laugh. "What did you expect, Margaret?"

"I don't know," she said lamely. "I've never seen an animal killed before."

Liam snorted, taking the dead thing from her arms, and grabbed her hands. "It's either them or us, Margaret. We have to eat." He wiped the tears that fell on her cheeks.

"I'm aware of that," Margaret snapped, her cheeks heating with embarrassment.

"I'll get you a fire started," Liam said, brushing off her annoyance.

argaret had refused to allow Elizabeth to help her with any of the preparations or cooking, telling the older woman it was her gift for the New Year. She was basting the chicken pie with butter before turning it for the crust to cook evenly when a thought occurred to Liam.

He had gotten so used to having Margaret around that he would miss her. It would be the first time he had missed someone besides his parents and the Gollacks in a long while.

"Margaret?"

"Hmm?" Margaret turned, picking up her wine she had purchased in town for the evening.

He looked over her face, cheeks warmed not only by the fire but by drink. "I would like to ask you something."

"You know that you can ask anything," Margaret said when he hesitated.

Liam swallowed, a sheen coming to his forehead as sweat started to gather. "Why Silvica?" he asked lamely, losing his nerve for his original question.

Margaret looked at him perplexed, a single eyebrow raised. "Pardon?"

"If you have all of Dorcia to reside in," —Liam thought quickly, not knowing where he was going with his line of questioning— "why settle in Silvica?"

"Silvica was where my father was born." Margaret shrugged. "I thought he would be more comfortable there in the end."

"Ahh." Liam poured himself a mug of beer, drinking it down in large gulps.

Margaret gave him a half smile, a single lighthearted grunt escaping her mouth. "You seem nervous," she told him.

"Anxious to leave, I suppose." He took another large gulp before filling his mug again.

"You know you'll be safe in the winter from soldiers," Margaret reminded him, her face falling at the mention of his leaving. "And you said that you would stay through winter."

Liam took encouragement from the subtle change on her face. "Winter will soon be over. I can't stay here with you forever." He ran his hand over his face. "Besides, you heard about the skirmish up north that brought soldiers to the border. I don't want to risk being here if they come down."

"There's still two months left of it." Margaret frowned at him. "You can think about that later."

Another large gulp was taken. "Would you—" His gut clenched, quickly changing his mind again. "Would you consider traveling back to Dorcia instead of going to the king?"

"I must go to the capital, Liam, no matter how dangerous it is," Margaret said. "I need to ensure my lands are not taken from me."

Liam drained his cup for the second time, his cheeks warmed from the alcohol. He grabbed her hand in his before he lost his courage a third time. "Why not come with me? I can keep you safe, and you will have no need to worry about the dangers that await you in the king's company."

Margaret's fingers curled tightly around his. "Liam…"

"I can keep you safe if you come with me," he told her hastily. "I cannot follow you to the capital."

She let go of his warm hand, putting hers in her lap, a look of regret on her face. "I can't go with you, Liam."

Liam watched the look on her face deepen as silence fell between them. Was it a look of regret for disappointing him, or for wanting to go but not being able? He didn't know, but he still had all of Jamonat and possibly Femonat to change her mind.

Liam would let it lie for now, but he would not give up.

19

Margaret went into Marbon proper with Elizabeth to see Susanna Laphar for dress fittings. With the snow, it had been nearly two months since Margaret had been able to visit the seamstress. The ground yielded easily beneath their feet as they walked the damp earth. Their journey was silent, contradictory to their usual unreserved conversations as they made the twenty-minute walk to the town.

"Is something the matter, Margaret?"

Margaret inhaled sharply, waking from her thoughts. "Hmm?"

"Are you all right, dear?"

Margaret smiled at her. "Yes, thank you."

She fell back into her distracted silence, her mouth turning to a subtle frown.

Susanna was with a customer when they entered the shop. Margaret brightened at sight of the fabrics on the dress forms throughout the large room. The majority of them were styles too grandiose for any Marbonite to wear.

"M'lady Margaret!" Mistress Laphar called excitedly once her customer had left.

Margaret smiled. "Mistress Laphar, I'm sorry I haven't had the chance to come here more often."

Susanna waved away her apology with the flick of her wrist. "The snow keeps us all at home, m'lady."

"Quite right," Elizabeth agreed, coming away from the sewing mannequins.

"Were you able to get any of the fabrics in from Jalmar?" Margaret asked, looking around at the partially completed dresses.

"The snow has kept those away, too, m'lady." Susanna frowned at her admission. "Only a few were able to sneak through between snows."

Margaret's shoulders drooped. "So production will be delayed."

"Unfortunately, yes, m'lady," the seamstress told her. "Let's get you fitted in the dresses we do have, though."

"Of course." Margaret followed one of the girls to the back room.

"So, m'lady," Susanna said with pins between her teeth, "has your gentleman friend recovered?"

Elizabeth looked at Susanna sharply. "Gentleman friend?"

"She means Liam, Elizabeth," Margaret said. "I came here while I was waiting for Healer Williamson to make his draughts."

Elizabeth's pinched face relaxed as she was mollified. "He's recovered nicely and should be on his way by the end of Femonat and resume his travels."

Margaret turned her head to the side, examining herself in the tall looking glass. She smoothed the cool navy silk gathered at her hips. There were pins still sticking into various parts of the skirt and bodice to keep the silk in place.

"He asked me to go with him, you know," Margaret said casually.

"He what?" Elizabeth squawked.

Margaret nodded. "I told him no, of course," she said, keeping her casual tone.

"Why would he ask you to go with him?"

"He claims for protection." Margaret pressed her lips together tightly. Her brows furrowed as doubt built in her. He had been different toward her ever since he rescued her from the blizzard.

Elizabeth looked at Susanna briefly before turning back to Margaret. "Perhaps we should speak about this at home."

Margaret nodded, remaining silent until she was spoken to.

The fittings lasted two hours more, Margaret having missed several appointments to inclement weather. With nearly a dozen new young ladies working under Mistress Laphar's tutelage, a few of the simpler dresses were already completed. There were too many boxes for the two women to carry back themselves.

"Will you have these delivered, Mistress Laphar?" Margaret turned to stout the woman before she and Elizabeth gathered their things to leave.

"Of course, m'lady." Susanna bobbed a small curtsey as they left.

Elizabeth waited until they were out of earshot of the town before she spoke again. "For protection?"

Margaret nodded. "So he said."

"Protection from what?" Elizabeth demanded.

Margaret hesitated before saying, "You're aware of Liam's situation, yes?"

Elizabeth's own mouth tightened. "Yes, I am aware."

"Then if news of my helping him reaches the capital and I arrive to trumpeters and announce my presence, I could be imprisoned to the end of my days, or I could be executed before a crowd as an example," Margaret said blandly.

Elizabeth stopped walking, her face slack with shock. "If you return to the capital, you could be executed?"

Margaret turned when she realized Elizabeth had stopped. "Yes."

The older woman grabbed Margaret's hands quickly. "You can't go back, Margaret."

Margaret was surprised at the strength in Elizabeth's hands. "I don't have much choice, Elizabeth."

"You do have a choice," she almost yelled before quieting her voice. "You could choose to go with Liam and let him keep you safe, or you could stay with Aram and me, and we can keep you safe."

Margaret smiled at Elizabeth patiently. "I don't have a choice, Elizabeth, not truly. If I don't, the people I am responsible for in Dorcia, the people my father loved and cared for, where would they be?"

"But you—"

"No matter how much I would or would not like to go with Liam and forget all this ever happened, I have no choice in the matter," Margaret said.

"You would be risking your life," Elizabeth tried to reason with her.

"And if I left, I would be risking theirs," Margaret countered. "The matter has already been settled, Elizabeth. I will return to the capital when the time comes, and I will face the consequences, whatever they may be."

20

Liam watched Margaret from the doorway, much like he had in her home in Silvica. At times, he still had trouble believing Margaret was comfortable living well below her station. The Gollacks' home was a poor one, but Margaret did not let on that she even noticed. Liam knew better, having traveled with her, that she noticed every detail about her surroundings.

Margaret was making their morning meal for them, forcing Elizabeth to rest, who had recently become more tired in her daily tasks. Margaret, as well as Healer Williamson, thought it was the vestiges of winter taking its toll on her body. Liam thought it sweet that she was concerned for Elizabeth's well-being. He was starting to see Margaret's true self was the caretaker rather than the haughty countess.

Liam watched as she flitted from one thing to the next. It was like a dance, her dress flowing behind her when she moved, blossoming out when she twirled around. She was captivating; Liam's eyes were unable to leave her.

Liam smiled when Margaret caught him staring, a bright blush erupting on her cheeks. The more time he spent with her, the more endearing he found her. Margaret averted her eyes and went back to her work. When Liam saw Elizabeth intently staring at him with her brows raised high, his own blush crept up his neck. There was a knowing look on Elizabeth's face, slowly looking him over. Liam cleared his throat and went into the kitchen, sitting next to the older couple. Margaret set the food on the table and smiled at Liam.

Her smile warmed him, and he found himself easily smiling back. Liam quickly stood and pulled out Margaret's chair. He pushed it in, seeing the looks exchanged between Aram and Elizabeth. Margaret kept her eyes down, avoiding eye contact. When she dared to look up, she caught him still staring. He could not help himself—Margaret fascinated him. She went from overly confident to a demure, subservient woman as soon as attention was on her. Was that the way all noblewomen were taught to behave?

Aram watched Liam intently when Elizabeth and Margaret cleared the table of dishes. "Do you have any intentions for that girl?" he asked with a surprising intensity.

Liam blanched. "Intentions?"

"You seem to be very interested in dear Margaret there," Aram told him. "And I don't want to see either one of you hurt."

"I wouldn't hurt her," Liam said, "not after what I've already done." He had done many things in his life, but ruining Margaret's would be the one he most regretted.

Aram left Liam in the kitchen with a shake of his head.

Liam pulled Elizabeth aside when Margaret left the room. "Beth?" he asked quietly, touching her elbow.

"Yes?" she asked just as quietly.

"Would you prepare a picnic for Margaret and me today for the lunchtime hour?" he asked almost shyly.

Elizabeth raised her eyebrows. "You want to go on a picnic—in Femonat?"

"Yes." Liam grinned shyly. "It's been warm enough. Will you prepare one for us?"

"Of course," Elizabeth said. "It will be ready by the time you want to leave."

Liam kissed her forehead. "You're my angel, Beth."

Elizabeth patted his cheek like a son and walked away to find a blanket for the pair to sit on.

Liam walked slowly with Margaret to his favorite part of the river, a small curve with a large tree that provided shade for the entire bend. Liam had spent many hours under the massive oak, the river and shade relieving the weight off his world-weary shoulders. He knew it would be the perfect place for him to take Margaret on a picnic. Liam laid the large blanket down in the shade and helped Margaret sit.

"Are you comfortable?" he asked anxiously.

"Yes, thank you." Margaret adjusted her skirts over her feet.

Liam sat next to her with a grunt, opening the basket of food. Elizabeth had included some of his favorite sweets and a skin of wine. He laid out the cold meats and cheeses, putting a half a loaf of bread between them. "Elizabeth has outdone herself with this."

Margaret looked around. Liam had taken her by the river before, but this spot was new. There was a soft smile on her face. "This was a wonderful idea, Liam."

Liam smiled. There was an easiness about Margaret while they sat. She seemed content in taking in her surroundings. "You look relaxed."

"Very," Margaret confirmed, grabbing a sweet Elizabeth had made.

"Good," Liam said. "I want you to enjoy your time here with Aram and Elizabeth."

"I will," she assured him. "They're both so wonderful."

"Yes, they are, Maggie." Liam smiled. "May I call you Maggie?"

"You may." Her smile was almost embarrassed, a light blush dusting her cheeks. "You would be the only one to ever do so."

"Really?" Liam was surprised. "No one has ever called you Meg or Maggie?"

"My mother was very formal." Margaret shifted, her hands clenched in her lap. "She never allowed anyone to call me anything but Margaret."

"Well then, Maggie, you have to try Beth's cream rolls," Liam said as he quartered a small slice of the pinwheel cake with a cream center. He held it up for her.

Margaret daintily took it from Liam's fingers with her mouth. Her eyes lit up in delight as she ate the special sweet. "This is delicious!"

Liam grinned at her. "This is what you'll enjoy now that winter is ending, and supplies are easier to come by."

"I won't be able to fit into my dresses when I leave here!" Margaret joked, eating another slice.

When they were full, Margaret and Liam leaned shoulder-to-shoulder against the oak. There was a much different tone settling between them now than there had been while they traveled, particularly after Margaret cared for him. It was much more comfortable and relaxed, more companionable. On their trip, they had been aloof toward each other, only speaking when necessary and at night when there was no avoiding conversation. Liam sighed as he rested his head on top of hers.

Margaret sighed contentedly as she watched the river flow. The chirping of birds ringing in their ears like tiny bells. A gentle breeze tossed her hair from place to place, eventually blowing the tendrils into Liam's open mouth. She turned when he made an indignant grunt.

"Sorry," she said.

Liam gazed at Margaret. He leaned in closer to her, his eyes intent on her mouth. He still regretted not kissing her that day in the snow. "You know, Maggie, you could come with me when I leave."

Margaret moved away from him quickly. "We should go back to the house before Aram and Elizabeth worry about us."

"I couldn't give you the life you would have in the capital, but I could keep you safe," Liam told her. "Safer than you would be here. It isn't unheard of for nobility to run away with a commoner."

"Liam…" Margaret looked at him helplessly. "I can't leave my people again. What would happen to them if I were just to pick up and leave?"

"What would happen to them if you were arrested and the king took your lands from you?" It was a very real possibility if Oliphant had reached the capital with news of her betrayal.

"I don't know." Margaret sighed.

"I can at least keep you safe, and you can manage from Glessic or Salatia, or even Frasisca," Liam countered.

"Please, Liam," she pleaded, "I can't go with you."

"Maggie—"

"I can't!" she cried, standing. A tormented look crossed her face. "I can't," she repeated quietly to herself.

Liam nodded, standing himself. "As you wish."

Aram shook Liam awake on the first morning of Marmonat. There was an annual fair to celebrate the thawing of the ground, with all manner of goods and livestock for purchase or trade. This year, Aram intended to make several purchases.

"Wouldn't Margaret and Beth like to go?" Liam groaned, trying to find any excuse to delay his waking.

"They," Aram said in a sing-song voice, pulling away the sheets to drag Liam from his bed, "are going to join us later in the day."

Liam leveled him with a baleful glare. "Why do we need to go so early?"

"I want to look over the livestock before everything picks up," Aram said excitedly. "Now up!"

With a groan, Liam followed Aram into the kitchen. Elizabeth was sitting next to the fire in the kitchen, chatting idly with a tired-looking Margaret. Aram kissed them both atop their heads before he sat and grabbed a corn muffin, heavily buttering it and stuffing half hungrily into his mouth.

"When will you be leaving?" Elizabeth asked, buttering another muffin for him.

"As soon as we've finished eating," Aram said, the sound muffled with his mouth full.

Margaret went to the pan at the fire and dished out two plates of eggs for Aram and Liam. Liam sat unceremoniously at the table and shoveled food into his mouth without speaking a word to any of them.

Elizabeth raised her brows at him, looking to Aram for an explanation.

"He's none too happy about the early hour."

"It *is* fairly early," Elizabeth agreed. "The sun isn't even up." There was barely any light peeking out behind the distant landscape.

Aram grinned at her. "Better to get there early than late. I want to get the best deals."

"And that couldn't have been done a few hours later?" Liam demanded between bites.

"It's bad luck to pass on your first customer," Aram said. "Get there early enough, and no one can say no to you."

Margaret looked amused. "It seems our dear Aram has a ruthless side."

"As a mouse," Elizabeth teased.

Aram rolled his eyes at the two women before he stood and clapped Liam on the shoulder. "Come along, my boy."

Liam snatched a corn muffin before following after the older man.

There were already several people at the fair by the time they arrived.

"See?" Aram pointed to the other men examining the livestock. "No one wants to miss the first deal."

"What are you planning on buying?" Liam looked around to see what was available. He saw everything from cows and goats to donkeys and horses. He followed Aram to the pig pens where no one else was.

"A few pigs, a goat or two, and maybe a few chickens," Aram said excitedly. "It will help provide more now that we have more mouths to feed."

"I will be leaving soon," Liam told him. "I should have already left."

"That's what you said in Demonat, and then in Jamonat and Femonat after the new year started." Aram's brows were raised tauntingly. "Are you sure you'll be leaving soon?"

"I have let comfort keep me where I am," Liam admitted, "but I will be leaving soon."

"You mean you let Margaret keep you where you are," Aram corrected. "Beth and I see the way you look at her."

"And what exactly is it you think you see?" Liam raised a brow at him. It was unlike Aram to be so confrontational.

"A man who has found something that is shiny and pretty and he wants to keep it close." Aram squatted to look at a pig.

"I don't see Margaret as some sort of bauble to possess," Liam snapped. "I certainly don't see her as mine."

"Good." Aram let the subject drop. "Now let's find the owner of these pigs."

Aram thumped Liam on the arm with the back of his hand to get his attention. "The ladies are here."

Liam saw both women were in new dresses, the usual earth tones replaced by soft pastels. It was very fitting for the spring celebration. "They look lovely."

Aram's face was luminescent looking at his wife. "That they do."

The women joined them, Elizabeth wrapping her arm around Aram's waist. "Did you get what you wanted?"

Aram grinned at her. "Oh, yes. We, my dear, are the proud owners of ten pigs and two goats."

Liam did not miss the shocked look on Elizabeth's face. It had been more than what the older couple could afford, but Aram had somehow managed a payment plan with one of those money lenders who circled the fair like vultures. They would be paying off the purchase for some time. Liam hoped it would not be for the rest of their lives.

"Where will you put them?" Margaret asked, tucking a strand of hair that had been loosened by the wind behind her ear.

"Behind the house." Aram gripped Liam's shoulder. "Liam will help build a paddock with me."

Liam offered his arm to Margaret, ignoring the stern glance from Aram. "May I buy you a sweet, Maggie?"

"You may." Margaret smiled, taking his arm.

"You look beautiful today," Liam said once they were out of earshot.

Margaret demurely lowered her lashes. "Thank you. You seem to be in better spirits than this morning."

"I'm more awake now," Liam explained. "And there was coffee."

"Coffee?" Margaret's brow furrowed. "I've never heard of coffee."

"It's a drink for the poor, my lady," Liam said.

The corners of Margaret's mouth tightened into a frown, pulling her arm away from his. "You mean it's something I wouldn't dare drink because I'm above everyone?"

"I'm not saying that, Maggie," Liam tried to defend himself. "I'm not saying that at all."

"It's what you meant," Margaret argued. "You think I think I'm too much of a snob to associate with the poor."

Liam stopped her with a gentle hand. "I know that isn't the case, Margaret. You wouldn't be thriving here if you were."

Margaret was only slightly placated. She took his arm again as they walked deeper into the celebrations. Children ran around a celebration pole, wrapping the long ribbons down the tall pole as they danced around it; giggling endlessly as they twirled. It was a charming sight, one Liam didn't get to see often.

Liam stopped at one of the vendors that had set up shop closest to where the children would be playing. There were several different types of sweets.

"Which one would you like?" Liam asked her.

Margaret caught her bottom lip between her teeth, looking over the treats. "I don't know…"

The vendor picked up a molasses chew, offering it to Liam. "A sweet treat for your beautiful lady?"

Liam looked at Margaret side-face, his crow's feet crinkling in amusement. He paid the vendor a drica for the chew, handing it to Margaret. She popped it in her mouth, letting out a pleased moan at the sweet taste.

"Good?" Liam led her away from the vendor to see the other festivities the fair had to offer.

"Delicious," she said, laughing childishly when she accidentally sprayed golden spit.

Elizabeth came to stand beside Liam. They watched Margaret with her skirt tied between her knees in the paddock he and Aram had built for their new purchases. It was large enough they could not see some of the pigs at the furthest reaches of the pinned in area. It had taken them almost a month to build the paddock and shelter, leaving the building open-faced. Margaret had a trail of pigs behind her while she was bringing fresh hay for their bedding. Elizabeth could not help but laugh; the pigs were following her like she was a mother duck and they were her ducklings.

Margaret threw the new hay down to replace the old, smiling when she looked back to see the pigs following behind. She would need to make many more trips to refill their shelter with an appropriate amount of bedding. She went for the small haystack they had purchased and slipped on the mud, going down with a cry that soon turned to laughter. Her trailing pigs were soon nosing her all over to check her state.

Liam laughed when he saw Margaret's face on her return trip. Her cheeks were muddy with pig kisses, and she continued on her way to their bedding.

"Have you been kissing the pigs, Maggie?"

"No, but they've certainly been kissing me!" Margaret called out to him lightheartedly.

Elizabeth laid her hand on Liam's arm and squeezed it. "I love this girl," she said, looking up at Liam. "Thank you for bringing her to us."

21

Margaret sighed as she looked at the river. Liam would be leaving the day after tomorrow. She had settled in better than she expected. It was like slipping into silk—easy and enjoyable. The Gollacks had shown her nothing but kindness; it was as if she had been their own child come home from coming out at court. She was sitting on a blanket in front of the river. Liam had suggested having another picnic to talk to her alone. It had become their place to talk privately when Liam took a break from working with the livestock or fixing the house.

Margaret looked Liam over—he cleaned up very nicely. His hair had been cut short by Elizabeth, and his face was now neatly covered by a beard that lined his jaw. He looked almost as healthy as he had been at the trial. Liam had stayed quiet the entire way to the river, looking deep in thought. He was staring at the river without blinking.

"What are you thinking about?" Margaret was curious as to what made him so silent.

"Where I'm going to go next." Liam looked over at her. "You look very relaxed today."

There had come between them an easy attitude of companionship since Margaret nursed him back to health. She always had a comfortable air about her when he was near, easily smiling at him whenever he looked at her. There could have been a much different feeling between them, had they met under different circumstances.

"It's the river." Margaret sighed, closing her eyes and lifting her face to bask in the sun that came out from behind the clouds. "It's soothing."

"It is very soothing," Liam agreed.

"And where is it that you'll be going next?" Margaret asked.

"Salatia, I think, with a few detours." Liam leaned back against the tree they were sitting under. "It's the only place Anatalian soldiers are not welcome."

"Aren't you worried about being found out as an Anatalian there?" Margaret had heard stories of Anatalian merchants being beaten on the roads of Salatia for simply being a national of their enemy country.

Liam looked her over. "Are you worried for me?"

"Yes, I'm worried for you," Margaret snapped, a blush creeping onto her cheeks.

"No, Margaret," Liam soothed, "I'm not worried. I've spent more than enough time in Salatia, hiding from my fellow soldiers and countrymen, to know how it's done."

"Is there nowhere else you can go?" Margaret asked him. "Can you not travel to Glessic instead?"

"Salatia is closer to you if you get yourself in trouble again," he replied with a mischievous look on his face.

"If I get myself in trouble again," Margaret said with a raised voice. "I do believe you're the one who brought me the trouble."

Liam wrapped his arm around her, pulling her into his chest. "Hush," he said. "I want to stay close if you ever need me."

Margaret looked up at him with a furrowed brow. "Why?"

"You refuse to come and make a new life with me," Liam told her seriously. "I've grown quite attached to you, Maggie."

Margaret blushed brightly, tingles going through her chest to her stomach. She eyed the river before she smiled like a happy child; her shoes and stockings were off in a hurry. She was up in a moment, her dress tied around her knees, walking toward the edge of the river. She boldly stepped into the river without hesitation. It had been unseasonably warm for the last two weeks and was the only reason she dared going in the river after her last attempt.

Margaret took in a sharp breath and let out a small cry before laughing. "It's so cold!"

Liam chuckled. "What are you doing?"

"I'm enjoying myself, Liam." She looked at him over her shoulder, giving him a playful look. "You should try it."

Liam rose to the challenge she had issued, moving as Margaret kicked water at him. He took his shoes off and rolled up his breeches. Liam joined her in the river, only to be assaulted with more water. He bent and scooped water in his hand and flung it at her. He laughed as she screamed, watching her move away from him.

"Come back here!"

Margaret screamed again when he chased her, laughing when Liam caught her about the waist. She turned around in his arms, resting her hands on his chest.

Liam stopped, studying her face. Margaret looked up at him with her lips slightly parted. He grabbed her face in his hands and kissed her hard. Liam wrapped his arm around her waist, pulling her against him. His other hand snaked its way behind her head, tangling his fingers in her hair.

Margaret clenched his shirt in his fingers for a moment before pulling away. She took a step back from him to put a gap between them and put her fingers to her still tingling lips. Her eyes were wide as she looked at him, her stomach still fluttering with butterflies. "We shouldn't have done that."

Liam cupped her cheek gently with his hand. "There's nothing wrong with kissing, Maggie." He stepped closer, gently pressing his lips to hers again.

Margaret relaxed into him, enjoying the tenderness he was showing her.

Liam slowly broke the kiss after a few moments. "You know, it's not long before I'll be leaving… It's not too late to change your mind and go with me."

Margaret nodded solemnly. "I know." She had grown more attached to Liam than she should have over their time together, but she could not give up her plans. "You know I can't."

Liam guided her out of the river, a serious look on his face. "I don't think you should go back to the capital."

Margaret sighed, exasperated. "Liam, the capital is where I belong. What's going to happen to all of what my father worked for if I don't?"

"And what if Oliphant made it back there and there's a warrant for your arrest?" Liam snapped.

"I have to, Liam, I really do." She looked over his face, seeing the disappointment in his eyes. It made her chest tighten—she didn't like seeing him disappointed in her. "I have to try and carry on my father's legacy, or else what meaning did his life have?"

Liam sighed, pulling her tightly to him. "I can't protect you there."

"You can't protect me here, either." It was more cruel than she intended for it to come out. Margaret gently touched his cheek.

Liam kissed her again, and she let him.

Liam pulled Margaret to him after Aram and Elizabeth had gone into their home. "Margaret, you can still change your mind and go with me. I'll wait for you."

Margaret gently squeezed his arm. "Liam, you know I can't," she said with a sigh. "Do you have to go to Salatia?" Worry nagged at her that he would be caught in Salatia, or hurt in some way.

"Would it make you feel better if I went somewhere else first?"

"Where would you go?" Margaret asked.

"Somewhere in Anatalia, maybe Glessic." He shrugged. "I won't go to Salatia until you leave for the capital."

"Thank you," she said quietly.

Liam tenderly took her face in both hands. "I'll write to you when I get to where I'm going."

"I would very much like to know you're safe and well," Margaret said.

"I'll come back before you leave here to make sure you are well and safe," he promised. "Maybe you'll change your mind by then."

"Liam—"

Liam kissed her soundly to quiet her arguments. "I'll be back for you, Margaret," he said before climbing atop Ashka and riding away from her.

It had upset her more than she thought it would to see him ride away on the stolen horse. Margaret watched the road until she could no longer see him. She looked around, the world seemingly more quiet now Liam wasn't there with her. She had no idea when she would see him again. Margaret wished she had told him of his family history when she had the chance, but every opportunity she had tried was interrupted.

Margaret went inside to find Aram and Elizabeth at their table with three cups of tea waiting. They gave her a knowing look.

"He'll find you again," Aram said.

"He can't go where I'm going," Margaret said sullenly.

"Then stay here with us, dear," Elizabeth said.

Margaret mustered a halfhearted smile. "Only until what I've commissioned is finished. I don't want to be a burden on you."

"You could never be a burden to us." Aram smiled at her kindly. "You've done more for us than we could have ever expected—more than we deserve."

Elizabeth was particularly melancholy with Liam leaving. She admitted to Margaret he reminded her of her son she had lost more than a decade ago in a boat accident while fishing on a particularly rough section of the river. The Gollacks had only been able to have one child, and his loss had been hard on the couple.

"He was such a sweet boy, just like Liam. Tall with dark hair, took good care of his parents," Elizabeth told her. "If Liam could stay with us as our son, we'd be the happiest people in all Aratia."

Margaret sighed as she sat alongside the couple. She unconsciously looked to the door for Liam to come in.

Aram smiled at her sympathetically, patting her hand gently. "He'll be back here. He always comes back."

22

Lord General Crompton sat across from a rugged-looking man, Adrian Markle. "I'm going to need more men."

"There are as many men as you need, Your Grace—under one condition. My master has instructed me to tell you he wants to see action soon, or he will be withdrawing support from you."

As though he hadn't tried. Crompton suspected his cousin managed to conscript a spy from his entourage—or Sorren had made a deal with Beelzebub himself. Every single attempt he'd ordered had failed. Every poison detected, every assassin apprehended. It was easier to convince a foreign ruler to toss away hundreds of thousands of lives than it was to kill that man.

"There will be action when my cousin travels with his court in the summer," Compton said sharply. "It will give us the greatest opportunity to attack and take Jalmar."

"My master needs it to be sooner," Markle commanded.

Crompton slammed his fist on the table, making their wooden steins shake. "It cannot be sooner!" he yelled, stooping lower as he quieted his voice to continue. "Sorren cannot be taken unawares while he's on his throne. He is always surrounded by advisors and a plethora of elite guards. Even poison will not work—he has tasters for his tasters. The king is a paranoid man, Markle. The only hope we have for taking the throne from him is to wait and take the capital in his absence."

Adrian frowned. "Are you certain there is no other way?"

"Don't you think I haven't tried other ways?" Crompton demanded, his voice harsh. "I have been trying for ten years to kill the bloody idiot, and nothing has worked. This is the only option left. You tell your master that, or I'll find someone else to bring my deal to."

Crompton could feel the deal starting to slip through his fingers. He stared down Markle as the messenger debated his next move. He had as much at stake as Crompton did.

"I will tell him," the rugged man said before he left.

Crompton stayed to finish his ale. This was a long time coming. He had been trying to rally enough troops to gain the Anatalian throne since the war between Salatia and Anatalia had started, and now it was finally coming together. He didn't care who sat on the throne as long as the lecher Sorren would be put where he belonged.

In a grave.

23

iam looked back at the road. He could no longer see the town of Marbon, unsure where he was going next, but he knew he had to get as far away from the town as possible. He could not risk getting too comfortable with Margaret and the Gollacks. The last time Liam had gotten comfortable, he had accidentally led soldiers into the town he was staying in. The soldiers had killed townspeople until someone told them where Liam was. He would not risk the same fate for the people of Marbon, and especially not Margaret.

Liam had grown far too attached to the younger woman. He had found in the time they had spent together at the Gollacks' that Margaret was actually a kindhearted young woman who truly cared about people. Over the last six months, he had been able to watch her sweet side emerge. She was not just the spoiled countess who got what she wanted when she wanted it. Margaret had refused to be idle in the Gollacks' home, taking on the majority of the chores that were no longer easy for Aram and Elizabeth to accomplish. He had watched as she looked at them tenderly, unabashed at the thought of having to do work for them.

Liam was amazed at how comfortable she was to do her part. She had even enjoyed feeding the newly purchased pigs Aram had penned behind their home. He did not want to think of this woman being arrested or killed because of him.

It was a complete contrast to how she had behaved on the road with him, playing the spoiled brat, giving orders, and complaining. It had worn at his nerves to the point he had fantasized about leaving her in the woods and going on his way. Liam had gritted his teeth and stuck with his plan to take her to the Gollacks, and he was glad he had. He wouldn't have been able to see the kindness she had shown him in Silvica again if he had abandoned her.

That line of thought gave him his next destination. He would make his way back to Silvica and investigate the state of the house they had left. Liam didn't know what he would find when he got there, but he owed it to Margaret to see. It would take him half the time to return to Silvica without Margaret with him. Liam had taken a more delicate pace with her. He would go through the home and bring her anything of value that remained.

It took Liam only a week to reach Silvica and the country cottage Margaret and her father had resided in. He immediately put Ashka in the stables and rubbed him down. When Liam went to the side of the house, he saw Margaret's garden had withered and died without her care, turning a putrid brown. When his eyes traveled further, he saw the door was slightly open. Liam entered the house cautiously—there were leaves and dirt gathering in the corners. It didn't look as though anyone had entered the home since they vacated in Omonat. Straightening his back, Liam went to the room where Margaret's father had been stabbed.

With a sinking feeling, Liam saw the body was where they had left it. He had held on to a small bit of hope that the soldiers chasing them had taken Margaret's father into the town's healer. He had obviously been dead for the entirety of their absence. Had no one cared enough to check on them for six months of hearing nothing? The smell had not been obvious in the rest of the house with the door having been left open, but in the bedroom, it was vile enough for Liam to cover his nose and mouth with the crook of his elbow. The body was starting to lose its hair, and the skin was taut on the face and hands. Liam wanted to bury him before continuing his search of the house. Waving away the flies, Liam wrapped him in the bedsheet he was laying on before taking him outside.

There was an oak tree behind the home, much like the one he and Margaret would sit under in Marbon. It seemed appropriate to lay the man to rest under the shady tree. He set down the body before going to the stables to search for a pick or shovel to make the grave. It took Liam the majority of the day to dig and refill the resting place.

To him, the grave looked plain. Breaking branches off the tree, Liam shaved off the smaller twigs before fastening three of them together in a simple six-pointed sun. He jabbed the cross at the head of the grave with a grunt.

Liam leaned against the tree with a sigh. He didn't know when he would be able to tell Margaret about her father. He would spend the night and go through the house tomorrow. It was starting to darken outside, cooling the air around him and bringing out the firebugs. He stood for a moment and enjoyed the simple sight before he remembered the bathhouse attached to one of the hallways and a smile came to his face. He would be able to relax his sore muscles. Liam went to the unusual luxury and lit the fire under the water pump.

He soaked for hours, thinking of all that had happened over the last six months. Liam could not get Margaret out of his mind. He closed his eyes and remembered the first night they had stopped. Liam could still smell her hair and feel the softness of it on his fingertips. He was hooked there and then, and she had been reeling him in since. The longer he stayed with her, the more beautiful he found her. Liam could not afford to get involved with her and drag her along on the road, always running. No matter how much he wanted her to go with him, she was right to deny him. He sighed before lifting himself out of the tub and going to one of the bedrooms.

Liam looked around the room and saw a family portrait. The Doremis family looked like a proud one. Father stood behind wife and daughter, his hand on

Margaret's shoulder. Margaret's mother was dressed in a magnificent gown of red and gold, layered in jewels. Her chin was upturned and had a look on her face that dared someone to contradict her authority.

On the other side, Margaret was in a beautiful gown, but not as extravagant as her mother's. She had a more timid look that made Liam want to reach out and put his arm around her to give her some comfort.

The next morning, Liam woke early to explore the home. Upon further inspection, it seemed no one else had entered the home in their absence. Only his musings had disturbed the order of things. How had no one checked on them in Margaret's absence—did they not care she had disappeared? He didn't understand—even if they had ignored her father, no one had even thought to come in and steal the jewels left behind?

Liam looked around Margaret's room, wondering where to start. Margaret had already commissioned new clothing, so he decided he would only bring her the jewels that had been left behind. Liam was surprised they were even still there—had no one at all come to the house? He found several compartmented chests filled with multiple different colored gems in necklaces and rings. He marveled at the amount of money that would have gone into commissioning those items. After placing all her jewels in a satchel, he went in search of any money to take with him.

Before he left the country home, he took some clothes from her father's bureau and took another look around the house. He would take a detoured route back to Marbon and enjoy some time alone again. He deserved the distraction. Liam hoped the long journey would help him take his mind off Margaret.

24

Feeling the distinct absence of Liam, Margaret preoccupied herself with almost daily visits to Marbon proper to have dress fittings once the finer fabrics reached the seamstress' shop. Aram suggested she get to know some of the townspeople, and she had heeded his advice. Margaret had stumbled upon a scantily clad child that had broken her heart to see. There was the smell of snow in the air—a late occurrence; spring had already begun to bloom—and the child had on what could barely be considered shoes. The leather on his feet was barely held together by strings, letting in the cold air and any water on the ground. He stared longingly into the baker's shop, which had just made fresh bread.

"Come here, child," Margaret said when he looked at her. She held her hand out to him.

The young boy shook his head, edging closer to the bakery.

"Come here," Margaret snapped, her mouth pursing.

The young boy looked frightened but came to her nonetheless. He did not take her hand, looking up at her with wide eyes.

"What's your name?" Margaret stooped to his level.

"Torryn," he said with a distinctly southern accent.

He had probably found the way with or without his parents from somewhere near Manolt at the Hook of Hamuel, a town that had kept the accent of the original immigrants of Tyradrica. The Hook had been named after explorer Tristan Hamuel, who had landed at the Hook in 1583—next year would be the seven hundredth anniversary of his landing and founding of Anatalia.

"Where are your parents, young man?" Margaret asked.

"I haven't got none." He snuffled and wiped his nose with a dirty sleeve. The boy would be sick by the day's end.

Margaret stood, dusting off her dress. "Where are you staying then?"

Torryn pointed to a run-down building not too far away from them.

"There?"

The boy nodded dumbly.

Margaret grabbed Torryn's hand, going to the building. "Excuse me?"

She looked around and saw dirt gathered in the corners and trash strewn about the room. The windows were covered with wood, letting in only small amounts of light where the boards had rotted through. There were several piles of rags and blankets on the floor with sheets filled with holes covering them.

"Hello?"

A boy, not much older than fifteen came into the room, looking at her suspiciously. "What are you doing here?" he asked abrasively. "Get out!"

"I'm looking for whoever is running this…" —Margaret looked around with disgust at the condition— "establishment." She didn't know what she could even call the rundown building. "Or whoever is taking care of this boy."

"He's mine," the teenager said. "All the children here are mine." He crossed his arms as if daring her to challenge him. He was a lanky young man with pale skin. He was almost a foot taller than Margaret. The teen's dirty blonde hair hung down in his blue-green eyes, nearly covering up his thick, dark eyebrows.

Margaret looked over the teenager critically. "What's your name, boy?"

"Jonathan," the teen snapped.

"Did you realize your 'son' is barely covered? There's about to be snow on the ground." Margaret gave him a disapproving look. "He'll freeze to death, running around outside with hardly any clothes on."

"I do what I can for my children." Jonathan looked shamefaced when he cast his eyes on Torryn's condition. "I got eight boys and two girls. I can't afford to put clothes on them all."

One of the two girls ran out and hugged Jonathan's legs. She was much cleaner than Torryn and Jonathan were themselves. It was fairly obvious he spoiled his daughters—or at least whom he perceived to be his daughters.

"Papa!" She lifted her arms for Jonathan to pick her up and rewarded him with a squeal when he did. Jonathan's face lit up when the young girl wrapped her arms around his neck.

Margaret let go of Torryn's hand, and he eagerly went to Jonathan's side, hiding behind his leg. "How long have you been here?"

The teen shrugged. "We move from place to place until we're told to leave," he said. "Me and my babies never stay very long in one place."

Margaret felt her stomach turn. "Do any of you have parents?"

"They got me," Jonathan said flatly. "That's all they need. Now if you would kindly leave?"

"Not just yet." Margaret walked further into the building. There was a rather unfortunate smell coming from the inner sanctuary of their home. Her mouth twisted in distaste.

"I want you out of here," Jonathan yelled, his face reddening.

"Have you thought of an orphanage?" Margaret asked, turning to face him. "There are several in the larger cities."

"We don't need an orphanage," Jonathan told her hotly. "I'm all they need."

Margaret let out an ambiguous noise from the back of her throat. She looked around critically. "I'll be back here tomorrow to see you and your babies."

"No, you won't!" Jonathan yelled after her as she left. "You're not welcome here!"

"Are you all right, my dear?"

"Hmm?" Margaret inhaled deeply, turning her attention to Aram. She had been staring at the door, lost in her own thoughts from the day.

"Is there something wrong?" Aram repeated.

"No," Margaret smiled at him. "Just lost in thought."

"Thinking of Liam again?" Elizabeth set a cup of tea next to her.

"No, actually." Margaret was surprised at herself—she usually was. "I came across a group of orphans today."

"Oh?" Elizabeth raised her eyebrows. "I didn't know we had an orphanage here."

"There isn't one."

"Then how did you know that they were orphans?" Aram asked her.

"Torryn, one of the children there, was barely clothed and staring hungrily into the bakery," Margaret told him. "I got him to take me to his 'father,' and there are eleven of them, including the young man who cares for them."

"Eleven?" Elizabeth looked shocked.

Margaret nodded. "I suggested an orphanage to the young man, but he seemed not to like that idea."

"It's his business if he wants to take care of those children," Aram said.

"They'll starve if they don't get any help." Margaret sighed, rubbing her cheek as she thought. "How is no one else helping? Everyone here has been so friendly to me, and now they let these children starve?"

There was a long silence before Aram spoke again. "You could help them, Margaret."

"Me?"

"Yes." Aram nodded. "You could help them, and it would give you something to take your mind off of Liam."

"I don't have Liam on my mind," Margaret said indignantly. But she was lying to herself, and to them. It was rare when Liam *wasn't* on her mind.

Elizabeth gave a knowing look to Aram before turning her gaze back to Margaret. "As you said, they'll starve if they don't get help."

"I think it would be good for you to help them," Aram told her.

Margaret chewed on her bottom lip as she thought. "I suppose…"

Margaret sighed as she went to see the orphans she had found yesterday. Her stomach was tight with nervous tension, wanting nothing more than to turn around and return to the Gollacks' home. She had told Jonathan she would return today, and she did not want to break her word, even if he didn't want her there.

Margaret knocked on the broken door tentatively. "Hello? Jonathan?"

Jonathan wrenched the door open. "What do you want?"

"I'm here to see the children," Margaret said pleasantly, despite the irritation on the young man's face.

"I told you yesterday that you aren't welcome here," Jonathan said tartly. "Now go!"

Margaret tried to enter the home. "How are they today?"

Jonathan blocked her way into the home, putting his hand firmly against the jamb. "They are none of your business. I don't even know who you are!"

Her lips pursed irritably. "My name is Lady Margaret."

"Well, Lady Margaret, you are not welcome here," Jonathan seethed, "and I want you to leave."

"But—"

"Leave!" Jonathan yelled in her face.

Margaret's livid glare should have quelled the furious young father, but she imagined his own ignorance aided in his defiance. She stepped away from him before turning her back to him, returning to the Gollacks in a huff.

"That petulant little… Argh!" Margaret slammed the door behind her, rattling the wall it was located on.

Elizabeth raised her brows. "My goodness, Margaret. What has gotten you in a fit?"

"Jonathan," Margaret growled.

"Who?"

"The orphans' father." Margaret fell into her seat with a growl.

"What happened?" Elizabeth's brows were still raised, looking over Margaret's slumped form.

"He refused to even let me in the home to see the children," Margaret complained irritably. "Told me I wasn't welcome."

Elizabeth shrugged slightly. "If he doesn't want you around them, there isn't much you can do."

"But they're starving, Elizabeth!"

"It's an unfortunate fact of life, Margaret," Elizabeth said. "You can't help someone who doesn't want to be helped."

"I can't allow those children to starve." Margaret sat up, gripping the arms of the chair. "I would feel responsible, because I had the opportunity to help and didn't."

"You aren't responsible for all of Anatalia, my dear," Elizabeth told her. "You don't need to feel that way."

"I'm going to go back to them tomorrow," Margaret said, ignoring Elizabeth. "I *will* see them tomorrow."

Margaret stopped at the door to the orphans' run-down home. She purchased several blankets to replace the rags the children had been sleeping with, as well as enough food for the children to eat for a few days. Margaret had no idea what to say to the petulant young father. She hoped that this time, with supplies for the children, he would welcome her back.

Margaret steeled herself. Picking up the baskets, she banished all self-doubt. She would help them whether they wanted her to or not. She shook her hair off her shoulders as she walked into the decrepit building. "Jonathan?"

"Didn't I tell you yesterday you aren't welcome here?" Jonathan demanded, coming to the common room. "Get out!"

Margaret held up the baskets in offering. "I have food for the children and blankets for when they sleep."

Jonathan paused, his face still pinched with irritation.

"Food?" a young voice called from the doorway. "Papa, is there food here?"

"Yes, there's food here," Jonathan said reluctantly. "Go get your brothers and sisters, and we'll eat something."

Margaret smiled to herself, proud she was able to get her foot in the door this time. She laid out one of the blankets and started setting out the food. When she looked up, the children were shyly standing on the other side of the room.

"What's the matter?" Margaret furrowed her brow. "Come and eat!"

"They're scared of you." Jonathan looked almost pleased.

"There's no reason to be scared, little darlings," she tried to say reassuringly, holding out a hunk of bread in offering. "I have food for you."

Margaret could see the hunger in their eyes, but none of them moved to take her offering. She looked to Jonathan for help, finding him smirking happily. She set down the bread, standing irritably.

"I just want to help all of you." Margaret's voice was almost a whine. "I can't, in good conscience, let these children starve."

Jonathan looked taken aback. "Come back tomorrow then, once the children have had a chance to fill their bellies."

Margaret's face lightened. "Really?"

"This doesn't mean I like you," Jonathan told her firmly.

"Just wait," Margaret said with a grin.

Jonathan resisted rolling his eyes. "Now will you leave? The children would like to eat."

Margaret looked back at the children, who were slowly edging toward the food now that she was no longer seated next to it. "I will see you all tomorrow then," she said. "There are enough blankets for everyone, and enough food for at least a few days."

"Fine, now go," Jonathan said with a wave of his hand.

25

L iam decided he would take his journey back to Marbon around the coast. He went first to the Hook of Hamuel. He loved the water—it took away all his troubles. He loved it ever since his escape into the ocean from his dungeon cell. Water would always mean freedom to him. It took him nearly a week to get to the city of Hamuel at the Hook—ironically, it was on the opposite side of the cliff face that actually hooked inward. Liam had only been there once before. It had been one of the more relaxing places he had visited. He had been able to walk freely through the city with no one paying him any mind. Hamuel was a large town deeply rooted in its history. A bronze statue of Tristan Hamuel, starting to oxidize, turning a bluish-green with crusted white splotches, stood in the center of the town square. The streets were cobblestone, the clopping of horses echoing off the buildings. Hamuel was the original capital city of Anatalia when the Tyradricans had come to colonize Hamuel's discovery.

While the rest of the continent had been sparsely populated and on the verge of innovation, the Tyradricans had brought with them things they had never seen before. It sped up the development of their industry and government exponentially. The countrymen set up a monarchy for the soon-to-be Anatalian people, getting rid of their tribes led by chieftains.

Along the blunt cliff face was a castle sitting in ruins, a perfect defense against attack but not age. He had not been there before, but he had been told it was a beautiful place to take young ladies to woo them into bed. Liam almost scoffed at the idea, picturing an acne-pocked young boy trying to use his surroundings as an aphrodisiac. With a laugh, he shook his head clear of the thought.

Liam went to one of the seedier inns in the town, luckily still having a stable for Ashka, and rented a room for the week. He was ready for food and to thoroughly acquaint himself with the drinks on tap. He stashed Margaret's jewels under the hard bed and grabbed a small change purse, going to the tavern he had seen earlier. He sat at a table in a secluded corner, partially obscured with a wall. He ordered a dark ale and requested they keep coming. He put down a two tholar with a pointed look to the barmaid. She grinned at him before she went to get his ale.

A bright-eyed young woman sat across from him unabashedly. "You gonna buy me a drink?"

Liam looked over the woman. She had flaming red hair and a fully freckled face. She obviously spent the majority of her time in the sun. She wore barely any clothing, and Liam immediately knew her profession. He raised his hand to call over the barmaid. "Pick your poison."

The fireball grinned at him. "I'll have a mulled wine," she said to the woman who came to take her order.

Liam let his eyes rest on her mouth. "What's your name?"

"Cassandra," the red-headed girl said. "Or whatever you want it to be."

"Cassandra will be fine." Liam told her.

Cassandra would be the perfect start to forgetting his affection for Margaret. With the distance, Liam was able to see Margaret would reject him whenever he asked her to come with him, no matter what her feelings could be. She belonged to the nobility, not to the likes of him. It would only cause him heartache if he continued to pine for her.

The fiery-headed woman sucked down her mulled wine and stood in front of Liam, leaning forward to expose her breasts. "How about we go back to your room?"

Liam grinned. He grabbed her hand and took her back to his room at the inn.

He was on her at once, his mouth greedily against hers. Liam pulled her against him, and he could feel her arms wrap tightly around his neck. He lifted her up, putting her on the bed.

The next morning when he woke, Cassandra was gone, along with the money purse he brought with him to the bar the day before. Liam sighed, glad he had only taken a small amount of coin he had from Margaret. Liam pulled a few tholar from the pouch under the bed before he left his room. He returned to the tavern from the night before and ordered a hearty breakfast. Liam was trying to remember what Hamuel had to offer as he ate. After he finished eating, he went to a shop to pick up a fishing line.

"Mornin', sir," the shopkeeper called out when he entered.

"Morning," Liam replied, looking over the spools of fishing line on the wall opposite the counter.

"You lookin' to go fishin'?"

"I am," Liam said. "Do you happen to know a secluded place to go?"

"Sure do." The shopkeeper eagerly got out a piece of parchment to draw him a map. He handed it to Liam with a heavy line. "My favorite place to go. Seas aren't too rough and you can get several bites."

Liam paid him for the line, hooks, and bait. "Thank you kindly, sir."

The map led him to a small cliff face he could easily fish off. He'd have to leave before the tide came in—the salty stains above his head told him the sea completely covered this cliff. Liam could hear the waves crashing against the rocks before he could see them. The white foam fizzled away after it hit the rocky terrain. He deeply inhaled the tangy ocean air, rolling up his sleeves to his elbows. It would be nice for him to clear his mind. Liam found a long piece of driftwood and tied his line and hook to the end. He cast it into the water and lay back to relax, waiting for a fish to bite. He hooked his feet in two divots so he would not be pulled over the edge unawares if a fish tugged too hard. Liam easily fell asleep under the warm sun, listening to the gentle crash of the waves.

Liam found himself in the great hall at the palace in Jalmar, dressed richly in a black and gray doublet, vaguely familiar faces filling the crowd. He was unsure of what he was doing there. Liam turned to face the doors that opened at the back of the hall, seeing a woman in a golden gown coming down the aisle. He turned to look around the room and saw there was a priest at the head of the hall.

Confused, Liam looked for a groom to accompany the woman in gold and found none. He realized once the woman reached his side and held her hand out to him that he was the groom. Liam took her hand in his, taking her up the small set of stairs where the priest waited. He felt himself saying vows to the woman but heard nothing come from his mouth. Liam could see the veiled woman's head moving as she emphatically said her own vows, but as with him, he heard nothing.

"You may kiss your bride," the priest told him, gesturing with a hand toward the woman in gold.

Liam lifted the woman's veil, finding a bright-eyed Margaret under the opaque fabric. A jolt went through him as she expectantly looked at him for a kiss to seal their contract. He leaned down to kiss her, only to be awakened by a violent tugging at the makeshift pole in his hand.

He shook his head to clear it, nearly letting go of the driftwood when another tug came.

Why couldn't he get Margaret out of his head? There was no reason for him to be obsessing over her. She'd turned him down on multiple occasions and made it clear she couldn't have feelings for him. He'd never in his life been so captivated by a woman—her no should have been more than enough to end his infatuation.

As he reeled in his line, Liam hoped the more distance he put between him and Margaret would rid him of her hold.

<h1 style="text-align:center">26</h1>

argaret entered the seamstress' shop. The front room was empty, but she could see Susanna through the doorway to the back room where all of the sewing happened. She had pins stuck between her teeth, pulling one out as she shook the fabric to urge it into a smooth pickup. She quickly pinned it to the mannequin before she called, "I'll be right with ye!"

"Mistress Laphar," Margaret said pleasantly. "It's wonderful to see you."

She bobbed a curtsey, smiling widely. "M'lady, we don't have an appointment until later this afternoon."

"I know," Margaret said quickly, "I know. I have a proposition for you that will make you even busier than you are now."

"I can hardly be busier!" Susanna cried. "I am already working to my limit!"

"I'll make sure it's worth your while, Mistress Laphar," Margaret assured her. "I came across some orphans here in the town, and I would like to commission some clothes for them."

Susanna made a sympathetic noise in her throat. "I've seen them here and there."

Margaret was hesitant for a moment. "It would be all right if you," —she cleared her throat, looking uncertain— "delayed production on my gowns to accomplish the task."

The seamstress' eyebrows shot toward her hairline. "Are you certain, m'lady?"

Her lips pressed together to form a thin white line. "Yes."

Susanna rubbed Margaret's arm with a smile. Margaret thought she looked proud, but she wasn't sure why. "All right then," the seamstress agreed. "How many are there?"

"Ten young ones." Margaret smiled thinking of how happy they'd be to have new clothes. "Plus, a teen who fashions himself their father."

"How many are boys and girls?"

"Two young girls, no older than four or five, and the rest are boys," Margaret said.

"Have ye got someone to do their shoes?" Susanna asked.

"Not as of yet," Margaret admitted. "I didn't know if there was a cobbler here in Marbon or if I would have to send for one in another city."

"Were ye not going to commission shoes for court?"

"I was going to commission them when I got to Jalmar," Margaret said slowly. "Shoes are easier to hide for longer than gowns."

Susanna nodded. "There's one that just came here not too long ago. I can take ye to him if ye'd like."

"That would be wonderful." Margaret supposed she could commission a pair or two for herself while she was there so she would have time to search for the best cobbler in Jalmar.

"Come along, then." Susanna grabbed her cloak before walking out. "We'll go see him now."

Margaret followed the stout seamstress a few shops down. She could see it was not completely set up. The previous name of the shop, The Pin Cushion, still hung over the entrance. Margaret's face fell slightly, looking at it. "Was this a seamstress shop?"

"It was," Susanna told her. "She went out of business with all the business you've brought me. All the ladies want their work done by the woman who does the Lady Margaret's dresses."

"But surely you can't handle that load all on your own?" Margaret looked at the sign critically. "She still could have made plenty of money."

"Her girls came to work for me when less and less work showed up." Susanna looked up at her. "She couldn't afford to pay them."

Margaret's face fell. "So I really did put this poor woman out of business?"

Susanna shrugged nonchalantly. "Her own stubbornness did. I offered Claire a position in my shop, but she refused. It's the way of life, m'lady. She'll probably go to another town and start a new shop there with the money Master Schlect paid her and the money I paid for her inventory."

Margaret followed her inside, looking around with her nose wrinkled. There were tools and shoes everywhere left in unorganized chaos. "How long has he been here?"

"A few weeks," Susanna told her quietly, calling out louder. "Master Schlect?"

A tall, white-haired man came out of one of the rooms, recognition crossing his face. "Mistress Laphar, what can I do for you?"

"I'd like to introduce ye to the Lady Margaret of Dorcia." Susanna stepped out of the way to reveal a full view of Margaret.

"My lady." He bowed his head in her direction. "A pleasure to meet you."

"The pleasure is all mine, surely," Margaret said.

"The Lady Margaret has a proposition for ye that will surely help yer business flourish."

"Oh?" Schlect turned an interested eye on Margaret. "What is your proposition?"

"I would like to commission shoes for the orphans here in Marbon," she said. "It would be a good deal of work, but I will pay you handsomely."

"No," he said bluntly.

Margaret shook her head, blinking rapidly, almost as if his words had slapped her. "No?"

"I do not like children," Schlect told her. "So, no. Thank you for considering me, Lady Margaret."

"If you do the work for me on behalf of these orphans, I will also personally commission an unseemly number of shoes for my return to court." Margaret had to entice him somehow, even if it meant paying more than he deserved. "I will also pay enough gold tals for you to hire more workers to help."

"Ye would be wise to take her offer, Daniel," Susanna told the cobbler. "She's made me a very rich woman, and ye will become a rich man in her service."

Master Schlect paused. "I will need to think about this."

"Think quickly, Master Schlect," Margaret urged. "I would like to keep my business within Marbon, but I will reach out elsewhere if you are unwilling to do the work."

"You will have my answer in two days," Schlect assured her.

"I look forward to hearing from you then." Margaret turned with Susanna and went back to her shop. "If you don't mind, I would like to have my dress fitting now," she said quietly. "I would like to speak to you about Master Schlect."

"Of course, m'lady," Mistress Laphar said, going to the back room. "There are some of your dresses ready for a fitting."

"Do you think the cobbler will take up my task?" Margaret asked, her brow furrowed.

"He doesn't have the money to turn ye down, m'lady," Susanna told her, helping her into her dress. "He just wants to make it seem like ye need him more than he needs ye."

"I see." Margaret rolled her bottom lip between her teeth. She wasn't used to people behaving like that. In Jalmar, no one said no to the Doremises. "He seems like he'll be a difficult man to work with."

"We shall see," Susanna said before sticking pins between her teeth to have at the ready.

Margaret entered the postmaster's building, a written advertisement in hand. She looked over it briefly to ensure she had made no errors.

Seeking: Skilled governess.
Must be willing to care for several children.
Payment will be discussed upon hiring.
Please send inquiries to Lady Margaret in the care of Postmaster Fraser.

It was short and to the point, but Margaret knew there would be at least a few interested in gaining a position that would last for more than a decade.

Inhaling deeply, she approached the postmaster. "Mr. Fraser," Margaret said pleasantly, smiling at him. "I would like to put an advertisement in your window."

Fraser nodded, holding his hand out for it. "It'll be a drica per day the advertisement is in the window."

"A drica a day!" Margaret balked, wondering how anyone in this town afforded such a price. She looked back in the window, noticing there were only two slots of the window taken.

"That is the price, my lady," the postmaster said firmly. "Most only have the advertisement for a day or two. How long would you like it to run?"

"For the entire month of Mamonat." Margaret sighed, knowing she had no other choice but to pay the price. "Or until the position is filled."

"Will that include the last few days of Amonat?" Fraser raised an eyebrow. "It would be thirty-four days of service. Two tholar and ten drica."

"I would also like to have copies sent to other postmasters for them to advertise," Margaret told him.

"Two copies per drica, plus their advertisement fees." Postmaster Fraser turned to grab his book that had the other postmasters' fees. "Where would you like them sent?"

Margaret sighed, "Where would you recommend?"

Fraser looked over the advertisement. "For a governess? Bishop, Fradure, perhaps even Zuev if you're willing to bring in a Glessican."

"Bishop and Fradure will be fine." Margaret didn't think Jonathan would appreciate someone who wasn't from Anatalian. "Two copies, then, and their advertisement fees for the month of Mamonat."

Fraser's finger slowly slid down the open book, pausing at a name, and the other hand writing down the price. The postmaster hummed softly to himself as he calculated the amount of money he would charge her. He scoffed slightly and crossed out some of his work, starting over. Margaret's brows impatiently slid toward her hairline.

"Your total, my lady, will be one gold tal and three tholar if you choose to use the services. Keep in mind, I will also have to provide money for the horse and rider to stay at an inn to rest and resupply."

Margaret knew his game, her mouth pursing with her eyebrows still raised. She set down two gold tals on the counter. "I'm sure this will cover the expenses needed."

"It will, my lady." Fraser nodded, quickly snatching up the money.

"Good," Margaret said shortly. No doubt she was charged more simply because she could pay the price.

"Your advertisement will be sent presently." Fraser bowed his head.

"Thank you, Mr. Fraser." Margaret nodded to him before going to the door. She stopped with her hand on the knob, turning back to the postmaster. "Mr. Fraser, you don't have any relation to the Widow Fraser in Silvica by any chance, do you?"

He let out a low chuff. "That old bag is back?"

Margaret furrowed her brow. "What do you mean?"

"She took my brother across the sea not long after they married." He crossed his arms over his chest, his face settling into a scowl. "I thought she'd stay there after he died. At least she didn't come back here."

Margaret tried to smile to diffuse the tension. "She was a great help to me in Silvica—she taught me a lot about gardening while I cared for my father."

Mr. Fraser glared. "She would, the old witch."

Margaret plastered a smile on her face, unable to think of anything else to do. "Thank you again, Mr. Fraser. I'll be back soon to check for responses." She hurriedly opened the door and left, letting out a frustrated noise when she was out of earshot. She doubted there would have been any pleasing Mr. Fraser when it came to talk of the Widow Fraser, but he didn't need to be so rude about her. Margaret had enjoyed the time she had spent with the widow.

Margaret walked the short distance to the bakery, smelling the sweet aroma of fresh bread. She would bring a few loaves of bread to the orphans.

Mr. Brunsik was covered with flour, wiping his cheek clean of the white powder when she entered. "Lady Margaret, what brings you in today?" he called when he saw her. "More food for those orphans?"

Margaret smiled pleasantly. He was a welcome reprieve from Mr. Fraser's sour mood. "Of course, Mr. Brunsik. Four loaves, as always."

The baker nodded, grabbing four fat loaves, still letting off heat. He tore off a large sheet of baking paper, putting the loaves on it, folding the paper around the bread to keep the heat in. He tied it closed with a length of twine.

"Will there be anything else, my lady?" Mr. Brunsik asked, sliding the loaves toward her.

Margaret put her hands atop of bread, basking in the heat of it with her eyes closed. "Perhaps a few sweets for the children? It would be a nice treat, I think."

The baker nodded, going into a closed room where he kept the sweet treats and cakes so they would not be stolen. He came out with a parcel wrapped in more baking paper. "A dozen cookies, then, my lady."

"Thank you, Mr. Brunsik." Margaret smiled at him, handing him a tholar.

He tucked the money into his pocket. "A pleasure as always, my lady."

Margaret took her goods and walked to the home the orphans stayed in. She was pleased to see the dilapidated building was starting to look cleaner since she started visiting.

"Jonathan?" she called out, walking into the large room.

One of the girls, the older one, peeked her head around the corner, looking hesitantly at Margaret. "Papa isn't here."

Margaret came further in, setting down her bounty on their makeshift table. "Where is he, little darling?"

She shrugged one shoulder, keeping close to the door jamb. "I dunno."

Margaret stooped down, holding out her hand. "Will you come here to me, darling?"

The child teetered, rolling on her foot in contemplation. She finally made up her mind, coming close to Margaret's extended hand. The child grabbed three fingers—all that she could fit in her tiny, grimy hand.

"What's your name, my darling?" Margaret asked, picking her up as she stood.

"Claira," she said shyly.

"That's a beautiful name, Claira." Margaret smiled at her.

Claira leaned away from her, looking unsure of the woman holding her.

"Would you like a cookie?" Margaret asked.

"A cookie?" Claira asked excitedly. "You have cookies?"

Margaret set her down. "I do. Go and tell your brothers and sister, and you can all have a cookie."

Claira ran out the door, calling for her brothers. Margaret tried to remember as many names as possible: Daren, Christopher, Marcus, Henry, and Paul were all yelled before Margaret started to lose track of the names. It would take her quite some time before she would be able to remember all them, she knew. In the interim, Margaret opened the package with the cookies, finding there were, in fact, two dozen sweets for the children.

Margaret smiled to herself, spreading out the paper and laying twelve piles of two cookies, two for each child and Jonathan, with some left over as a special treat for the father to have later. She heard the patter of feet slapping against the wooden floors. When she turned, Margaret saw eighteen hungry eyes staring at her.

"Can we have our cookies now?" Claira piped up, stepping in front of her brothers, holding her hands up for her prize.

"Yes, you may." Margaret handed her two cookies. "Each of you must tell me your name before you can get your treat."

One boy, who looked to be the oldest, shoved his way forward. "Daren," he said shortly, holding out his hand.

"Henry," said the next oldest once Daren got his treat, holding out his hand just the same.

"Paul."

"Christopher."

"Charles."

"Marcus."

"Daniel."

"Torryn."

Margaret handed each child their cookies in turn.

"Where is the other girl?" she asked, looking at the children. "There are only nine of you here."

"Sarah Beth is with Papa," Claira said, her cheeks stuffed to the brim.

"When did your papa leave?"

"In the morning," Henry informed her. "Sarah Beth is sick."

"Did your Papa go to the healer then?" Margaret asked, untying the twine holding the bread together. She started to tear it into chunks for the children to have later.

Henry nodded, stuffing a whole cookie in his mouth.

Margaret pursed her lips. "Take care of one another," she said. "I will be joining your Papa with Sarah Beth."

Margaret left the children to their own devices, guilt niggling at her stomach as she walked away from their home. She walked quickly to the apothecary, immediately spotting Jonathan upon entry.

"What are you doing here?" Jonathan demanded.

"The children told me Sarah Beth was sick," Margaret told him, seeing she was not in his arms. "Where is she?"

"With Healer Williamson," the teen father said. "Not that it's any of your business."

She resisted the urge to roll her eyes. "And how did you plan on paying for Healer Williamson's services?"

Jonathan remained silent. Margaret could almost feel his hackles raise, the air tensing around them.

"You hadn't planned on paying him, had you?" she demanded.

"No."

Of course, Healer Williamson found this the most opportune time to emerge from behind a curtain. "Lady Margaret," he said, surprised to see her. "Is there something I can do for you?"

Margaret smiled at him gently. "You're already doing it," she told him. "I am with this gentleman and the child you're examining."

Williamson seemed surprised at the news. "With…*them*?"

Jonathan bristled. "'*Them*'?"

Margaret laid her hand on Jonathan's arm, squeezing it. "Yes, Healer Williamson. They are soon to be under my care. I trust you are giving Jonathan here no issue with Sarah Beth?"

Healer Williamson cleared his throat. "Of course not, my lady. I was just about to instruct the father on how to administer the proper medication."

"Good. I would like to hear it as well." Margaret smiled, looking at Jonathan pointedly to keep him quiet.

"Of course, my lady." He bowed his head to her. "He is to give Sarah Beth a spoonful of a draught I will make for her in the morning and the evening until her cough ceases. She will also need plenty of warm milk to keep her stomach from upsetting with the draught."

"And how long do you expect for her cough to last?" Jonathan asked. "And where is she?"

"Sarah Beth is still in the back room," Healer Williamson said quickly. "She should stop coughing within a week."

"I would like her back now," Jonathan told him, standing to his full height. It was an ineffective intimidation tactic as the teen was not taller than the healer.

Healer Williamson raised a brow at him, then went to get the adopted daughter. When he returned, he immediately put Sarah Beth in Jonathan's arms.

"If you would like, I will wait here for the draught and bring it to you," Margaret suggested to Jonathan. "She will probably be more comfortable in a familiar environment."

Jonathan nodded, shooting a glare to the healer before he left.

Margaret settled in to wait, sitting on the plain bench next to the door for Healer Williamson to make the draught she had no doubt he had no intention of making before she attached herself to Jonathan.

27

Liam rubbed his growling stomach. He needed to eat something, and his supplies had run low not long after leaving Hamuel. There would be another town coming up soon where he could buy some rations and treat Ashka to some oats instead of him grazing in the fields. He might even treat himself to a quick ale.

When he entered the town, Liam found a tavern with a stable attached to it. He tossed a coin to the stable boy, with instructions to water and feed Ashka. He sat in the corner, his back against the wall. Any time Liam stopped anywhere in Anatalia, he never sat where he could be caught unawares. It was fairly empty, but it was still early in the day for a dinner rush.

The inside of the tavern reminded him of The Whistling Squire in Jalmar, the smell of seared lamb making him long for the old days where his life hadn't imploded. He hadn't thought about that life in so long. He slumped against the wall, covering his face with his hands. Would this life on the run ever end for him? He should have listened to his mother and never joined the Anatalian military.

"Can I get you somethin'?"

Inhaling deeply, Liam pulled his hands from his face. "Whatever you think tastes best here and a strong ale."

She nodded and walked away.

By the time she came back with his food, the tavern was starting to fill. Mectnora was the nicest town he had stopped at in a very long time. He'd have to eat quickly to ensure he didn't spend too much time there. He didn't want his stomach to get him in trouble a third time over. Liam put a bite of the seared lamb in his mouth and groaned. It was just like The Whistling Squire.

Jorren would have loved it.

Goodness. He hadn't thought about Jorren in even longer. He wondered what Jorren would be doing now if they'd never met and hadn't transferred into Liam's regiment to serve together in the war. He'd probably be married with eight children and serving under his father.

Liam sighed into his ale before taking a long gulp. All the things he'd like to be doing. Maybe one day. Maybe with M— No. He couldn't let himself go down that line of thinking.

When he looked up, he caught a table looking at him—the men looked away from him quickly. His stomach sank.

He had to play this smart. He couldn't run. The chase would start much sooner with no chance of his escape if he ran right away.

Liam swallowed hard, cutting up more of his meat. It turned to lead in his mouth, sinking heavily into his stomach, weighing him down.

When the other patrons started whispering to each other, he gripped his knife until his knuckles shone white though his skin. He would need to leave soon. Liam looked around the room, looking for an exit other than the one he had come through.

Liam swore under his breath.

There wasn't one.

He didn't know this town well enough to make an escape plan. If he could get to Ashka, he could ride the gelding hard until they found somewhere to hide. Maybe Manolt? He'd really have to push Ashka, but no one in Manolt would help the soldiers. They were a law unto themselves and didn't appreciate interference.

His breath caught when a pair of soldiers came into the tavern.

Liam looked to the men who'd spied him and found them staring once again. The larger man at the table looked between him and the soldiers. Acid pooled in Liam's throat as the large man rose, moving toward the soldiers.

The serving girl walked past, and Liam grabbed her hand. "Is there another way out of here?" he asked quietly.

She furrowed her brows. "Only through the kitchens, but I can't let you back there."

Liam tried to smile at her with all the charm he could muster. "My brother-in-law just walked in, and he still blames me for my wife's death. I don't want to get into it with him in here."

The serving girl looked back to the entrance, then back to Liam. "I'm sorry, sir." She pulled her hand from his and walked away.

Liam looked back to the soldiers and found them walking toward him. He clenched his fists. There would be no easy escape. He'd have to make his own. Liam only hoped it wouldn't end the same way it had with the two soldiers who had tried to prevent his escape from the dungeons in Jalmar.

When the soldiers approached, Liam remained seated. "Can I help you?"

One of the soldiers gestured to the table behind them. "These gentlemen say that you're a wanted criminal."

"Am I?" Liam feigned surprise. "That's news to me. What did I do?"

Neither soldier looked amused.

"They say that you're Liam Fulton, the man wanted for treason these last eight years," the other soldier said, his brown eyes narrowing on Liam. "Said they saw you on a wanted poster in the town square."

Fuck.

Liam didn't know there were wanted posters of him still circulating. This was going to make it even harder for him to escape now. "Is that so?"

The brown-eyed soldier put his hand on the dagger at his side. "It is. Would you stand?"

Fuck.

He swallowed, standing slowly. This was his chance. Liam eyed the table. He didn't have enough ale to throw into their eyes to distract them. He'd have to use fists. He didn't know if he could still throw a punch that would incapacitate.

If he could take one out of the fight, he could get to the stables to get Ashka. He hoped.

"What happens now?" Liam tried to keep his hands relaxed at his side until it was time.

He scanned the room. All eyes were turned on him now. There were a few men in the tavern who looked like they'd be able to overpower Liam if they were so inclined. He hoped they would remain bystanders—every crowd was different. Some helped, some didn't.

Most didn't.

"Now we take you to Jalmar to confirm whether you are Liam Fulton."

This was it. His stomach tightened as he inhaled deeply. Liam clenched his fist and brought it to the brown-eyed soldier's jaw next to his ear.

The soldier's eyes glazed, and he slowly sank.

Liam didn't wait for him to hit the ground before he ran.

"In the king's name, I command you to stop!" the other soldier yelled, following after him.

Liam felt sick. How many times had he said that exact same thing to criminals when he was in the Third?

Men stood to stop him. Liam shoved past them, not caring whom he knocked aside. He would not be brought back to Jalmar for his execution. Not when he wasn't guilty.

Not when he had to go back to Margaret.

Liam made it to the stable attached to the tavern, pausing in the doorway to look for Ashka. He was in the back stall furthest from the door.

Of course, he was.

Liam looked over his shoulder and found the soldier coming toward him. He wouldn't have time to get on Ashka before the soldier caught up to him, but he could get the stall open to get Ashka out easier when the time came.

Blessedly, the stable boy hadn't unsaddled him. Liam's hand fumbled with the lock as the soldier approached.

Liam grunted when he was shoved against the wall.

"With the authority of the King of Anatalia, you are under arrest for treason and will be brought—"

Liam brought his head back against the soldier's mouth. He closed his eyes tightly at the sharp burst. The soldier stumbled backward, and Liam unlocked the stall and pulled the door open.

If he could—

Liam let out a yell as he was pulled backward, the soldier shoving him to the ground.

"With the authority of the King of Anatalia, you are under arrest for treason and will be brought to the royal magistrate to receive your punishment," the soldier said, his knee in Liam's back.

Liam reached back, grasping for anything he could. His fingers found the belt around the soldier's boot, and he grasped it tightly. He took several deep breaths—as deeply as he could for the soldier's knee being in his back—and pulled sharply.

His stomach quivered as he felt the soldier's knee in his back dislocate.

The soldier screamed, falling back from Liam. The soldier held his thigh above his knee, his eyes tightly closed.

Liam pushed himself from the ground and grabbed Ashka's reins. The horse pranced anxiously, the whites of his eyes showing. He pulled Ashka to the doors of the stable and mounted quickly.

He didn't have time to calm the horse down before they fled. Liam barely had to tap his heels against Ashka before he bolted.

Liam held on tightly, his stomach unclenching the further they got from Mectnora.

28

Two weeks had passed since Margaret put her advertisement in the window. She did not want to seem overeager by checking each day she went into Marbon proper. Her stomach constricted with nervous excitement as she tied Duchess to the post in front of the postmaster's building.

"Mr. Fraser," Margaret greeted pleasantly. "Have there been any responses to my advertisement?"

"Plenty of them, my lady," the postmaster told her, grabbing several sealed letters addressed to her. "Fifteen by my count."

Margaret excitedly snatched them from him. "Thank you, Mr. Fraser." She curtly nodded before she nearly trotted to Duchess. Once they were out of the city proper, Margaret gave Duchess her head and allowed her to gallop to the Gollacks' home to open the letters.

She unsaddled Duchess, letting her loose in the paddock. She could use the time outside. Margaret brushed past Aram quickly in her effort to get inside.

"What's the hurry, Margaret?" Aram asked, his hand shooting out and grabbing her before she could go inside.

Her eyes twinkling, she held up the letters in hand. "Responses for the governess advertisement!"

Margaret didn't let him respond before she went into the kitchen and set water in the kettle to heat. She set the letters on the table, keeping the stack neat and tidy, before she went to grab a sheaf of parchment. Margaret poured the hot water over a pinch of tea leaves, letting them steep as she broke all the seals on each of the letters.

She opened the first one excitedly.

> *Lady Margaret,*
> *I was pleased to see your advertisement.*
> *I have included references for your review and am looking forward to hearing from you in the future.*
> *Your Obedient Servant,*
> *Elizabeth Whiret*

Margaret looked over the references with a critical eye. They were good references, but Elizabeth only taught three children, maximum, at once. She took a sip of her tea and thought of her return letter, her nose scrunching at the bitter taste; Margaret had forgotten to add honey. She grabbed the honey pot and drizzled it into her cup.

Miss Whiret,
I regret to inform you that we have not chosen you as the children's governess.
I wish you the best in your endeavor of finding employment.
Lady Margaret Doremis

Margaret wrote and sealed several such letters, her excitement dying slowly the more letters she read. She sighed as she picked up the last letter. It was considerably lighter than the other applications. Margaret sighed once more. No doubt, she would be writing one last rejection letter.

My Lady Margaret,
I regret that I cannot send you any references along with my application, but I will happily detail my experience:
For the last six years, I have been serving as a governess at an orphanage in Frasisca until the last orphan came of age to leave of his own free will. At maximum there were fifteen children, though there were other governesses there to aid in instructing the children.
I was to take a position as governess to a prominent family within Bishop, but upon my arrival, I was told that their child had fallen ill and died. I was thrilled to see your advertisement and wish sincerely to gain employment with you.
Your Humble and
Obedient Servant,
Evangeline de Clement

Margaret sucked in her breath excitedly. Finally, a worthy candidate for the position! She nearly knocked over her teacup as she reached for the parchment to reply.

Miss Clement,
I am very pleased to offer the position.
If your experience is as you say, you will make a perfect governess for the children, as they are also orphans.

I have enclosed a small fare that will cover the cost of your journey from Bishop to Marbon. I very much look forward to your arrival and working with you and the children.

My Greatest Thanks,
Lady Margaret Doremis

Margaret sealed the letter more thickly than the others, ensuring the tholar she enclosed would not be taken. She returned to Marbon proper as quickly as she could on Duchess. Margaret nodded to the people who called out greetings to her, smiling faintly.

"Mr. Fraser," she said upon entry.

He was packing things away, readying to close for the evening. "I'm sorry Lady Margaret, the post is closing. You'll have to come back tomorrow."

"These letters need to be sent out immediately, Mr. Fraser," Margaret protested.

"That's unfortunate, my lady." Fraser didn't even bother to look at her.

"If you ensure these go out tonight, then I will not even ask for the tal back for the remainder of the time that advertisement would be up," Margaret said, trying to tempt him into doing her bidding.

The offer made Fraser pause, looking at her contemplatively. Finally, he held out his hand. "I will send them tonight."

Margaret smiled at him brightly. "Thank you, Mr. Fraser," she said pleasantly. "And I trust you will also have your messengers tell the postmasters of Bishop and Fradure to remove the advertisement?"

"Of course, my lady." The postmaster bowed to her as she left.

Margaret arrived at the orphan's hovel with Mistress Laphar and Master Schlect—he finally agreed to her urging to take the job. It seemed all the children were there. She was thankful Jonathan had listened to her request to have all the children at home for her visit. Margaret looked around, wrinkling her nose when she saw some of the children were running through the room with no clothes at all.

"Jonathan?"

Jonathan came out of another room, his sleeves rolled up to his elbows, suds dripping from his long fingers. He must have been bathing one of the younger children.

"What?" he demanded crossly.

"We're here for the children's fittings. They'll be measured for clothes and shoes today so they can be made by the end of the week." Margaret gave the cobbler a hard stare when he blanched at the time constraint she had put on him.

She saw the look of sympathy on Susanna's face, glad the kindhearted woman would be more likely to work quickly for her. Margaret could see Master Schlect would be as much trouble as she thought.

"I can't pay for that. Send them away." Jonathan glared at her before he turned to go back to the child he was bathing.

"I'm financing this project." Margaret looked at the children. "And as soon as I can find somewhere, you'll be out of this hovel and in a more suitable home. Children, please line up to be measured."

Jonathan gave the children a nod to do as they were told, a hesitant look on his face. Margaret had gotten the children more comfortable around her, but none of them, including Jonathan, were at the point of obeying her without question. It would take much more than cookies and bread to win them over. She sighed as Jonathan returned to his task, leaving her alone with the children.

All nine in the room lined up in two rows, with one to be measured for shoes and the other to be measured for clothes.

Mistress Laphar knelt in front of her line of children, smiling gently at one of the young boys. "And what's yer name, laddie?" she asked as she pulled out a long rope with knots tied in small intervals.

"Henry," he said as she measured him quickly and wrote down the measurements.

"A fine name that, Henry." Susanna patted him on the cheek. "To the other line, aye?"

Margaret smiled at the gentle interaction between the seamstress and the children, looking to the cobbler. He roughly grabbed Claira's foot, causing her to cry out. Margaret went to her side, kneeling next to the child. "You will be gentle in your touch, sir, or I will terminate your employment with an immediacy that will leave you reeling," she whispered harshly to him.

Margaret held Claira's hand to help balance her. "Are you all right, my darling?"

Claira nodded emphatically but stayed quiet. The child watched Master Schlect trace her foot, then the other, on a piece of parchment using a similar rope to Mistress Laphar to measure her ankle and calf.

"Away with you." The cobbler waved his hand toward Mistress Laphar's line.

Margaret gave him a hard glare, holding her hand out for the next child. Master Schlect finished his work first, rushing to get away from the children, barely taking the time to measure Sarah Beth, who tottered into the room as he was readying to leave. Standing in the doorway, he looked at Margaret expectantly.

"You may go, Master Schlect," Margaret dismissed.

"Thank you, Lady Margaret." The cobbler bowed, retreating quickly.

"Remember, one week!" she called after him, sighing when she received no recognition she had spoken.

Margaret turned to Susanna with the children, a small smile on her face as she watched the attentions of the seamstress. She caught sight of Jonathan coming into the room to watch his children intently. He was trying to catch any hint of wrongdoings on the stranger's part. It was obvious he was very protective of them.

Claira came up to Margaret with big eyes. "Are you gonna be our Mama?"

Margaret knelt, holding out her arms to the orphan girl. "Come here, Claira."

Claira went into Margaret's arms, wrapping her tiny ones around Margaret's neck. Claira gave her a big, toothless grin.

Margaret stood with the girl in her arms. "Well, my dear, to answer your question, I am not going to be your Mama, but I will be around to help your Papa for a little while."

Claira looked back at Jonathan with an inquiring look. The young father gave Margaret a suspicious scowl, only giving a slight nod to the pair.

With Claira still in her arms, Margaret turned to Mistress Laphar. "Remember, I want two outfits and two pairs of shoes by the end of the week. Will you remind Master Schlect that it is indeed two and not one? He has assured me he's capable of the work because they're smaller."

"Yes, m'lady," Mistress Laphar said to her with a small curtsey before walking out of the lackadaisical building.

Margaret waited for the seamstress and cobbler outside of the orphan's home. Her stomach roiled with excitement as she watched Susanna come toward her with several young girls in her wake. They all held wrapped packages for the children, their own smiles taking over their faces. Margaret could hardly wait to see the children's excitement when they received their new clothing.

"Where is Master Schlect?" She did not see him among the herd of women coming toward her.

"I told him we were goin' over now," Susanna said irritably, "and he shooed me away, sayin' he wasn't done."

Margaret shared the seamstress' irritation. "I told him he needed to be done today!"

"I know, m'lady," the seamstress agreed. "I kept tellin' him ye'd told him one week."

Margaret let out a frustrated noise from the back of her throat. "I'll speak with him later. For now, these children need their new clothes."

Susanna clapped to gain the attention of her workers. "Each package is labeled with the children's names. The oldest ones can dress themselves. Ye'll help the others into the clothes and move on to the next."

Margaret smiled, letting them flood into the orphan's home.

"My darlings, I have a surprise for you!" Margaret called out. "Will you come here please?"

Susanna smiled as they heard the stampede of feet coming from every direction in the dilapidated building. "Line up, ladies," she commanded.

The children paused in the doorway, seeing the unfamiliar women lined up with packages in hand. Doubt plastered their small faces.

Margaret took one of the packages from the women. She read the name on the box. "Daren? Come get your new clothes."

The oldest boy came forward cautiously, snatching the package from her hands. He retreated to the back of the room before opening the box, holding up the newly constructed clothing.

"Henry, Christopher, Charles," Margaret called them, motioning toward the women that held their clothes, "you can also dress yourselves."

Claira came to her side, pulling on her skirt. "Where are my clothes?" she whined.

"Who has Claira's package?" Margaret asked, taking hold of the orphan's hand.

"I do, m'lady." Susanna handed it to Margaret.

Claira let go of Margaret's hand, reaching greedily for the box that contained her goods. Her tiny fists opened and closed in eager anticipation, making Margaret bark a short laugh. Margaret knelt in front of the orphan girl, letting her rip open the box. She saw there were, in fact, three outfits instead of two in the box.

Margaret shot Susanna an appreciative glance, mouthing 'thank you' before she helped Claira into one set of her new clothes.

29

Liam arrived in Manolt, the city on the opposite side of the Hook of Hamuel, as the noon bell tolled. It was drastically different from the historic Hamuel. The city was not as clean as the old capital city, or as large. Manolt looked like it once had cobbled streets, but they were now only against the front of the buildings and in the mostly unused alleyways. The people in Manolt were uncaring about a person's situation as long as they didn't stay around to cause trouble. Soldiers never came to this town—when they did, they were harassed until they left. What was the point of going when the city made its own law? He'd stay a few days to rest Ashka and gather supplies for the road since he had been unable to in Mectnora.

Liam shook his shoulders out, letting loose a heavy breath. It had been too close a call in Mectnora.

He found the only inn with stables, more upscale than the previous one in Hamuel. Liam doubted he would find any prostitutes coming to his table here. He found the proprietor of the inn, setting down a few Tholar.

"How long of a stay will this get me?" he asked, wanting to see if he could bargain his way into a longer stay with little money.

The proprietor, a severe-looking man with white hair, looked him over with a raised brow. "Two days."

"Two days!" Liam exclaimed, flabbergasted.

"It includes the stables and feed for your horse, your room, and two meals a day," the proprietor told him. "Take it or leave it."

Liam's lips pressed together in a thin white line. He set down the same amount of Tholar next to his original pile. "Fine. I need a room."

The proprietor quickly snatched up the money, handing Liam a key hanging on the wall behind him. "Room seven."

Liam nodded, going to the room to hide Margaret's jewels before someone else walked off with them. The room was decent enough, with a bed and a nightstand in the corner. There was a basin and pitcher with cold water on the opposite side of the room and a small rug in front of the bed. Not much to the room, but it was sufficient for his needs.

He took only a few coins with him before returning to the common room for a meal. He could smell a chicken roasting over the fire, periodically sizzling as grease dripped.

A serving wench came to his table. "What'll ye have, sir? Chicken or porridge?"

"Chicken," Liam said quickly. It was the more appetizing choice. "And ale."

She nodded, looking him over appraisingly before going to fetch his dinner. It was quickly brought back to his table. The chicken was cut into thick slices, juices flowing freely from the fresh cuts. She poured a thick brown gravy over the chicken and the smashed potatoes.

"I gave you the freshest meat we got, sir." She looked at him suggestively.

Liam couldn't keep the half-grin from his face. "Thank you kindly."

She nodded once before walking away.

He ate heartily, enjoying the savory taste of his meal. The food alone, he could see, would be well worth the price of the inn. Liam looked up when the serving wench came back to his table. She had a plate and a pitcher in her hands.

"How are you enjoying your meal? I brought you another plate." She took away his near-finished one. "And a pitcher of ale just for you."

"Do all the customers get such special treatment?" Liam raised an eyebrow at her, examining her as closely as she had examined him earlier.

She was not an unpleasant woman to look at. She was pudgy around the stomach, her breasts overlarge, and her cheeks ruddy from the heat in the room. The serving wench had plain, mouse-colored hair, not nearly as lustrous as Margaret's deep brown. He immediately banished thoughts of the young woman he had grown far too attached to.

"Just the ones I like," she told him.

"What's your name?"

"Lydia," the serving wench said.

"Lydia," he tested it on his tongue. "That's a very nice name, Lydia."

Her cheeks reddened even more. "Thank you, sir."

"Liam."

"Thank you, Liam," she corrected, lowering her lashes at him flirtatiously.

"Would you care to join me for a drink?" Liam asked, taking note for the first time there were only two or three other patrons in the common room.

Lydia's eyebrows raised, a smile playing on her lips. "I'll grab a cup."

Liam poured himself more ale as he waited for Lydia to return. He could hear the scraping of chairs on the floor, soft chatter between patrons as they enjoyed their meals. Liam looked back when he heard the rattle of cups and plates. One greasy-haired man had passed out on top of his plate, smashed potatoes creeping up to his hairline.

Lydia sat across from Liam, her own plate in front of her. She smiled, her hair let down around her shoulders.

Liam filled her cup, looking over at her appreciatively. He could see her interest in him plainly, her shift untied to show her bust more clearly. "Are you spoken for, Lydia?"

"Not as of yet." Her lashes delicately lowered.

Liam took a sip of his ale. "I leave in a few days, and I wouldn't be able to take you away from here."

Lydia shrugged. "I don't particularly feel like leaving."

"What are you expecting?" he asked, taking another sip of his ale.

She looked at him directly, a small twitch of her mouth making her smile. "Just a bit of fun."

Liam finished his ale, clearing his throat. "I'm in room seven, for whenever you're done with your work," he said, standing. "I'll leave the door unlocked for you."

He returned to his room, not locking the door as promised. Liam lay down on the bed, sighing as he waited. He hadn't bothered asking how long until her shift was over. His mind wandered to Margaret, unbidden, thinking of how he turned her life around. It was no wonder she refused any offer he made to take her with him. It was for the best that she had stayed where she was.

Liam reached under the bed, pulling out the small chest that contained Margaret's jewels. They were expensive enough, he probably could have bought the whole town and still had money left over to buy another. He put it back quickly when he heard a knock on the door, Lydia coming in shortly after.

"Liam?" she asked, almost timidly.

He held his hand out to her. "Come here, Lydia."

Lydia took it, sitting next to him. She looked nervous now, biting her bottom lip.

"You don't have to do this," he told her, squeezing her hand. "I won't force you."

"I want to," she said, kissing him.

When they had finished, Lydia laid against Liam, her head on his chest. "Who is Maggie?"

"Hmm?" Liam inhaled sleepily, his eyes barely opened when he looked at her.

"Maggie, the woman's name you called out," Lydia reminded him.

"Someone I would like to forget." He pulled her closer to him. "Now go to sleep."

Liam smiled at a somber-looking Lydia. She had taken residence with him for the entirety of his stay, showing him what sights her city had to offer. It was not much, mostly only a few good fishing holes and a place to dive off cliffs. He rummaged through the saddlebags on Ashka, pulling out a large diamond and pearl brooch.

"I want you to take this," he said quietly, putting it into her hand. "I doubt I'll be back this way for quite some time."

Lydia gasped when she opened her hand. "Liam! Where would you have gotten something like this?"

"Think nothing of it," Liam put his hands on her shoulders. "I want you to use it…just in case."

"Are you a noble?" Lydia demanded, clutching the brooch tightly to her chest.

"No." Liam almost laughed at the prospect. "I am not a noble."

"Did you steal it then?" Her eyes were wide. "Are you giving me stolen goods that could get my cheek branded?"

"I assure you, the lady will not miss it," Liam tried to reassure her. "She left them behind when she moved far, far away."

Lydia's eyes still held her skepticism, though the brooch was not so tightly clutched to her chest now. "You're sure?"

"I'm sure." He kissed her forehead, mounting Ashka.

"Do you have to go?" she asked, her voice raised a third higher than usual.

"I do." He smiled at her gently. "I made a promise to someone I intend on keeping."

He bowed to her at the waist before he urged Ashka into a trot. He was looking forward to being on the road again. Liam's true joy was being on the road, having no rules but his own. He didn't think he would stay in another city as he made his way toward Glessic.

"I'll miss you, Liam!" Lydia yelled after him when he was nearly out of sight.

He turned Ashka to wave back at her once. Liam would think fondly of her for some time. He traveled his way along the coast, stopping at each town only to get enough supplies to reach the next. He took a slow pace toward Glessic, where he would spend a month out in the open without worry, sleeping on the beaches with a large bonfire from the driftwood he found.

30

Margaret entered the poorly constructed building Jonathan Lerosen and his babies lived in. "Jonathan?"

Jonathan came out from the backroom, the permanent scowl on his face. "What do you want?"

Margaret frowned. Jonathan had been giving her a harder time than the children had. He was suspicious of anyone trying to help him since no one else would bother looking his way. "I wanted to see how the children were liking their new clothes."

"They like them just fine." Jonathan nearly sneered at her. "Is that all?"

Having heard Margaret's voice, Claira ran up to her. "Maggie!"

Margaret picked her up with a smile. "Hello, my darling." She kissed the young orphan on the forehead.

"Well?" Jonathan asked. "Is that all?"

"No," Margaret said firmly. "We are going to get you fitted for new clothes and look at the better accommodations I've picked out for you."

"We're just fine here," the teen said stubbornly. "And I can't afford new clothes."

"Jonathan," Margaret snapped irritably, pointing a finger at him, "I think we should establish something right now: I *will* be helping you, whether you like it or not, for the sake of these children. You will be receiving better accommodations for yourself and the children. You will have a new wardrobe, there will be a governess for these children to have a proper education, they will learn manners—and you along with them—and you *will* show me the respect that I am showing you."

Jonathan hands balled at his side, knuckles white, as he silently stared at her.

"Do you understand me?" Margaret asked as Claira hugged her around the neck, burying her face in Margaret's hair. The little girl obviously did not like the tone between the two.

"Yes," he snapped at her.

"Yes, Lady Margaret," she corrected.

"Yes, Lady Margaret," Jonathan said through clenched teeth.

"Good." Margaret set Claira down for her to go to Jonathan. "Now that we understand each other, I would like for you to come with me to Mistress Laphar's shop for you to be fitted for clothes and then look at a new home I've found."

"What about the children?" Jonathan asked. "They can't stay alone for that long by themselves."

"I have their new governess waiting outside, who arrived yesterday to watch them while we're gone," Margaret informed him with a smile.

Jonathan growled, crossing his arms tightly over his chest. "You think of everything, don't you?"

"Everything," Margaret confirmed with a satisfied smirk.

"Bring her in," Jonathan sighed. "I'll go with you."

"Evangeline, please come in here," Margaret called toward the door.

"She's Frasiscan?" Jonathan asked, surprised.

"All the best governesses are," Margaret told him offhandedly.

"Yes, my lady?" Evangeline asked when she entered the room. "Where is it that I will be with the children?"

"Right here, Evangeline," Margaret told her. "For now, at least."

"Here?" the Frasiscan woman blanched. "Truly, my lady?"

"Yes," Margaret said. "We won't be gone very long."

"Yes, my lady." Evangeline reluctantly curtsied.

"Come along, Jonathan," Margaret called as she walked out the door.

Jonathan followed Margaret out of the home and to the seamstress' shop, brooding silently.

Margaret entered the shop with a smile. "Mistress Laphar? I have another task for you and your girls."

"M'lady, ye'll work us until all that's left of our fingers are bare bone!" The seamstress complained.

"And they will be very rich bones," Margaret told her. "Jonathan here needs a new wardrobe."

"While I measure the lad here, I want ye to try on the dress we just finished," Mistress Laphar told her.

Now that all the fabrics had arrived from the capital, the seamstress and her girls, old and new, had been working tirelessly to finish her commission as quickly as possible. The ten of them had managed to finish a dress almost every day. The seamstress had told Margaret she would have to hire another two girls to ensure Margaret had the highest quality possible.

Margaret smiled brightly at the woman. "Mistress Laphar, you're far too good to me!"

"Yes, I know," the seamstress cooed. "Now let's go and put yer dress on."

One of the girls measured Jonathan while he waited for Margaret to come out in her dress. He was sitting on a bench when Margaret came out. He stood when he saw her, a shocked look on his face. "Lady Margaret…"

Margaret smiled at him. It was a daring dress for court, but nonetheless an amazing gown. She had given Susanna liberty to create some of her own designs instead of following the court fashions. The gown was made of emerald-colored silk in a diminutive ball gown style. The top was a tightly fitted corset with gold embroidered knots at the bust that extended out to the arm cuffs that were not attached to the dress. The cuffs fitted tightly to her upper arms so they would not slip. The bottom had a diaphanous fabric that trailed halfway to the ground.

"Beautiful, m'lady," the seamstress told her. "A perfect fit, don't you think, boy?"

"It is the finest thing I have ever seen," he said almost breathlessly.

"Thank you, Jonathan," Margaret cooed sweetly. "Will you have this dress sent to the Gollacks' home for me, Mistress Laphar?"

"Of course, m'lady," the seamstress told her, leading her back to change out of the garment.

Margaret returned to the front of the shop, where Jonathan was waiting for her. "Are you ready to see the house I've picked out for you?"

"There are no homes here in Marbon that can fit all my children," Jonathan told her.

"It's not within the town's limits," Margaret informed him. "It's about a twenty-minute walk from here."

Jonathan sighed as he followed her out of the shop and along the main road of the small town of Marbon. He walked silently next to Margaret. She enjoyed the quiet, for once not having Jonathan yell at her to stay away or frustrated over something she was doing for the children. She understood he wanted to do things on his own, but taking care of that many children was beyond his capability.

Margaret wanted to help them, to leave something good behind in Marbon the way she had in Silvica, helping the villagers as often as she could. Her father would be proud of her doing this, and certainly wouldn't begrudge her the money she had spent on the orphans' new home.

The home they walked up to was three stories high, made with red brick, mostly covered with climbing ivy. The roof was slate and coming out of it were six chimneys, three on each side of the original portion of the house. Attached to the middle, the original portion, were the east and west wings which each had twelve windows between the three levels. The center part of the construction had six windows between the three levels and a roof higher than the east and west wings. A simple pediment decorated the front of the higher roof. The manor home was two bedrooms deep, giving the children twenty bedrooms to choose from, each bedroom having two windows to let light in.

The ground level of the home housed a small library, a large dining hall, and a drawing room for entertaining. There was a small kitchen on the east side of the house. The house had been left by the previous owner with all the furniture still in it. Each room was fully furnished with a bed and accompanying necessities, some with paintings still on the walls and others with the shadows of the paintings taken with the previous owner.

"I won't be here forever—I'll be leaving once I can get all of my purchases finished to go back to the capital, but I want to make sure you're all taken care of," Margaret said. "I went to the banker's bench and started a fund the estate will be able to draw from to keep it running and provide for you and the children. It should last well beyond the time the children leave."

Jonathan said nothing, only stared at the house.

She shifted awkwardly. "Some of the decorations like the drapery and the bedding will need to be replaced before it's suitable for you and the children to move in here, but there is more than enough room for all of you and others in need to live comfortably," Margaret told Jonathan with a sidelong glance.

He stared at the manor house in disbelief. "Why are you helping us?"

Margaret shrugged. "I suppose I'm somewhat of an orphan myself. My father is gone, and my mother left us when he got sick."

"This is too much for us, Lady Margaret." Jonathan looked back at the house.

"It's already purchased, and there are new beds and bedding on their way here so you and the children can move in by the end of the month."

"So everything is all settled whether I approve of it or not?" Jonathan sounded almost helpless.

"Yes," Margaret admitted. "I'm not accustomed to the word 'no,' Jonathan."

"I can tell," Jonathan said. "Can we go back to my children now?"

When Jonathan and Margaret arrived back at the dilapidated living space, the toys and blankets were strewn about the room.

"My lady," Evangeline called out to her desperately, her hair undone and the sleeve of her dress torn. "My lady, I cannot do this. I cannot be their governess. The children…they're monsters!"

"Evangeline, wait!" Margaret called after the governess, watching the Frasiscan woman throwing her hands up in the air with an indignant huff.

"I think you just got your first 'no,' Lady Margaret," Jonathan said with an amused smirk.

31

Glessic was Liam's second favorite place to go when he felt the need to leave Anatalia, the first being Radovan, where he spent the majority of his exile. The country to Anatalia's southeastern border took great pride in keeping its cities and towns clean and orderly, along with having the fewest homeless citizens. Liam inhaled deeply as he entered the city of Zuev, looking around. There were flowers planted in the front of every shop to ensure the city always smelled sweetly; there was no trash or waste in sight in keeping with the country's clean reputation.

Liam openly strolled the streets, looking for an inn. They were more expensive in Zuev than any other city in Glessic, but they were impeccable. Liam would normally have to work for his stay in the stables, but with the money from Margaret's home, he could relax. He should feel bad taking the money from her, but he knew she would have told him to support himself comfortably and given it up freely anyway.

Liam heard a minstrel singing in the common room of The Maiden Fair. A serving wench immediately offered him a mug of beer when he sat to listen. He thanked her, took a sip of the drink, and continued listening to the minstrel. He was singing in a light falsetto about the beauty and charity of the baron's daughter. Lord Iesos Stelios owned the surrounding lands and city of Zuev. From what Liam could gather, the lord's daughter had golden hair like the sun and eyes as blue as the sky, with a smile that could banish any darkness. He also learned from the singer that the daughter gave alms to the poor every day. Liam wondered how a baron's daughter could afford such a charitable endeavor. After the song ended, Liam decided he would pay for a room at the Maiden Fair for the next week.

Liam cleared his throat to get the attention of the proprietor.

"Yes sir," the tall man said when he turned around. "What can I do for you?"

"I'd like a room for the week." Liam set down two gold tals.

The innkeeper picked up the tals, examining them closely. "Anatalian money? Is this your first visit to Glessic?"

"Not a first visit, no," Liam told him. "Is my money acceptable?"

"It will be acceptable," he said reassuringly, grabbing a key from the drawer in front of him. "Will there be anything else, sir?"

"That will be all, thank you." Liam took the key from him.

"Room two, on the second floor."

Liam thanked him, climbing the stairs two at a time. He was anxious to put Margaret's jewels in a safe place.

He unlocked the door, entering the fresh-smelling room. There were flowers on the table next to the window, the vase sitting on a crocheted doily. Liam went to the four-poster bed, letting out a relaxed sigh when he sat. It was feather, and well worth the money he spent on the room. Liam looked around for a place to hide the jewels, finding the only place he could safely put them was in his own pack under the bed. He would need a better method of hiding the treasure horde, and soon.

Once his things were locked away in his room, Liam decided to explore Zuev. It was a beautiful city. Fleetingly, he thought Margaret would enjoy visiting one day. Liam could smell the fresh river air as he walked through the city, courtesy of the Zuev River. The water rushing past was a relaxing sound that made him want to spend his time near the banks. Liam picked a petal off one of the many flowers in the window boxes that all the shops had to beautify the city, sighing as he thought of Margaret.

Liam decided to explore the city further than his initial search for an inn. As he strolled through the spotless city of Zuev, Liam saw a crowd gathered at the end of the street he was on before he heard someone yell, "Fire!"

The hairs raised on the back of his neck, and Liam jogged to the crowd, seeing a bucket brigade trying to put out the flames licking up the side of the large home. A man standing at the front of the crowd, his hair in disarray from running his hand through it, yelled in a panic at anyone who would listen. "My daughter is in there! Help her, please!"

Liam looked around and saw no one was making a move to enter the burning home. He lingered for a moment, his hackles rising, knowing if no one helped the trapped girl, she would die. Liam bounced impatiently on the balls of his feet, waiting for any sign of movement before rushing into the burning building.

The heat of the fire assaulted him, smoke stinging his eyes, making them water to near blindness. Liam heard a weak cry above the whoosh of the flames. Crackling seemed to come from every direction, the smoke refracting the sound. He covered his nose and mouth with the crook of his elbow as he tried to navigate his way through the smoke, avoiding the flames licking up the walls, listening to the cries of the trapped woman.

"Where are you?" Liam yelled over the roar of the fire, his body wracking with coughs when the smoke invaded his lungs, its long tendrilled fingers forcing their way down his throat.

A responding round of coughs came from somewhere in front of him. "Here!" she yelled with as much strength as she could muster. "I'm here!"

"Keep talking to me!" Liam wiped away the tears gathering in his eyes, searching through mere slits for anything not ablaze.

"I'm here! Please!" she called out between loud coughs and choked crying.

Liam jumped back with a strangled cry when a burning pillar crumbled next to him. He searched with renewed fervor. The house could collapse on them any minute, and both would be killed if he did not find her soon. "Say something!"

"I'm in here! I can see you!" She let out a relieved cry, nearly laughing with joy. "Through the doorway!"

After searching for what seemed like hours in the smoke, Liam finally found the pleading man's daughter under a fallen beam. Already light-headed from the smoke, Liam was thankful the room she was in had the least amount of smoke clouding his vision. He tried to lift the beam off her.

"It's too heavy." The trapped woman let out another round of coughs. "It's why the servants left me behind."

"I'm not leaving without you." Liam struggled with the beam, searching for any space he could wedge his fingers under.

He braced himself and took hold, grunting as he pulled it toward him. Liam's neck bulged, veins popping vividly on his neck and forehead as the weight of the beam rested on his shoulders. With a spectacular effort, Liam lifted the fallen beam and hefted it backward, the offending object landing with a thunderous crash.

"Thank you," she cried breathlessly, tears making clean tracks on her ash-streaked face.

Liam picked her up, throat burning from smoke inhalation. He struggled to navigate to an open exit, stumbling on fallen debris. Liam stopped short as he heard a beam from the ceiling crack and fall close to his side.

"Hold on!" Liam yelled as the house began to rumble.

Liam burst forth through the entrance of the home as the roof collapsed in on itself, blowing smoke out like a gust of wind toward the scattered crowd.

"My daughter!" the disheveled man cried, rushing to the sooty pair. He took the woman from Liam's arms and held her close to him.

Liam doubled over, breathing in deeply, letting out a round of coughs. He had townspeople patting him on the back for saving the woman. The worried father went to him once he had examined his daughter to make sure she was not seriously injured.

The father helped Liam stand up straight. "Thank you," he breathed. "Thank you. Anything you desire is yours."

"I require nothing," Liam told him, coughing once more, getting clapped on the back by the man in front of him.

"There must be something," the man told him. "Money, women, anything you want."

"There is nothing I require," Liam repeated.

"I am the lord of this town. Anything you want is yours," Lord Stelios informed the ash-covered man. "Even the hand of my daughter Lady Adelena."

"My lord, truly, I require nothing," Liam told him once more.

The baron clapped him on the back one last time. "Get this man new clothes and a basin to wash from. He will be dining with us tonight," he ordered his servants.

"My lord," Liam started.

"I will hear no more of it," the baron said, putting his hand on Liam's shoulder.

32

Jonathan tied the last string on all the children's outfits. He was proud to see all his children in well-fitting clothing for the first time since he had adopted them. He would be even prouder, he imagined, had he been the one to provide them instead of Lady Margaret.

Jonathan wasn't sure how to feel about that woman. She willingly paid for his children to prosper in a way he would never have been able to provide. For all she was doing for them, she was bossy and demanding. She ordered him and everyone around like servants because she had the money to. It drove Jonathan to madness to put up with her haughtiness. If it weren't for his children needing more help than he could give them, he would have had nothing to do with her.

He went to the makeshift kitchen to make their breakfast. "In here to eat, lambs!" he bellowed to ensure his voice was heard throughout the building.

Jonathan's jaw set as he watched his children eat. It was another thing he had not provided for them, unable to afford the luxury.

There was a light knock on the door, and the person entered without permission. No doubt it was the *benefactor* that forced herself upon them. She was the only one with the audacity to treat the sanctity of his house as such. Jonathan sighed, hearing the click of her heels on the floor as she searched the building for them. It had been nearly two weeks since he had seen her, though he had found deliveries of food and supplies at his door every other day.

"Jonathan?" she called out tentatively. "Where are all of you?"

"In here," he reluctantly answered.

She smiled when she found them. "I have a wonderful surprise for you."

"I love surprises!" Claira yelled, her mouth full.

Margaret gave her a disapproving look. "We don't speak with a full mouth."

"What is your surprise?" Jonathan interrupted her scolding.

"Today is moving day!" Margaret beamed at him, clapping her hands in excitement.

"Not today," Jonathan told her. "We aren't ready to leave."

Her smile stayed plastered on her face, though he could see her eyes turn icy. "I have everything ready for all of you. All you have to do is walk there."

"We aren't ready to leave," he repeated.

"Jonathan," she said, smile sharp as a blade, "anything and everything you need is there. You don't even need anything from here."

Jonathan shrugged one shoulder, raising a brow at her in challenge.

"Are you being deliberately difficult?" Margaret demanded. "To what end? To be in control?"

"You have come in here and taken control of everything and given us zero choice in the matter," Jonathan snapped at her. "We will leave when we are ready to."

Margaret's brows rose abruptly. "And you think that making the children stay here in this…hovel when there is a perfectly good home that is fully furnished because I'm telling you what to do?"

Jonathan felt the conviction in his chest fade. "I am their father. I tell them when we are moving, not you."

She shrugged at him irritatingly. "I'll be waiting for you at the house whenever you're ready to act like an adult, where there's a cook, a housekeeper, and new clothes for everyone and toys for the children."

She left without another word.

Jonathan growled low in his throat. She had an infuriating ability to get under his skin. He looked over his shoulder at his children, happily shoving food into their mouths. Sighing heavily, he turned to them.

"Finish your breakfast, lambs, we're going to take a trip," he told them, resting a hand affectionately on Charles's shoulder.

"Whhhere awwe goin' Papa?" Sarah Beth kicked her legs in excitement, bouncing on her seat.

Jonathan smiled at her, his eyes crinkling affectionately. "It's a surprise."

"A supwise?" Her eyes turned big.

"Right after you all finish eating," Jonathan told them. "What do you think about that?"

Sarah Beth tried to shove an entire roll in her mouth in response.

Jonathan stopped in front of the house, holding Claira and Sarah Beth's tiny hands. He looked back, the rest of his children were hand-in-hand walking in what he assumed was their attempt at a straight line. Their gait reminded him more of a snake slithering rather than the order he asked for.

"Wassat?" Sarah Beth pointed at the manor home, looking up at her father.

"That, my love," —Jonathan picked her up, holding her on his hip— "is our new home."

"Really, Papa?" Henry asked, looking at the house in disbelief. "This is ours?"

"Thanks to Lady Margaret." Jonathan nodded. "She bought this for us."

Claira gasped loudly and over-exaggeratedly. "Maggie bought us a *house*?"

"Can we go in, Papa?" Charles asked, looking at the home in wonder.

"You can." Jonathan was barely able to say before the children were rushing the door.

He followed them, smiling when he heard their giggling as they ran through the house. They happily explored the home, running through each room. Jonathan found Margaret in the library, a book in hand.

"So you decided to come today." She didn't look up from her book.

"I did." Jonathan tried not to let her get under his skin for the second time today. It was not going to be easy; she was the most annoying person he had ever met.

"Good. Call the children in here, please." Margaret set down her book.

Jonathan could hear the faint patter of tiny feet in the upstairs rooms, the children yelling to each other to come look at this or come look at that.

"Lambs!" He yelled up to them, the tendons in his neck standing out in the effort to be heard. "Get down here!"

By the time he returned, Margaret had gathered two other women into the library. She smoothed her skirts as Jonathan walked in, flashing him a bright smile.

Jonathan gave her a tentative one back, lining the children up as they came to him.

Margaret waited for them to quiet before she spoke. "Welcome to your new home. You will be welcome here until you come of age to start your own lives, or marry, and your father will be staying here as long as he likes." She paused, looking over the children. Their eyes were already glazing over, the amount of information small as it was. "You will be taught to read and write here, and anything else your governess, when she arrives, sees fit to teach you. In the meantime, I will start to teach you what I think is important for you to know."

The children stared at her blankly, and Jonathan was happy to see her bluster fading rapidly.

Margaret cleared her throat, turning toward the two other women in the room. "This is Gretchen, your maid—whom you will not make extra work for being messy—and Matilda, the cook, who will make you three meals a day. You can call them Miss Gretchen and Miss Matilda."

"And what will we call you?" Jonathan asked.

"Miss Maggie will be fine," she assured them. "Some of the children already call me Maggie anyway."

They all stood there, shifting on their feet, waiting for any other instruction from their benefactor.

"You may go." Margaret clapped her hands at them. "Explore, pick your rooms, enjoy yourselves. You will be called for lunch when it is ready."

Jonathan shooed the children away, staying in the library to see if there was anything else he needed to know.

"I would like to show you your rooms personally, Jonathan." Margaret came and laid a hand on his arm. "If you'll let me."

Jonathan nodded. "Lead the way, Miss Maggie."

She led him to the third floor to the room for the master of the house. It spanned the entire center of the home. There was a large bed, an area blocked off by privacy screens to change, and a small writing desk on the wall furthest from the door. Four rugs met on the floor, attempting to look like one large continuous rug. The room was left sparse to allow him to decorate as he wished.

Jonathan walked to the center of the room, turning around slowly. "All of this for one person?"

Margaret nodded. "It's for the master of the house, which will be you since you are the children's father."

He shook his head. "This is too big for one person. Six children could sleep in this room comfortably."

"There are nineteen other rooms for the children, and there are only ten of them. You have the opportunity to take in other children who need your help now," Margaret told him.

"Where will Gretchen and Matilda sleep?" Jonathan was confused.

"In the servant's quarters." Margaret had her own look of confusion. It must have seemed obvious to her that's where they would sleep.

"I see."

"They have plenty of room down there," Margaret assured him. "It's fitted for up to twenty servants, and there are only two. I've given them leave to hire more as needed. Matilda has already asked for five helpers, and Gretchen would like time to see how the children behave before settling on her number to hire."

"I don't know how to handle servants," Jonathan protested.

She smiled. "You'll learn."

Jonathan glanced about the room.

"I'll leave you to get acquainted with your new lodging," Margaret told him, heading for the door. "Let me know if you require anything else in the room."

Jonathan nodded mutely.

<h1 style="text-align:center">33</h1>

Margaret woke early, sitting next to the glowing embers of the fire for warmth. She was sipping tea when Elizabeth came into the kitchen. She smiled tiredly at the older woman. Margaret was rarely up before the sun.

"Would you like a cup of tea?"

"You're up early," Elizabeth commented, grabbing a cup from the cupboard. "Couldn't sleep?"

"I want to get to the children early this morning." Margaret took another sip.

"Any word on a governess?" Elizabeth sat across from her, pouring milk in first, letting the tea mix itself when she poured it over.

"Not yet," she sighed. "I'll be giving the children their first lesson today."

"What will that be?"

Margaret shrugged. "I have no idea. Maybe writing their names?"

"Do they know their letters?" Elizabeth sounded doubtful.

Margaret sighed again, rubbing her cheeks in frustration. "More than likely not."

The older woman patted her hand lightly. "You'll have your work cut out for you."

Margaret drained her tea, standing. "I should leave."

"You shouldn't be walking around while it's still dark. There were raiders seen outside the village down river yesterday," Elizabeth warned her. "I'll wake Aram to walk you."

"Let him rest. I'll take Duchess there," Margaret told her. It had been far too long since she had ridden her mare. "It won't take me long with her."

"Just be careful." Elizabeth stood to walk her to the door.

Margaret unsaddled her mare when she arrived, giving her a quick rub down before going into the house. She hadn't seen anyone else out on her ride in, thankfully. The children were trickling in one at a time, bleary-eyed and yawning, to breakfast. Jonathan carried in a platter of rolls, setting it on the table before he noticed her.

"Miss Maggie." Jonathan sounded surprised. "What are you doing here?"

Margaret smiled at him. "I wanted to get here early for our first lesson together," she said with a small shrug.

"What will you be teachin' 'em today?" Jonathan put the dish down on the table, turning to pay attention to her.

"Do they know their letters?"

"No." Jonathan's mouth turned to a hard line.

"Then I'll be teaching them their letters, and maybe to write their names," Margaret told him, feeling hopeful as she looked at the children. "Or just their letters, depending on how the day goes."

Jonathan nodded, an odd smile on his face. "Good luck."

Margaret didn't get the chance to ask him what he meant by that. Jonathan returned to the kitchen to carry in more food. Shrugging to herself, she grabbed a roll before going to the library where their lessons would be held. In preparation for the governess, Margaret had purchased a large rotating chalkboard, both sides easily used.

She picked up the bone-white chalk, biting her lip nervously. Margaret carefully wrote out each letter, A to Z, in both lower and uppercase to show the children the difference. On the opposite side, she wrote each of the children's names.

Margaret looked over her work carefully, making sure every letter was perfect. She let out a pleased noise when she saw they were. Returning to the dining room, she smiled when the children hastily swallowed to say hello. Even Jonathan seemed pleased to see her for the first time since their meeting. Not wanting to spoil the moment, Margaret sat in the only empty chair at the long table. There was barely any food left, but there were several rolls she could snack on.

"Do you have everything all ready for the children?" asked Jonathan after swallowing a large gulp.

She nodded, her own mouth full.

Margaret grew more and more frustrated as she tried to teach the children the sounds of their vowels and consonants in conjunction with how the letters looked. Unused to listening for more than a few minutes at a time, the children were shifting in their seats and whispering to each other.

Margaret's lips pursed tightly as the children giggled. She turned on them quickly, finger poised to scold them when she caught sight of Jonathan in the doorway. His eyebrows were raised at her, as if to challenge her decision to discipline the unruly children.

"Jonathan, can I help you?"

Jonathan pushed himself off the jamb, going into the library. "How 'bout givin' the children a break?"

"Of course." Margaret waved her hand at the children. "Go play outside. I'll have Matilda fix a small snack for them."

The children nearly ran Jonathan over to escape their lesson.

Jonathan's lips twitched in amusement. "I see your first lesson is going well."

Margaret gave him a bland look. "It could be going better."

He pushed a short burst of air through his nose, the amused look still on his face. "I'll tell Miss Matilda to make them something."

"Thank you, Jonathan." Margaret smiled at him.

He nodded to her before he went to the kitchen.

Margaret felt a hand slip into hers, looking down to see Henry's blond head already tousled with grass. "Yes, my dear?"

He was looking at her with wide eyes. "Is that yer horse out there?"

She smiled at him. "It is. Her name is Duchess."

"Can we ride her?" Henry asked, his eyes glowing with excitement.

Margaret hesitated, unsure of how her mare would react to the children swarming around her.

"Pleeease, Miss Maggie!" Henry begged.

"All right." She squeezed his hand. "Go tell your brothers and sisters."

The child delightedly yelled, nearly ripping Margaret's arm off her shoulder as he forgot to release her hand before he ran to tell the others.

Margaret smiled to herself as she tidied the room. She hoped Duchess would take the children in good spirit. Margaret went to the stables to saddle the mare, finding all the children were gathered in front of her stall. She raised her brows, her mouth turning with amusement.

"Can we ride her now?" Claira asked loudly, reaching her hands up to climb over the stall in her impatience to reach her equine prize.

"Duchess needs to be saddled first, my darling." Margaret grabbed her under her raised arms to pluck the young child off the gate. "Otherwise, your backside will be sore for days."

A collective whine went through the children, though they did move away from the door for her to get to Duchess.

Margaret quickly prepared the horse for riding and led her outside. "Who will be first?"

"Me!" Came the chorus of replies from all the children.

Margaret was relieved when Jonathan came outside to join them. The children gathered around Margaret, each one with their arms raised eagerly, all wanting her attention. She didn't know how Jonathan dealt with them constantly on his own— just a few of them were too many to keep track of, much less ten.

Margaret helped Daren—with some difficulty, as he was only an inch shorter than herself—on the horse, turning to swoop a giggling Sarah Beth and place her in front of her older brother.

"Hold on tight to her," Margaret reminded him before she grabbed the reins, leading Duchess in a circle.

Jonathan waded into the crowd of children. "What's going on here?"

Claira grabbed his hand excitedly. "Papa, can Miss Maggie be our Mama?"

Margaret turned her head sharply at the question. She wouldn't be here long enough to become anyone's mother, surrogate or otherwise.

Jonathan picked her up, a surprised look on his face. "You want her to be your Mama?"

The young child nodded vigorously, swinging her head to look at Margaret, a delighted smile on her face.

Margaret could only see him whisper something into Claira's ear as he watched her intently, kissing the girl's temple. Margaret wished she could have heard him, furrowing her brow at the pair.

Margaret spent every day with the children, getting to know each one's personality. With no governess yet, she stayed often enough to warrant having her own room made up for whenever she wanted to stay the night. Margaret already interviewed several governesses at the manor house, all coming to the conclusion there were too many children for them to handle as an individual and refusing

Margaret's proposition to hire another governess to help. She was getting more frustrated after each applicant turned her down.

She generally tried to teach them their letters and how to read, but currently, Margaret was trying to teach the children table manners. They were all gathered at the long table with the place settings all put out. There was a different course on each of the children's plates to demonstrate which utensil would go with which portion of the meal, as well as sides and dressings for the meal.

"How many courses do we have set out?" she asked the children.

"Who cares?" one of the older children answered her.

"Six!" Claira answered her excitedly.

"Thank you, Claira, for taking your lessons seriously," Margaret told her, giving a hard look to the boy.

"Take this seriously!" Daren yelled at her before throwing the chicken covered in brown gravy on her dress.

Margaret gasped, recoiling at the stain already forming on her bodice. "You… You little monster!"

Henry, the next oldest boy followed suit and threw the sautéed onions at Margaret.

Margaret gasped again. "Little monsters, all of you!" she yelled at them.

Daren continued to throw what was left on the table, encouraging the others to take part.

"Little monsters!" she yelled before scooping some potatoes that had been mashed and flinging it toward the two boys.

The children stared at Margaret in shock before they all retaliated, throwing the remainder of the food on the table at her and each other. When there was no more food to catapult, the children rose and rushed her, all giggles. Margaret let herself be tackled and brought down by the small beings.

"What is this?" Jonathan boomed when he came in from fetching eggs and milk for Matilda.

The children were silent at once, looking up at their father, shamefaced.

"We're learning table manners, Jonathan." Margaret wiped food off Daren's cheek with a smile. "Can you tell us if we were successful?"

The children giggled again, and Jonathan shook his head. "Up, all of you, and get to straightening the room so poor Gretchen doesn't have to clean it all on her own."

Margaret was helped up by Jonathan as the children grumbled, moving slowly to do their task. "Thank you, Jon."

"There's a Claudette here, Miss Maggie," he told her, gently wiping potato off her jaw and neck. "She said she's here for the governess position."

"Oh!" Margaret excitedly grabbed his hands and squeezed them. "I forgot she was coming today!"

"She's in the library."

Margaret wiped off some of the food the children had thrown at her dress, going to the library to meet the potential governess. She was a petite blonde, cheekbones jutting out of her thin face.

"Claudette, I'm so sorry to come to you in such a state. We were trying to learn table manners."

Claudette curtsied to her. She was equal in height to Margaret when she stood. "It's all right, my lady. I'm the oldest of ten children. I've looked like that on more than one occasion."

Margaret smiled. "Oldest of ten?"

"Yes, my lady," the short blonde woman confirmed. "Mostly boys."

Margaret smiled even wider. "There are eight boys and two girls whom you would be teaching and looking after," she told Claudette. "And most of them are unruly, as you can see."

"That won't be a problem for long, my lady," Claudette said confidently.

"If you choose to take the job, you will live here, and your salary will be twenty gold tals a year for as long as you choose to work here. Does that sound adequate to you, Claudette?"

"Adequate?" Claudette blanched. "My lady, it's triple my previous salary!"

"When can you start?" Margaret asked her.

"Now, my lady," Claudette said quickly. "If that's all right with you."

34

The servant escorting Liam chatted all the way to the baron's home, giving Liam every detail he could remember about the city and the family. Liam had not realized he had been saving the woman in the song at the Maiden Fair. When he arrived, the servant took him to change and clean the soot from his face and hands.

Liam learned the house that burned down was not the home of the baron, but another of the wealthier residents in Zuev whom the baron and his daughter were visiting for the day.

Liam was given a blue vest with vines and leaves embroidered in a creamy yellow to go over his stark white shirt, paired with a jacket and knee-length britches of the same design. To finish the outfit, he had white hose and soft black leather boots—the boots didn't go well with the outfit, but he figured they were the only shoes on hand that would fit him. The baron had even given him a silver brooch of a finely detailed lion's head with a filigree background. Liam marveled that there were even silver whiskers placed on the brooch. He looked himself over in the mirror. He had never seen himself looking so refined. It made Liam uncomfortable, knowing he could easily ruin clothes worth more than half a year's salary in the Anatalian military.

Another servant escorted Liam down to the dining hall. It was filled with a fourteen-foot solid oak table that was plain on the top, but the sides were engraved in a floral scene with scrolling vines throughout the expanse. The back of the chairs were carved out vines, leaving enough of the back for the occupant to comfortably rest against. The table was heaped with food, including roast duck, an entire rib cage of an elk decorated at the center of the table on an enormous platter, a large bass on the other side of the main dish and several side dishes interspersed on the table. Liam was amazed there was even room for the plates.

Liam's stomach growled at the smell, his mouth watering. He'd had hot meals at inns since he left Margaret in Amonat, but never had he imagined he would dine on a meal such as this. Would it always have been like this if he had been born noble? The common foot soldier would not be invited to the grand feasts as the knights were, and Liam would never have had an opportunity to see such a display. Liam was guided to a seat next to the baron and across from Lady Adelena. It was a seat of honor, surrounded by the wealthiest men and women in Zuev.

The baron stood before the meal started, holding up his glass. "A toast to my daughter's savior!" he exclaimed, raising his glass higher.

Many scraping chairs filled the hall as the rest of the table stood, calling out "Hear, hear!" in response before drinking deeply from their cups.

Liam drank along with them, his cheeks coloring with their praise. He ate quietly next to the baron, not wanting his accent to reveal he was Anatalian. He had spoken to the baron earlier, but he hoped in his harried state, the baron wouldn't have noticed.

"Tell me, Liam, what brings you to our city?" Lord Stelios asked. "You're Anatalian, if I'm not mistaken."

"You are not mistaken, my Lord Stelios." Liam examined the nobility in front of him. So much for keeping his heritage a secret. "I'm taking a leisurely coastal tour on my way to return to a dear friend of mine."

The baron seemed intrigued. "Where is this friend of yours?"

"She is staying in Marbon bordering Salatia until she returns to the capital," Liam said.

The baron's daughter had been intently listening to the conversation. "Your friend is a woman?" Lady Adelena asked, surprised. "Is she quite plain, then?"

Liam raised his eyebrows at her question. "Margaret is not plain, but she is not as beautiful as you are, Lady Adelena." He noted the small puff of her chest at the compliment. "Do you not have male friends, my lady?"

"Men are only interested in my dowry and a beautiful bride," she said bitterly.

"My daughter has no need of male friendships other than that of her husband and her sons," Lord Stelios interjected firmly, giving Liam a warning look for trying to put foreign ideas in her head.

Liam disagreed with the baron but said nothing. He thought the baron could gain more alliances through friendships of his daughter than parading her around as only a marriable object. The stubborn look on the lord's face told Liam the subject was finished even if he had wanted to give a rebuttal.

When the dinner ended, the baron stood. "Shall the men go to the drawing room for a drink?"

The other men, obviously accustomed to an after-dinner drink, stood and made their way to the drawing room. Liam brought out the pocket watch Margaret gave him to check the hour. "It's late, my lord. I should be going."

Iesos looked at the pocket watch, raising his eyebrows. "May I see that?"

Liam hesitantly handed him the watch, carefully watching the lord as he handled the precious gift.

Lord Stelios examined the timepiece carefully. "This is a very fine piece," the baron said surprised. "How is it that you came by this?"

"The woman I told you about in Marbon bought it for me as a gift." Liam held his hand out for the timepiece.

"A very fine gift indeed." Iesos gave Liam back his watch. "Pray, how did she afford such a gift?"

"She's the Countess of Dorcia," Liam said quickly as if to defend her.

The baron raised his eyebrows once more. "You may go if you wish. Come back tomorrow. I wish to introduce you to a few more people."

"As you wish, my lord," Liam said before leaving.

He went back to the Maiden Fair, ready to be out of his fancy clothes. He went to his room, finding the gold he had paid the clerk at the inn for the week. Liam went to the clerk with the gold in hand. "This was in my room." He set the gold down on the counter in front of him.

"I was the one to put it there," the clerk told him plainly.

"Are you putting me out?" Liam demanded.

"You saved Lady Adelena," the clerk said quickly. "You stay here for free."

"No." Liam pushed the gold tals forward.

"No one will take your money in this city after what you did," the clerk told Liam. "No one."

"Then use this to pay for the next person," Liam said firmly. "There must be need for this money. Think of it as a donation."

The clerk stuffed his hands in his pockets stubbornly, a challenging look on his face.

Liam frustratedly threw his hands in the air, leaving the gold on the counter when he went to his room for the night. He did not want to stay on the charity of the townspeople.

Liam ventured into the town the next morning to purchase more comfortable clothes to go to the baron's home. He found a tailor in the side streets of Zuev and entered the shop warily.

"Master Tailor, I'm in need of new clothing, and quickly," he called out to the man behind the counter.

The tailor came around with a rope knotted in increments. The man quickly measured Liam with a swiftness of a practiced tailor. "What will you be in need of?"

"A leather vest, pants, and a bloused shirt," Liam told him. It was the style he had seen on the men around the city.

Looking over Liam, the tailor went into a back room and returned with the requested items. "Put these on." He handed the clothes to Liam, pointing to a room for him to go in.

Liam came out in the premade clothes. The vest fit snugly across his chest, and the pants were surprisingly well fitting. The shirt was larger than he would have liked, but with the vest, the only part of the shirt that was largely noticeable were the heavily bloused sleeves.

"Here." The tailor pointed to a raised platform for the customers to stand on.

Liam stepped onto it, looking at himself in the mirror. He would be able to blend into the city without incident in these clothes.

The tailor quickly had a needle in the sleeve of the shirt, pinning it to a more appropriate size. "Go change, and come back in one hour to pick up your clothes."

He changed clothes and left the shop to have lunch at the Maiden Fair. The inn offered a wide variety of classic Glessican meals. There was a slow-cooked boar over a spit, many different baked fish, seafood chowders, roast chicken, and duck. Liam ordered a clam chowder topped with crusty bread. It was quickly brought to him by the serving wench, along with a drink. The chowder was perfectly creamy, and the bread was piping hot from the oven, wafting a delicious aroma toward him.

When he was finished, Liam put a tholar on the table and left so he could not be denied again when trying to pay.

He returned to the tailor to pick up his clothes. "Master Tailor?"

The tailor came out of the back room with the clothes in hands. "Ahh, yes, three gen."

Liam laid two tholar on the counter. "Will this be enough?"

"Anatalian money?" The tailor asked, surprised. "You are the one who saved Lady Adelena!"

"Is it enough?" Liam asked again, ignoring the statement.

"I will not take your money, sir," the tailor said. "Please, take these clothes as a gift."

Liam sighed. He needed the clothes for the baron that night. "Please let me pay you, Master Tailor."

"No." The tailor put the clothes in Liam's hands. "It is a gift from me to you."

"Thank you," Liam said with another sigh. "I will pay you back."

"No, no," the tailor said hurriedly. "It is my pleasure to give these to you."

Liam dressed in his room at the Maiden Fair. There was a knock on the door as he was pinning on the Lion's-head brooch. "Enter."

The clerk came into the room, holding the tholar Liam had left on the table. "I told you no one in Zuev would take your money, and I meant that."

"I'm well aware," Liam said irritably. "The tailor I pur—" Liam let out a small growl before he corrected himself "—got these from refused my money as well."

"You are the hero of this city, sir," the clerk said plainly. "No one will take anything from you."

Liam sighed. He would need to find a way to repay the people of Zuev before he left.

He arrived early to speak with the baron as requested. He was brought into the library by the butler. "My lord, Mr. Liam Triburn to see you."

Liam had not given the butler his criminal name, but the one he was born with, to hide his transgressions. He was unsure if the household of Lord Stelios would have heard of the 'traitor' Liam Fulton, and did not want to risk being returned to Anatalia. He was already garnering too much attention for his taste.

The baron stood when Liam was announced. "Liam, it's wonderful to see you again."

"You as well, Lord Stelios." Liam gave him a small bow.

Lord Iesos Stelios straightened Liam. "Please. I should be the one bowing to you after what you've done," he said with a peculiar look on his face. "And call me Iesos."

"Iesos," Liam said slowly.

"Please sit, Liam." Iesos motioned to the seat across from him as he sat.

Liam looked around the room, sitting across from the baron. "What is it that I can do for you?"

Lady Adelena entered the room, looking surprised when she saw Liam. "I'm sorry, Father, I wasn't aware you had company."

"Adelena," Iesos called fondly. "Come join us."

Lady Adelena sat next to her father in one sweeping motion, smiling at Liam. "A pleasure to see you again."

"And you, my lady," Liam told her, turning back to the baron. "You have such a generous city, my lord."

"Iesos," the baron corrected.

"Iesos," Liam repeated. "The clerk at the Maiden Fair refuses to let me pay for a room or meals at the inn, and I've been gifted clothes by one of the tailors here."

"Surely it's in thanks for saving me." Adelena smoothed out her skirts.

"It is, my lady," Liam said. "I would like a way to repay the kindness of the people here."

"There's no need to worry yourself with that," Iesos said. "They're honoring you in the only way they know how."

"Are you joining us for dinner tonight, Liam?" Adelena asked indifferently, her face devoid of interest.

"He is," the baron answered for him. "I have a few things to settle yet. Adelena, will you stay with Liam?"

"Of course, Father." She smiled at Liam. "What is it that we should talk about?"

Liam looked over the baron's daughter. "Are you recovering well, my lady?"

"Very well, thank you," Adelena said pleasantly.

An awkward silence fell between them.

Adelena chewed her lip as she watched the man in front of her. "Are you enjoying Zuev?" she asked after several long moments more.

"This isn't my first time here in Zuev," Liam told her, "but this is the first time I've been treated so well."

"I hope that this visit has given you a brighter view of our dear city." Adelena examined her nails. Her face still held no interest in what he was saying, the conversation obviously boring her.

Luckily for the both of them, the baron did not take long to finish his business. "The other guests are being seated for dinner. Liam, would you go ahead so I can speak with Lady Adelena?"

When the baron and his daughter joined everyone in the dining room, Lady Adelena was all smiles, happily sitting next to Liam. She animatedly talked to him throughout the dinner, touching his hand and arm, hardly letting him get a word in edgewise.

Liam was surprised at the change in Lady Adelena's behavior from their private audience to the dinner, feeling uncomfortable with the attention she was giving him. The dinner dragged on longer than the previous night's. Liam would have preferred having a private dinner at the Maiden Fair than listening to these men talk about their accomplishments and how much money they all had.

Once the dinner was over, the baron once again invited the men for a drink in the drawing room. "Liam?"

Liam stood and held out his hand. "I'm sorry Iesos, I'm going to have to leave without that drink."

Iesos shook his hand. "Are you sure I can't convince you to stay for a while longer?"

"I'm sorry," Liam said. "It's been a long day, my lord."

"Iesos," the baron corrected once more. "Adelena will show you to the door."

Adelena linked her arm in Liam's. "Shall we go?"

Liam walked with the baron's daughter to the door. "I suppose I won't be seeing you before I leave for Anatalia, Lady Adelena."

"I wouldn't be so sure." She looked up at him with an almost adoring look.

"Oh?" Liam was surprised she would want to see him again.

Adelena rested her hands on his chest, standing on her toes to kiss him. "Yes. I think we'll be seeing more of each other. Goodnight, Liam."

"Goodnight, my lady," Liam said with a confused look, hurriedly returning to the Maiden Fair.

35

onathan accompanied Margaret and the three oldest children, Daren, Henry, and Christopher, to the main part of the town. The boys pushed through the crowd of people, chasing after one another and yelling. Many of the people yelled after the boys as they raced through the street. Margaret had asked them to come on her errands with her to see how it would be done once she left. Many of the Marbonites on the street started to whisper as they walked along. Jonathan waited for Margaret to scold the boys for being unruly, but it never came. At least, not from her.

"Keep those mongrels away from me!" a woman yelled out when Christopher came too close to her.

"You—" Jonathan started up before Margaret cut him off with a raised hand. He was livid someone would call his children mongrels.

Margaret placed her hand on Christopher's shoulder and stared down the woman intently. "These children are no more mongrels than you are a noblewoman," Margaret said coldly. "I wouldn't dare have these children around such a vile woman as you."

Jonathan smirked as he took the other two children's hands and followed behind Margaret, who had already grabbed Christopher, and went on her way to their errands.

The children behaved until they reached their first destination. Margaret herded them into the cobbler's workshop. "Master Schlect, I trust you have our order ready this time?"

David Schlect looked Margaret over with a bland expression. "No, my lady, they are not done yet."

"We have been waiting for over two months!" Margaret exclaimed exasperatedly. "Two *months*!"

"My lady, you have a very large order." Schlect shrugged as he lamely made his excuse.

"I am paying you enough money to get these done as fast as you can," Margaret scolded. "Why don't you hire someone to help you? Mistress Laphar hired nine new girls to help her with everything; the least you can do is hire one more person!"

Master Schlect handed her two pairs of shoes. "This is all that's done."

"That isn't good enough, Master Schlect." Margaret picked up the shoes. "They all need to be finished by the time I come back next week for them."

"It cannot be done, my lady," the shoemaker complained.

"Hire someone, then, and quickly," Margaret seethed as she headed for the door. She stopped before she exited the shop and turned to look at him. "And if they aren't done by the time I want them, then I will demand the return of my deposit back and bring all of my business, including my commissions, to someone willing to do the work he is hired to do!"

"Yes, my lady," the cobbler said with the barest of nods.

"Are you always this unrelenting?" Jonathan asked her.

"Yes," Margaret snapped. "I don't know when I'll be leaving, and I'm doing everything I can to make sure Marbon prospers while I am here."

"And after you leave?"

"I'll still be investing money here," Margaret told him. "I won't ever stop my patronage of this town. I won't let you go hungry again. Not ever, Jonathan."

Jonathan let a small smile through. He could tell by her bright smile in return that Margaret delighted in it. She was finally breaking through the walls he had put up. It had been easier for her to win over the children than him. All they needed was her affection, and they had delighted in her presence. Jonathan needed more than that. He needed a reason to trust her.

It was hard to trust anyone after all the times he had been kicked down when he had asked for help for his children. He couldn't have cared less if he had to go hungry for them to eat. He would work his fingers to the bone to make sure they were cared for.

They finished the rest of their errands without incident. It was like watching an artist work when Margaret interacted with the people of the town. The people who were unappreciative of her generosity, she attempted to charm until they relented, and if they didn't, they were party to her ire. The rest were treated as family friends, and Margaret made sure to ask about their families and themselves with an attentiveness Jonathan would not have expected of Margaret.

On the way back to their manor home, Margaret saw a man who had been on the street for as long as Jonathan could remember. He was someone no one wanted to go near. He was blind and severely scarred. He appeared as if he had been burned in a fire, half of his face looking like it had melted along with several splotches of his skin along his arms and legs. If anyone bothered to help him, they threw the food at him so they would not have to get near, or left old clothing next to him while he had been sleeping so they didn't have to talk to him.

"Water…" the old, crippled man begged in a dry croak. "Water…"

Margaret stopped when she heard his cries and stared at him intently. She handed Christopher a few drica for him to buy the man a few skins of water. While they waited, Margaret went to the suffering man with some of the food they had purchased in the city and knelt next to him. She grabbed his hands gently, causing him to jump, and placed some warm bread in his open palms. He ate voraciously and coughed when he had finished.

"Christopher," Margaret called when she saw the boy had returned. She held the skin up to his lips herself as he drank fully.

When he was done drinking, the cripple took her hands and held them to his face, closing his eyes. "Thank you," he breathed gratefully.

Jonathan stared in disbelief as Margaret kissed his melted cheek, and the crippled man savored her touch. "You're welcome…?"

"Matthias," the man on the ground told her.

"Matthias," Margaret said with a smile, cradling his cheek in her hand. "Don't worry, Matthias; I'll make sure you're cared for."

"Thank you." Matthias kissed both of her hands in turn. "Thank you beyond measure."

Margaret waited until he was done before she stood and rejoined Jonathan and the children.

He was amazed she had not wiped her hands free of his touch or balked in revulsion from it. "Miss Maggie," Jonathan said quietly. "You're good people."

❧ 36 ❧

Margaret leisurely strolled the Marbon with Elizabeth, spending quality time with her older companion for the first time since starting the orphanage. She had more time on her hands since hiring Claudette to teach and care for the children. They chatted with the townsfolk they passed, each exchanging polite pleasantries. Their first destination was the seamstress shop to visit Susanna Laphar, an occasion Margaret had not had much time for while taking sole responsibility for the children.

"My Lady!" Mr. Fraser, the postmaster, called out as they passed his shop. "My Lady Margaret!"

Margaret turned, her brow furrowed.

"Mr. Fraser," she said pleasantly, a small smile on her face. "What can I do for you?"

There was a bundle of thick parchment letters in his hand. "Several letters have come to post for you, my lady."

"Who are they from?" Margaret reached her hand out to snatch them.

Mr. Fraser pulled them away, holding out his empty hand instead.

"A Drica apiece, my lady," he said with a patient smile.

Margaret glared at him, pulling out her purse from a hidden pocket. "How much, Mr. Fraser?"

"Three Drica." He fanned out the letters.

Margaret snatched the letters from his hand, replacing it with the appropriate amount of money.

"Who are they from?" Elizabeth peered over Margaret's shoulder.

Margaret smiled brightly. "They're from Liam."

Elizabeth let out a delighted noise, a smile blossoming on her face. "How exciting!"

Margaret tucked the letters away for safekeeping with her money purse, nodding to the postmaster. "Thank you, Mr. Fraser."

Mr. Fraser bowed his head to her as the two women continued on their way.

Margaret entered the seamstress shop first, smiling when she saw all the girls at work.

"Susanna?" she called out, not seeing the plump woman.

"Is that you, Lady Margaret?" The seamstress waddled into the room, carrying dress boxes piled above her head.

"It is," Margaret confirmed.

"Let me help." Elizabeth grabbed the top three boxes, setting them down on the counter.

"It's been quite some time, my lady," Susanna told her, a concerned look on her face. "Has anything been wrong?"

Margaret smiled at her. "I have been spending all my time with the children."

"How are the little ones doing?" the seamstress inquired.

"Well," Margaret told her, "they have a governess now. The children seem to like her very much."

"Wonderful!"

"You seem to be busy here," Elizabeth commented.

Susanna gave the older woman a lopsided grin. "Every woman in Marbon wants to be seen by the same seamstress as the Lady Margaret."

Margaret's cheeks bloomed with color, a pleased smile on her face. "Do you have any more dresses ready for me, Susanna?"

"I think you will be here a while, my lady," the seamstress told her. "We have twenty dresses waiting to be fitted on you."

"Twenty!" Margaret's face was slack with shock. "How do you have twenty dresses nearly complete?"

"My lady, I have barely seen you since Mamonat when you came in with that young man," Susana reminded her. "We've had quite a long time to work."

"I suppose we should get the appointment started then." Elizabeth smiled at both women.

"You are my only appointment of the day," Susanna assured Margaret. "We have plenty of time."

Margaret and Elizabeth arrived home late in the evening.

"You go and read your letters, dear," Elizabeth told her, heading toward the kitchen. "I'll start dinner."

Margaret gave Elizabeth a grateful smile. "I'll be out as soon as I can to help you."

"Take your time." She disappeared into the kitchen.

Margaret went to her room, ripping the letters from her pocket. She broke all the seals and found the one with the earliest date.

Margaret,

I went to your father's house and took care of everything for you.
Liam

Margaret was disappointed with the brevity of the letter, a small frown creasing her brow. What did he mean by he took care of everything? She moved on to the next, hoping for more detail.

Margaret,
I've taken my travels along the coast.
I went to Hamuel and fished off the cliffs at the Hook.
I'm now in Manolt, and I plan to have my fill of relaxation. I'll write to you again when the opportunity arises.
Liam

The crease in Margaret's forehead deepened. This was not the friendly Liam she remembered. He didn't even seem to remember their earlier flirtation—not even a hint toward it. She wasn't even sure she wanted to continue reading the letters.

The last message from Liam sat staring at her, tempting her despite her disappointment.

Margaret,
I am now in Zuev, a city in Glessic. I can't help but walk around and think of how much you would love it here. It's a city modeled with your sensibilities—one that I hope you will see one day. I'll be returning to Marbon after I have finished my time in Glessic.
I hope to be with you soon.
Liam

Margaret set down the letter, a small smile returning to her face. At least she knew he did on occasion think of her as she thought of him.

Margaret walked into the manor home where the children were now fully settled. "Little monsters?" She looked around, hearing laughter coming from the drawing room. "Jonathan?"

Jonathan grinned at her when she entered the room. "Miss Maggie!"

There were a few children who broke away from him. "Maggie!" Their voices chimed.

Margaret knelt and smiled brightly at them. "How are my little monsters?"

Jonathan answered for them. "They're keeping up with their studies and learning their manners."

Margaret stood with the youngest girl, Sarah Beth, in her arms and smiled. Now that the governess had arrived, she didn't feel the need to come by every day.

"That's wonderful to hear. Has Master Schlect been by with the newest installment of boots and shoes?"

"He doesn't like the children, Miss Maggie." Jonathan's face hardened. "He doesn't come when he's 'sposed to and with not enough shoes."

"That dirt weasel," she muttered under her breath. "I'll let him know that we will be taking our business elsewhere." Margaret sighed, her expression quickly turning to an amused one. "Has Daniel stopped trying to bite poor Claudette yet?"

Jonathan chuckled. "No, Miss Maggie, not yet."

Margaret looked over the children affectionately. Sadness filled her as she looked over each face carefully.

"Somethin' wrong?" Jonathan asked her.

"Just thinking about when I leave."

"We made it once. We can make it again." Jonathan had a fallen look on his face.

"You'll always be taken care of as long as you choose to stay here, Jonathan." Margaret looked at him directly. Margaret would not allow her funds to stop like he assumed she would. "I mean that."

"Why do you have to go back to the capital, Miss Maggie?" Jonathan asked.

Margaret kissed Sarah Beth on the forehead, much to the child's delight. "Jon, I've already told you, I have to go back to finish what my father started. I leave next month, and Claudette already has her instructions for after I'm gone."

"You aren't your papa, Maggie," Jonathan told her plainly. "Stay here with me and our babies. Be their mama."

Where was this coming from? She had barely been able to get him to accept her, and now that it was coming time for her to leave, Jonathan wanted her to be the children's co-parent. Had Claira's question of her being their mother prompted some sort of desire in him? "Jonathan…" Margaret said slowly. "I can't be their mother, and I can't stay here."

"How can you just abandon us like this?" Jonathan demanded, a crestfallen expression on his face.

"I'm not abandoning you, or the children, Jonathan. I'm still going to provide for all of you," Margaret solemnly told him. "You'll never be forced into an abandoned building or have to worry about clothing and feeding yourself and your children again."

"Our children," Jonathan firmly corrected.

Margaret remained silent. How had he flipped from irritable teen to demanding she be the children's mother? It didn't sit well with her.

"I'll come back as often as I can," she said eventually.

"I need to collect the children for their lessons." Jonathan stalked out to the children playing outside.

Margaret sighed, rubbing her cheek in frustration. This was not a situation she was equipped to handle. She heard him snap at the children, and a chorus of groans followed his pounding footsteps.

"Jonathan," Margaret called out to him from the dining room. "Please come in here."

Jonathan ignored her summons, bounding up the stairs.

"Jonathan!" When he ignored her again, Margaret yelled after him, "Jonathan, we need to talk!"

"Talk about what?" Jonathan rounded on her. "How you have to leave to fulfill your father's legacy? How you need to go back to Dorcia and rule over your people?"

"Jonathan," Margaret started to placate him, "the people of Dorcia—"

"The people of Dorcia ruined my life, Margaret!" Jonathan yelled at her, his face red. "They are the reason I became an orphan!"

Margaret's face froze, her mouth open with her unsaid argument. "Excuse me?"

"My mother, father, and I went to Dorcia during the war for my father to find work," Jonathan was still heated as he spoke, though the angry look on his face diminished. "We came all the way from Bomack, and my mother fell ill on the way."

He remained silent for a moment, a faraway look on his face, remembering the time vividly. "When we made it to an inn, we were turned away because of my mother's sickness," Jonathan told her.

"Jonathan…did your mother have the plague?" Margaret asked quietly.

"Yes," he confirmed. "She died that night when we slept out in a field, and my father had to bury her before we went into the town to look for work, but he was already sick. He was turned away from every place he asked. He died the next night."

"Jonathan," —Margaret placed a hand on his arm— "I'm sorry that happened to you."

He ripped his arm away. "If you were, you wouldn't be leaving to go to the worst place of my life," Jonathan snapped. Running the rest of the way to his room, he slammed the door behind him.

Margaret stared after him, dumbfounded.

37

Liam climbed the stairs of the Maiden Fair, rubbing his full stomach contentedly. He hugged the wall as another came down the stairs, holding a chest. Liam did a double take and ran the rest of the way up the stairs and saw the door to his room was opened.

He barreled back down the stairs. "You!" he bellowed, pointing an accusatory finger at the man carrying his chest. "That is my property!"

The man stopped, startled. He turned to look at Liam. "Are you Mr. Liam Triburn?"

Liam stopped short of the man, furrowing his brow. "Yes?"

The man bowed to him. "Lord Iesos has requested you spend the remainder of your stay in his home and has sent me to retrieve your things."

Liam felt himself bristling. "I have not agreed to this."

The man gave him a sympathetic look. "No one says no to His Lordship, sir."

"Is there anything left in my room?" Liam asked with a sigh.

"This is the last of it," the servant told him.

Liam sighed again. "Tell Lord Stelios that I will be there by the evening meal."

"Yes, sir." The servant bowed his head to Liam before leaving him in the street.

Liam let out an aggravated noise. If he did not go, he would lose everything he had accumulated on his journey, including Margaret's jewels he planned on returning to her. The streets were starting to crowd with people, and Liam decided to return to the Maiden Fair to speak with the clerk. He was behind the counter, filling in the accounts. Liam cleared his throat.

The clerk looked up sharply. "How can I help you, Mr. Triburn?"

"I understand that I am being moved to the baron's residence," Liam informed him, pulling the key out from his vest, along with a few gold tals, setting them on the counter. "Thank you for all you've done."

"I cannot—" the clerk started.

"Thank you," Liam said again before he walked out of the inn.

Liam went to the baron's residence where the butler greeted him enthusiastically and showed Liam to the same room he had used to change the first time he came to the home. Not much was different, though the doors to the bureau were open. His clothes were hung up, and others were added to supplement his wardrobe.

A knock sounded on his door as he was exploring the room.

"Enter," he called.

Lady Adelena entered the room, almost shyly, standing by the door. "Are the rooms to your liking?"

"They are, my lady, thank you." Liam bowed his head to her.

Adelena smiled. "I will leave you to get settled." She walked further into the room and pulled aside a curtain to show him a lever. "Pull this if you need anything that requires a servant."

"Thank you, Lady Adelena." He felt uncomfortable at the thought of summoning someone for a service.

"I will see you tonight at dinner." She brushed her hand on his arm as she left the room.

Liam sighed once she was gone, looking around the room in trepidation.

A knock sounded on the door as Liam pulled an item of his new clothing out of the bureau.

"Enter," he commanded.

A man entered, looking at the floor, coming to stand in the middle of the room.

"Yes?" Liam raised his brows.

"I am to be your valet, sir," the man said, his head still bowed.

"I see… What is your name?"

"Bartolome, sir."

Liam cleared his throat uncomfortably. He could count on one hand the number of times he had been attended by a servant, and the majority of them in the baron's home. "And what is it that you will be doing as my valet, Bartolome?"

Bartolome's head snapped up, confusion on his face. "Sir?"

His cheeks colored, and Liam cleared his throat, embarrassed. "I have never had a valet—I don't know what they do."

"I will arrange meetings for you, draw your baths, help you dress and keep your clothes in top condition, and shave you if you so desire." Bartolome eyed Liam's heavy scruff.

"I think I can dress well enough on my own," he told the valet. "I've been doing it all my life."

"As you wish, sir." Bartolome bowed, holding out a folded piece of paper. "From the Lady Adelena."

Meet me in the library.

A

Liam looked up to see Bartolome still standing in the same spot, looking at him expectantly. "Yes?"

"I am waiting for you to dismiss me, sir," Bartolome told him.

"Yes, of course," Liam said, shifting uncomfortably, "you may go."

Bartolome bowed to him, leaving the room silently.

Dressing quickly, Liam went to the library, running a hand through his hair to straighten it. Adelena was seated in a tall wingback chair, with a book in her lap. The sunlight shone through her hair, giving her an ethereal look. He cleared his throat to get her attention.

She looked up at him. "Liam, you came!"

"You requested me, Lady Adelena."

Adelena came to him, resting a hand on his arm. "You didn't have to come just because I asked."

He resisted the urge to laugh at her, knowing had he not come, she would have been offended. "What did you want to see me about?"

"Just to make sure you were settling all right." She flipped her hand dismissively.

Liam furrowed his brow. She had done that when he arrived. Why was she being so attentive to him? "I am, thank you, my lady."

"You may call me Adelena if you'd like, Liam." A small pout graced her lips.

"If you wish," he said cautiously.

"Have you been shown around the home, yet?" she asked, linking her arm through his.

"Not yet."

She grinned at him, tugging him along. "I'll show you, then."

Adelena led him through the home, pointing out artifacts her family had acquired over the years and what had been given to them as gifts from other noble families. The information passed through one ear and out the other, him not particularly caring for the history of the gifts. He made the appropriate noises to keep her happy. They stopped in a hallway that looked like it was not in use.

"Is that all?" Liam looked around, his brows furrowed.

"Unless there is something else you would like to explore." Adelena looked at him suggestively.

"Ah, no," Liam hurriedly told her, "thank you."

She pouted at him but led him away from the empty hallway. "Dinner will be at its usual time," Adelena said over her shoulder. "I hope you will be more appropriately dressed."

"Lady Adelena."

She turned quickly, looking at him hopefully. "Yes, Liam?"

"Why have I been brought here?" He looked around at the opulence.

"A hero should be staying somewhere appropriate to his status. We thought you would be more comfortable here," she assured him. "Aren't you?"

"I couldn't tell you yet, my lady," Liam told her honestly.

Adelena smiled at him. "I hope you feel free to stay here as long as you'd like."

38

Lord General Crompton waited in the junction of four tunnels under the palace. He bounced on the balls of his feet to release his nervous energy, listening for any noise. His head snapped toward the light footsteps coming down the tunnel to his left.

"Your Grace?" a voice whispered, barely audible in the deafening silence.

Crompton strode into the tunnel, meeting the man halfway. "Are you prepared to do your duty to me?" he whispered intently to the smaller man.

The smaller man nodded, though his eyes looked doubtful.

"Do you have all you need?"

"Yes." The small man patted his side where he had a knife hidden.

"Good." Crompton nodded at him once. "We'll start our hunt at midmorning. Make sure you're in our party."

"Yes, Your Grace."

King Sorren breathed in the fresh air outside the palace. Crompton clapped him on the shoulder, a boyish grin on his face. "It's been some time," Crompton commented.

"Indeed, it has, Cousin," Sorren confirmed.

The party waited while servants waded into the forest, banging their wooden shields with thick dowels. Crompton stood by the king, catching the eye of the small man from the tunnel. He hoped the man was smart enough to wait until the party went into the forest to do his deed.

"It's going to be a good hunt," Sorren said. "I can feel it."

Crompton only grinned, clapping his shoulder again before going into the forest for the hunt. It would be a good hunt—a hunt for something royal. He could hear the boars squealing as they were chased out of their nests. Crompton stayed a safe distance from his cousin, spear at the ready for any unsuspecting boar.

Crompton froze when he heard growling behind him. A pig must have gotten around his back without him knowing. He turned slowly on his heels, his heart thundering in his ears. Sweat trickled between his shoulders as silence fell around him. The boar's maw was dripping with foam and slobber, kicking his hooves back in preparation. Crompton slid one foot back to brace himself for the inevitable attack.

The boar let out an angry squeal before he charged.

Crompton jerked his spear forward, letting the pig impale himself on the sharp tip. A cry that was not his own sounded as he was knocked down. Crompton struggled to get the flailing pig off him before his ribs were bruised, or worse yet, broken.

"The king!" Crompton heard someone yell. "The king has been stabbed!"

Crompton wrestled the pig off him, running toward the shouting.

Sorren was lying on the ground, clutching his side. His face was pale, sweat beading on his forehead. "I'm dying!" Sorren yelled.

"Get him back to the palace," Crompton barked. It was the last thing he wanted to do, but his part in this could not be discovered. He had to be just as worried as the rest of the courtiers, doing everything he could to ensure his king's safety.

A flurry of people surrounded the king, carrying him back to the palace. They brought him to his chambers, setting Sorren on his bed.

Crompton went to his side, clasping Sorren's hand tightly in his. "Everything will be fine," Crompton assured him, though he hoped it would not.

"I need to see Lillian," Sorren said, white-faced. "I'm dying! Bring her to me now!"

"I don't—"

"I need to see her now! Now! Bring her here!" Sorren yelled, his eyes wild with panic.

"I'll get her," Crompton assured him before turning to the rest. "Where is the healer?"

"He's on his way," one of the men attending the king said.

Crompton waited outside the queen's chambers while his wife, Duchess Cecily, requested Queen Lillian's presence.

"What do you want, Tobias?" Lillian demanded irritably at the door.

"His Majesty has been stabbed and is asking for you," Crompton said with a low bow to her.

"Where is he?" Lillian shrieked, the blood draining from her face until it was a pale white.

"In his chambers, Your Majesty." Crompton was barely able to get out before Lillian passed him.

His wife grabbed fistfuls of skirt to rush after the queen. He followed quickly behind. There was a crowd growing outside of the king's rooms as the yelling for his wife continued.

"Move for the queen!" Crompton boomed behind her as she reached the mass.

"Lillian!" the king yelled as the crowd parted for the queen. "Where is my Lillian?"

She fell to her knees next to his bed, clutching the king's hand until her knuckles were white. "I'm here, my love," she cooed. "I'm here."

"Lillian," —he turned to her, sweat pouring down his face— "I'm dying."

"Hush now," she told him firmly, wiping a wisp of hair off his brow. "You're not dying."

"I need to apologize." He swallowed hard, licking his lips nervously. "For what I've done to you."

"Out!" Crompton commanded, waving his arms in a shooing motion to rid the room of bystanders. "Give Their Majesties their privacy!"

Sorren watched the crowd warily as they retreated.

"What is it you wanted to apologize for, my love?" Lillian prodded as the nobles and servants left. Only the healer and Crompton, along with his wife Cecily, remained in the room.

The king kissed her hands fervently but did not speak.

"Go on," she urged, "there is no one here but us."

"For all the women," he quietly said, as though he were a child being scolded, "that I've had affairs with over the years."

Lillian's face turned to stone, pulling her hand away from his as he named upwards of twenty noblewomen—the places, the number times, and positions of his quick trysts. Crompton knew he left out only the details of his long-standing mistresses over their marriage and the servants he had assaulted over the years. She stood, her back rigid, and left without a word.

Crompton turned to his wife and nodded for her to go after the queen. Cecily's face held a dumbfounded expression as she turned and did as she was bid.

"Your Majesty," the healer said in the background, "you must let me examine you."

Crompton took the queen's place, kneeling next to the king. "You've said your peace, Your Majesty. Let the healer help you."

Sorren nodded, blinking slowly as he relaxed into the bed. "I'm ready to go now."

Crompton stood back as Healer Windsor moved Sorren's blood-soaked shirt. Windsor gently probed the wound, the king's face turning even whiter as he did so. The healer cleared his throat delicately. "Your Majesty, your wound is a superficial one," he said trying to hide his amusement—succeeding as well as anyone, Crompton thought—though it did break though. "You will not perish from this."

Another failed plot. Crompton was starting to wonder if he was the problem in killing his cousin. How could one man survive so many attempts?

But there was hope—the king had given him another means to undermine him.

Crompton rubbed his mouth to try to take the smile from his face. He would not die, but the nobles would be easier to turn against him when the lords found out how many of their wives the king had slept with. "Are you certain, Healer Windsor?"

"I have full faith in my diagnosis, Your Grace."

Realization dawned on Sorren's face as he understood what he had truly done.

39

argaret groaned, squinting against the light coming through the shuttered windows. It'd been some time since she'd been able to sleep past the sunrise. She and Elizabeth had a day planned in the town of Marbon visiting with Elizabeth's friends and more fittings for Margaret.

She was relieved she no longer had to worry about seeing the children daily. Margaret rubbed the sleep from her eyes. She didn't mind seeing them daily, but teaching them their lessons…it was enough to drive her insane. Claudette fit in with the children better than Margaret could have ever hoped. She was such a natural caretaker of them, she could have easily been their birth mother. It freed Margaret to do whatever she wanted during the day.

Groaning, Margaret got out of bed. She could smell breakfast on the hearth—she shouldn't keep Aram and Elizabeth waiting. She put on a simple dress she could wear in town without issue and went to the kitchen. Aram was already eating, buttering a fat square of cornbread.

"Good morning." Elizabeth set two more plates on the table. "I thought after breakfast we could go into town so you'd have the afternoon free for the children. It's been a few days since you've been."

Margaret stifled a yawn behind her hand. "Would you like to come with me to see the children?"

"That's all right, they're very…rambunctious."

Margaret laughed. "They are."

They finished their breakfast, then walked to Marbon proper. Margaret furrowed her brows, watching the women titter excitedly. She was sure Mistress Laphar would know what was going on. She'd ask during her fitting.

Margaret and Elizabeth had barely walked in the door before Mistress Laphar said, "Have ye heard what happened?"

"We haven't," Elizabeth said. "What happened?"

"There was a raid here yesterday," Susanna said, her eyes alight with the chance to gossip, "by the Salatians!"

Elizabeth gasped, grabbing Margaret's forearm. "Raiders?"

Margaret's stomach sank. Was this as Liam had predicted and she had attracted raiders with her flaunting her wealth in the small border town? "Was anyone hurt?"

Susanna shook her head. "They were stopped before they got too far into town by some of the farmers."

Elizabeth squeezed Margaret's arm before letting go, breathing out a sigh of relief. "Thank Theotes."

"Now, m'lady, let's get ye fitted." Susanna ushered her into the back room. "We've got three for ye today, and then we've only got two left to make."

"Only two?" Margaret was surprised they were so close to being done. Her dresses were the only thing keeping her in Marbon. At least, that's what she told herself. She didn't want to leave, but she would have to at some point. She couldn't leave things to chance for her people—or for herself.

Susanna nodded, helping Margaret into the first dress. "The girls have already started cutting the fabric on them. It shouldn't be more than two weeks more, m'lady."

"I see…" Margaret inhaled deeply. "I suppose that means I'll need to prepare for my journey to Jalmar. I think the beginning of Aumonat will do fine."

"What?" Elizabeth looked at her sharply. "Leave?"

"I have always said once I have everything I need, I'll be leaving." Margaret flinched when she was poked by a needle. "I'll need to hire a caravan with servants and guards."

"You don't have to leave," Elizabeth said. "Aram and I would love it if you stayed."

Margaret grabbed her hand and squeezed it. "Oh, Elizabeth, I wish that were true. You know why I have to leave."

When Susanna had finished pinning all the places that needed to be tightened, she took Margaret out of the gown and put her into the next.

"Susanna, you know everyone here." Margaret turned to look at the back of the dress in the long mirror. "Do you know of anyone who'd be capable of leading a party and providing security?"

"I do," Susanna said once she took the pin from between her teeth. "There's a Captain Vojvo that moved back here after the war. He'd be yer man for the job."

Margaret nodded. "I'll have one of the local boys summon him for me in a few days."

When all the fittings were finished, Margaret thanked Susanna. "You'll have to let us know if you hear anything more when we come back."

"Of course, m'lady."

"I'd like to stop at the postmaster's on our way home," Margaret said after they left the seamstress. "I'll need to leave an advertisement for a lady's maid."

"Will you have time to find one?"

"I should. Aumonat is still a month and a half away, and news always travels fast for a lady's maid position." Margaret linked arms with Elizabeth as they walked. "Don't worry—I'll be fine leaving, and so will you."

Margaret went to the postmaster and wrote a quick advertisement detailing the skills she would require, and a duplicate for the window. She smiled at Mr. Fraser. "If you could, please make sure these are distributed to the local pamphlets and surrounding posts."

The postmaster nodded. "Shall I send you your bill this time, my lady?"

"I think that would be easiest so that we don't hold up the line," Margaret said, leaving with Elizabeth.

They went back to the house, and Margaret went to the back where Liam and Aram had built a small stable for Duchess and Ashka when they first arrived. "I think I'll go now to see the children. Will you tell Aram for me?"

Elizabeth raised her brows. "You don't want to tell him yourself?"

"No." Margaret shook her head. "He'll react…poorly."

Elizabeth laughed. "That, my dear, is a very gentle way to put it."

The younger children played outside as Margaret rode up on Duchess, their squeals of delight having reached her long before she saw them. Their squeals grew louder as they ran up to her, surrounding Duchess as they walked to the stables.

"Where's your papa?" Margaret asked when she'd finished stabling Duchess. "I need to speak with him."

"He's inside with Miss Claudette," the oldest of the group said.

Margaret found Jonathan sitting with a book in hand, Claudette standing behind him to read over his shoulder as he slowly read the text. Margaret smiled. This would be good for Jonathan, though she doubted he'd do anything to thank her for it.

"Jonathan?" she asked when there was a long pause in his reading.

Both Claudette and Jonathan jumped from their positions. "Lady Margaret," —Claudette put a hand to her chest— "you scared us."

"I wanted to tell you some news, and I suppose it's a good thing you're here as well, Claudette."

Jonathan came to stand next to Claudette, his brows furrowed. "What is it, Miss Maggie?"

"Well…" Margaret didn't expect it to be this hard. "After some news today, I have decided that I'll be leaving at the start of Aumonat."

"Why?" Jonathan demanded.

"There isn't a need for me to stay here longer than that, and I have to make sure my people are taken care of." Margaret rubbed his arm, glad at least he hadn't flown off the handle like he had the last time she brought up leaving. "We've talked about this before."

"How can you just leave us?"

"I'll always take care of you and the children as long as you stay here." Margaret took his hands, squeezing them. She wouldn't let him make her feel guilty for leaving when she had always been clear about her terms. "And you'll have Claudette to help with the children."

<h1>40</h1>

Marius Vojvo brought his ax down on the trunk of a tree next to the road, felling it after three more strokes of the blade. He brought it back to his sheltered workshop, laying it down next to his bench. Marius cut off each branch before grabbing what he called the scalper, a sharp curved blade with handles on both sides. He squatted on the log, digging the blade into the wood. He pulled hard, leaning back as though he were rowing, peeling the bark in large strips.

Vojvo rolled the log over to the doorway of his shop, securing it on the wheeled device. He rolled it toward the blade mounted on the bottom of the doorway, squaring the log before cutting it in half. Marius gave the wood a companionable slap before going back to his workbench to rummage through his tools. A short knock sounded on his doorway, causing him to look up in surprise.

"Captain Vojvo?"

"How may I help you?" Vojvo asked, wiping his hands free of wood shavings.

"The Lady Margaret has requested you attend her," the young man, Thomas Raeburn, said.

Vojvo raised a single brow. "There aren't any peers in Marbon."

"Beg pardon, sir," Thomas started, obviously not wanting to contradict him, "but the Lady Margaret has been residing here for months now."

Marius was confused. "Why this pitiful town? Why not somewhere more befitting a lady?"

Thomas shrugged helplessly. "I couldn't tell you, sir."

"When is Her Ladyship wishing to see me?"

"Right away, sir," Thomas said. "I am to escort you to her."

Vojvo's mouth flattened. It had been some time since he'd had any dealings with the nobility—he'd forgotten their penchant for only their needs to be met. He wiped his hands once more to ensure there were no more splinters of wood stuck to his fingers. "Very well. Let's be on then," Vojvo said as he threw down his cloth.

They walked the distance to the manor-turned-orphanage, Vojvo wiping his face free of sweat. A barrage of children spilled out of the door as they entered, knocking the Vojvo and his escort out of the way. He scowled at them as they passed, straightening himself as the last one giggled his way out the door.

"This way, sir." Thomas held his arm out to allow the Vojvo to go in first. "The Lady Margaret is in the library on the left."

Vojvo hesitantly approached the library. He stood in the doorway, looking over the young noblewoman carefully. Her dark brown hair shadowed her face as she read the book in her lap.

He cleared his throat lightly, standing up straight with his hands clasped behind his back. "You've been expecting me, my lady?" he asked when she looked up.

"Captain Vojvo?" Lady Margaret inquired, standing.

"At your service, my lady." Vojvo bowed to her.

Lady Margaret smiled, closing the distance between them. "I am in need of those services."

Marius raised his brows in question.

"I will be traveling to Jalmar at the start of Aumonat, and I am in need of guards and an escort," she told him, pulling the rope to his left. "Please, sit," she added as she returned to her seat.

Vojvo sat as another young woman entered the room.

"Gretchen, please have Matilda send up refreshments for the good captain," Lady Margaret commanded.

The maid bobbed a curtsey and left as quickly as she appeared.

"My lady." Vojvo leaned forward, his face pinched. "I don't know if I will be able to help you. I have retired from soldiering and guarding."

Lady Margaret's smile was plastered on her face. "You came highly recommended to me as the head of an escort, Captain."

"And whoever it was was very kind to say so, my lady," Marius countered, "but I am retired."

She remained silent as Gretchen laid a tray with tea and finger sandwiches, her mouth pursing with irritation. Her eyes no longer held the friendliness they had when he had first arrived.

"Captain," Lady Margaret drawled slowly, as though talking to a child, "I'm not sure you understand me. I must have a capable escort to reach the capital, and you are whom I want."

"I've already said no, my lady," he said as he started to stand.

Lady Margaret was in front of him faster than he expected, grabbing onto his hands. "Captain, I absolutely must get to the capital—my father is dead, and no one leads our people now. I've built up some supplies here, but I have to claim my title in order to help my people. I can't leave them floundering."

"Lady Marg—"

She squeezed his hands, looking up at him with pleading eyes. "They will suffer without me. I can't be party to their downfall."

"Your Ladyship—"

"Captain Vojvo, I will pay you an incredible sum for three months' work, and you get to return home to whatever it is you do here in your retirement," Lady Margaret interrupted. "I will not take no for an answer."

His mouth became a flat line. He could see she would not give up before he did. "It seems, my lady, that you have your guard, then."

Lady Margaret's face lit once more with pleasure. "Wonderful, Captain!"

Vojvo sighed. "Will that be all, my lady?"

"I will give you a list of what I think will be required as well as the value of the items that will be transported with us," Margaret told him, fluffing out her skirts before she walked, Vojvo in tow, to the door of the home. "I trust that will be acceptable?"

"Very good, my lady." Vojvo bowed his head to her.

"I look forward to seeing you again soon, Captain Vojvo." She stepped back from the door to allow his exit. "Good day, sir."

Marius bowed to her before he left, his hackles rising the further he got from the home. He had let that woman force him into a job he did not want far too easily, and he was none too happy for it.

41

The Baron of Zuev, Lord Iesos Stelios, greeted the butler pleasantly when he entered his bedroom.

"My lord, these parcels arrived for you this early this morning." He set the packages on the bed next to the baron.

"Thank you, Heltz," Iesos murmured, wiping his mouth free of crumbs. "You may go."

Heltz bowed his way out the door, closing it quietly.

Iesos ripped into packages with a child-like glee as soon as his servant left the room. He did not want to show the servants his excitement over what had come. After seeing Liam's watch with the 'T' topped with a crown and him being introduced as a Triburn, Iesos had sent for any information available about the Triburn family in their time on the throne. He flipped through the titles—*The Fall of the Triburns of Anatalia*, *A Collective History of Anatalian Monarchs*, *Anatalia: A History*, *The Monarchs That Changed History*—three out of the four coming from Glessic.

Iesos dressed without his valet and went to his private study, closing the door firmly behind him. He laid the books out in a neat row, trying to decide what to read first. He closed his eyes and hovered his hand over the books, moving it across the line slowly before he laid his hand down on the leather binding. *The Monarchs That Changed History*.

Iesos skimmed over the words, looking for the Triburn name, flipping the pages quickly as his eyes could scan the pages. He had to flip back when he passed over the name, taking the time to read the passage.

> ...King Meridon of the Triburn line ordered his army into the lands of Adria and Zapha that had been absorbed by Salatia, now respectively Glessic and Mekhor, to hold Emperor Nadra at bay while Dukes Glessic and Mekhor rallied the men loyal to them. King Meridon was able to call the Frasiscan and Radovan kings to his side to aid the budding monarchs...

He quickly finished the passage and found that that was all there was on the Triburn monarchs. Iesos sighed, flipping through the rest of the book just in case.

He picked a new book, *A Collective History of Anatalian Monarchs*, and employed the same tactics. He scanned, boring quickly, and nearly let the book shut in his surprise when he came across a picture. The book had printed copies of monarchical portraits of the more notable, or assassinated, kings. The spitting image of Liam greeted Iesos when he looked at the page again.

He narrowed in on the text below the picture. King Ettien Triburn at his coronation in the year 2145.

Iesos sat back in his chair, wonderment running through him. He had only speculated Liam was a Triburn of *the* Triburn line, but the portrait confirmed it. It was as if the artist had Liam sit for the painting rather than Liam's great-great-grandfather King Ettien.

A gentle knock sounded on the door. Iesos flipped the book over to hide the picture. "Enter."

Adelena entered the room quietly. "Luncheon will be soon, and we haven't seen you all day. I don't know how much longer I can stand being around Liam." She sighed heavily. "He's such a bore. Why are you having me be so nice to him?"

Iesos beamed at her. "I have good news, Adelena. Very good news."

She raised a single brow at him, waiting for him to continue.

"That 'bore' is the rightful king to the Anatalian throne. He's a Triburn, my dear." He flipped the book over and held it open with three fingers. "Come look at this," he commanded her.

"I thought they were all killed?" Adelena asked, surprised. She came forward, peering over his shoulder. She let out a gasp as her eyes took in the copy of the portrait. "Who is that?"

"Liam's great-great-grandfather, or great-great-great-grandfather, depending on his forefather's quickness to procreate," he informed her. "Apparently, King Reuben didn't get all of them. Liam has a watch with the old Triburn sigil that one of the nobility of Anatalia gave him. And he goes by the Triburn name."

Adelena ran her fingers over the page. "Liam looks just like him. Do you think he knows?"

"I doubt it very much," Iesos said. "The Platiri family has taken great pains to eradicate all memory of the Triburns."

"Should we tell him?" Adelena asked, pulling her hand away.

"We'll tell him after you've married him and become the next Anatalian queen," Iesos mused. "So he does not feel the need to find a royal wife to make an alliance."

Adelena smiled brightly. "The next Queen of Anatalia," she said dreamily.

"Now go find him and woo him into wanting you," Iesos commanded, "by any means."

Her smile slackened. "Yes, Father."

Margaret was reluctant to admit she did not want to leave Marbon.

She had grown accustomed to her role in the small river town, bringing some degree of prosperity to Marbon. Margaret had been with the Gollacks for close to nine months. Margaret had refused to even think of leaving until Jonathan and the children were settled, but they had been settled for over a month now. Liam had not been back to check on her yet. She had no idea she would miss him so much— he had been her constant companion for almost six months, and she had grown more attached than she thought. She supposed somewhere in the back of her mind, waiting for him to return kept her there as well.

And the Gollacks—Margaret would miss the Gollacks beyond measure. Elizabeth had treated her like the daughter she never had, and Aram had been so charmed by her he could not say no to any of her whims. They were the parents Margaret wished she still had.

Margaret would leave for Jalmar at the beginning of Aumonat, and she was already in tears at the thought. She would have to send for Aram and Elizabeth to visit her in the capital. In all their lives, neither one of them had ever been to the capital city of Anatalia. Margaret would take great pleasure in being the one to show it to them. It was a beautiful city with grand mansions housing the great lords and ladies of Anatalia. Her father had once owned one of those mansions when they had lived there. Margaret smiled at the thought of the Gollacks wandering the capital with looks of amazement on their faces.

Margaret had invited Elizabeth to the manor home with her for her interview of lady's maids for her upcoming trip to the capital. There were several applicants who would be coming, the manor home being the most adequate place for them to hold the interviews. Jonathan sulked with his children as Margaret explained why she was using the library and dining hall.

"You don't need to do this, Miss Maggie," Jonathan said to her. "You don't have to leave us."

Margaret frowned, her brow furrowing. "Jonathan, you will always be taken care of, if that's what you're worried about."

"The children love you, Miss Maggie." Jonathan looked at her with sad eyes. "How are you going to explain to them why you're abandoning them?"

"I'm not abandoning them," Margaret said shortly. "Are the applicants here yet?"

Jonathan gave her his usual scowl. "There are a few waiting in the dining hall."

Margaret pointed Elizabeth in the direction of the library. "Please wait in the library, Beth. I'll be there in a moment," she said, looking in Jonathan's direction.

Elizabeth did as she was bid, pausing in the doorway, looking in wonderment at the number of books lining the walls.

"Jonathan," Margaret cooed at him.

"What?" he snapped.

Margaret laid a calming hand on his arm, rubbing it gently. "Why don't you and the children go outside and play a game of hide-and-seek?"

The teen father raised a single brow at her.

"You could bring Claudette along with you," she suggested, grinning slightly at his demeanor brightening. She had noticed shy glances between the two of them. No doubt once Margaret was gone, Jonathan would forget all about her. "I'm sure all of you would have great fun."

"If you insist, Miss Maggie," Jonathan responded coyly.

"I do," she said before she left him to join Elizabeth in the library.

"Is everything all right, dear?" Elizabeth asked.

"Just a small matter of attitude." Margaret pulled the bell mechanism to summon Gretchen.

Gretchen appeared as Margaret sat next to Elizabeth. "Yes, my lady?"

"Tell Matilda to make us some tea," Margaret commanded, "and bring in the first applicant, if you will."

"As you wish, my lady." Gretchen bobbed a small curtsey before leaving.

The first woman who arrived came into the library. "M'lady," she said with a curtsey.

"Please sit." Margaret motioned toward a chair. "What's your name?"

"Deborah Marerk, m'lady."

Margaret searched through the application letters along with references. Many looked like they had been written by a hired hand for someone who couldn't read and write.

"Deborah," she started. "You have some accomplished references. Why should you be my lady's maid?"

"I'm a very hard worker, m'lady," Deborah told her quickly. "And I need this job."

There was an awkward silence while Margaret waited for her to continue. "Thank you, Deborah," Margaret said when it was clear she would indulge no further. "I'll let you know by the end of the day."

Many of the interviews went the same way. The women were hard workers and they needed the job. Elizabeth rubbed her hands over her face. "Is it always like this?"

"No," Margaret told her. "Usually, the housekeeper does the first interviews to weed out the poor candidates and presents us with the top choice of girls."

"That sounds much more pleasant," Elizabeth commented.

"It is."

There was a gentle knock on the doorway to the library. "Are the interviews still going on?" a small voice asked.

"What's your name?" Margaret called, sitting up in her seat. She thought they had gone through all the applicants' letters.

"Sarah Essler, Miss," she said quietly with a slight accent.

"My lady," Margaret corrected her, motioning for her to sit.

"My lady," Sarah repeated. "I didn't send in a letter of application."

"Do you have any references?" Elizabeth asked her.

"No," Sarah said. "I have no references."

"Were you denied one from your last employer?" Margaret asked, surprised.

"No, my lady, I have no references that would mean anything to you."

"And why is that?" Elizabeth asked the pretty young girl.

Sarah pursed her lips. The sun shone through the window and landed on the prospective lady's maid, turning her brown eyes golden and making her dark amber hair gleam. Her face was a naturally darker tint, looking almost like she had spent most of her time in the sun, her face full of freckles.

"I'm not from Anatalia," she said. "I would have no references that would mean anything here."

"I see," Margaret started. Of course, she wasn't. There was only a slight accent, but it was there. Each of the countries had their own language, but most spoke in the common tongue that was primarily spoken in Anatalia. "And what brought you here to Anatalia?"

"I needed a change, my lady." Sarah shifted in her chair uncomfortably.

"And have you ever been a lady's maid before, Sarah?" Margaret asked, looking over the girl critically.

"I was a kitchen maid before I left home, but I'm a very fast learner, my lady, and I would so much like to work for you," Sarah said emphatically. "I will never have an opportunity to reach Jalmar or interview for another job like this otherwise."

Margaret smiled at her. "Thank you, Sarah. Are you staying here in town?"

"Yes, my lady, at the only inn in Marbon."

"I'll let you know by the end of the day, Sarah. You can go now." Once the prospective lady's maid left, Margaret turned to Elizabeth. "What do you think?"

"Sarah is the only one that stands out, my dear, simply because she is not a maid and has no references."

"I like her," Margaret commented. "She's different, and she didn't tell us 'and I need this job' like everyone else did."

"She isn't even a lady's maid, Margaret," Elizabeth reminded her.

"She can learn, and if she doesn't work out, then she'll be in the capital like she wants to, and then I can pick from any lady's maid in either the palace or the city," Margaret said. "I think Sarah will do just fine for me."

～ 43 ～

Crompton impatiently broke the seal on the letter from his informant, Donald Ruysdael, or better known to him as Gerrit Hackaert. Crompton had been waiting for news on whether he would get his army from the Salatian King to overthrow King Sorren.

When the news reached him that King Peralta's wife had died alone in the nunnery, Crompton immediately sent a letter to offer his sympathies and remind the foreign king that she would have died in comfort at home had it not been for Sorren. And that he was still looking for a chance to overthrow his cousin.

> *Your Most Esteemed Grace,*
>
> *Your inquiry of my family's health has been most appreciated, and pleases me most that you value their well-being as much as I. Your Grace's concern pleased Mrs. Hackaert so much and so thoroughly, she blushed prettily, and tears came to her eyes.*
>
> *I am obliged to tell you, sir, that your gift of twenty gold tals were too much, though most appreciated, and we wish to tell you that we cannot accept your generosity. Beatrice asks that she may present Your Grace with a gift that she has made for you. If you wish that we send it via the post, we will abide by them, as Beatrice is too sick to travel presently.*
>
> *We await your command most anxiously.*
>
> *Your Most Obedient Servant,*
> *Gerrit Hackaert*

Crompton clumsily opened a jar of foul-smelling liquid, jamming a brush in it quickly and spreading it on the paper. He watched in wonder—and it was wondrous no matter how many times he saw it done—as the unwanted letters disappeared.

Lord General Crompton let out a relieved sigh.

You have your army. Twenty thousand will be at your disposal. We await your command most anxiously.

He would finally have the resources he needed to overthrow Sorren. There would soon be a better Anatalia for all.

His attempt to anger the nobles by spreading the news of the women Sorren had affairs with had resulted in nothing. The husbands already knew—some had even bartered their wives in an attempt to gain better positions and favor with the king.

Crompton refolded the letter, stashing it away in his locked chest before he went to Theotes's chapel. He knelt in front of the altar, covering his face.

Once he had lost Peralta's support when the war was over, it had struck doubt in his heart that his purpose was truly in Theotes's name. But now that the Salatian king was behind him again?

"Forgive me for doubting you." Crompton lowered his forehead to the floor. "I see now that it was not your timing."

Crompton deeply inhaled as he rose.

With Theotes behind him, he could not fail.

44

L iam walked the city with Adelena on his arm. This was their third such walk this week. Was this what nobility did? Walk around cities and show themselves to the people, and then go home to epic feasts? What was the point?

He sighed, smiling when he had to as Adelena guided him through the swarm of people who fawned over their lady, calling her name as they passed. Adelena glowed in their adulation. Would Margaret have been the same way? He wasn't entirely sure—she might, but he thought she might be more genuine than Adelena. Adelena seemed like she would do anything for praise.

"I have a surprise for you." Adelena squeezed his arm, leaning into him.

"What would that be?"

She giggled girlishly. "You'll see."

Adelena led him to a part of the city he hadn't seen yet. A stage sat at the bottom of tiered stone seating. He didn't know Zuev had a public theater, but it didn't surprise him. She took him to the private seating surrounded by stone walls to keep other patrons from getting too close, centered several rows back for the perfect view. Several other people were already there.

"What are we seeing?" Not that he would know what it was anyway—he'd never been to a play in any country, much less Glessic.

"That's part of the surprise." She sat with a flourish, waving to the people who called out to her. "It'll be starting soon."

Liam wasn't a fan of surprises, but there wasn't much he could say while in the depths of the Stelios's hospitality. It wasn't long before actors filed on stage, the audience politely clapping. Liam furrowed his brow. Was that…?

He leaned forward, squinting.

It was!

One of the men on stage was a replica of his outfit when he'd arrived in Zuev.

Sinking as far as he could, Liam covered his face with his hands as the play was introduced: *Saving a Lady*.

This was going to be torture. It was all he could do to not groan as he uncovered his face to look at Adelena, whose face was split with a wide smile.

"Isn't this a wonderful surprise?"

It was not.

"It's certainly…surprising," Liam said slowly. "When would they have had time to write this?"

"Oh, it was started the day after you saved me," Adelena gushed, squeezing his forearm. "I wanted to show you how much I admire and appreciate you."

Liam looked at her sharply. "You commissioned this?"

She nodded rapidly, her smile widening. "They're about to start."

The play was two hours of torture, every minute an exaggeration of what actually happened. He wanted to leave the second it started. When it finished, the audience applauded not the actors on the stage, but him. Liam wanted to disappear—the attention made him want nothing more than to run through the crowd.

Instead, Adelena urged him to stand and lifted his hand. The crowd cheered louder. "Wave," Adelena whispered in his ear, "they're cheering for you."

Liam did as he was bid, hating every second of it.

Liam looked out his window, watching the dogs run through the yard with the Master of Hunt on their trail. He had been here much longer than expected—his week-long trip turning into a month-long sojourn in the splendid home of the baron and his daughter. He tried on more than one occasion to go out in the city on his own, and either Lady Adelena accompanied him with her trail of servants or his valet, Bartolome, went with him. The only time Liam had to himself was when he was in his bedroom.

He went to open his door to try and sneak away and found Adelena with her hand poised to knock. "What are you doing here?"

"I came to see you," she said sweetly, pushing into the room.

"I was just leaving, my lady," he replied curtly.

Adelena turned to face him, slowly unlacing the front of her dress. "Are you sure?" she drawled seductively.

Liam watched her hands for a moment before focusing his attention on her face. "This is inappropriate, Lady Adelena."

She sauntered toward him, fingers still pulling at the laces. There was a challenge in her eyes as she drew closer.

Liam cleared his throat, looking away from her. "Lady Adelena, does your father know where you are?"

"He wishes us to marry," she told him.

Liam's head snapped toward her. "Pardon me?"

Adelena eyed his lips as she stopped in front of him. "Father admires you greatly, Liam," replied the lady. "As do I."

He tried to reply, but Adelena had pulled his head down to kiss him. She kept his mouth to hers until he grabbed her by the shoulders and held her at arm's length. "My lady, you should go."

"Why?"

"This is inappropriate," he told her again. "Very inappropriate."

She pouted at him. "But if we are to be married, there is no harm."

"You have not even let me respond to this marriage proposal before propositioning me in my own rooms," Liam scolded.

"You don't want to marry me?" Her mouth slackened, realizing for the first time he might not say yes.

"I think you should return to your rooms, my lady," he told her gently. "Let me think."

Her cheeks colored deeply, quickly lacing her bodice closed. "As you wish," she said, her eyes down before she fled his room.

Liam let out a long breath through mostly pursed lips. He needed to leave, and soon. It was the furthest thing from his mind to marry the young noblewoman he had saved. There were many others he would put before her, and there were not many he thought would return the sentiment. He would wait until the evening meal to leave, feigning sickness to not attend.

〰️ **45** 〰️

Iesos sat at the head of the table, waiting impatiently for Adelena and Liam to arrive.

His daughter walked in, shamefaced, and sat next to him.

"Where is Liam?" he demanded.

"He is feeling unwell and will not be joining us for dinner, or taking dinner in his room," she said meekly.

"What did you do to him?" Iesos looked at her through squinted eyes.

Adelena remained silent, her cheeks coloring.

"Speak, Adelena," he commanded.

Adelena focused on her hands in her lap. "I tried to seduce him," came her quiet answer.

"You *what?*" Iesos stood, furious.

She looked up at him tearfully. "You told me by any means. I thought that's what you meant, Father."

He sighed heavily. "I will speak to him on your behalf."

Adelena said nothing, her eyes back on her hands.

Heltz entered the private dining room, his face flushed from hurrying. "My lord, Mr. Triburn has left."

"What?" Iesos demanded, shooting an accusatory look Adelena's way.

"Bartolome went to check on Mr. Triburn to see if he had an appetite, finding his room empty and the clothes he came with missing."

"Wonderful. Just—wonderful," Iesos fumed, sitting back in his chair and throwing his cloth napkin on the table.

"I'm sorry," Adelena said, not looking at her father.

"This is your fault, Adelena!" he yelled at her.

She looked at him, her forehead crinkled. "My fault?" Adelena demanded, her voice raising. "*My* fault? You were the one that demanded I woo him!"

"I didn't say, 'Act like a common whore.' I said *woo* him!" he seethed before stalking out of the dining room.

✦ 46 ✦

argaret finished hiring servants a few days before she was supposed to leave for the capital to help her prepare for her journey. She had eighteen all told: her lady's maid, Sarah; four grooms; twelve guardsmen, and Captain Vojvo to lead them. She thought twelve guards were excessive, but there had been reports of rebel soldiers attacking caravans on the road. Margaret's caravan would be small, but it would still be worth attacking. The majority of the guards would be sent back to Marbon with a hefty sum for their journey once she was settled in the capital. The servants she would have left would be adequate until she figured out where she would live in the capital. It was difficult adjusting to having servants again. Margaret was out of practice letting others do things for her and telling them to do it.

Margaret wanted to take her mind away from leaving Aram and Elizabeth; she put on a simple house dress and went down to the river. She left Sarah behind so she would have time alone to think. Margaret had grown fond of walking with either Aram or Elizabeth by the river that sustained the life of this town. She would occasionally walk the river by herself if the couple could not join her, enjoying the solitude. In an odd way, Margaret was happy Liam had dragged her here. The soothing rush of the water calmed her whenever she was close enough to hear it.

Today it had no effect.

Margaret pulled her wrap closer as she walked along the gurgling water. She thought of how she would not see Liam again before she left, and it brought a profound sadness to her. She touched her lips as she thought of one of the last days he had been with her. She had gotten a thrill in her stomach whenever she thought of that day. She had never experienced a kiss like that—and she doubted she would again.

Margaret's butterflies turned into a fearful tightening of her stomach as she heard a twig snap behind her. Her thoughts went to the previous year when soldiers sought to capture her and Liam. Margaret turned around to see what had broken the stick, and her vision was flooded by a man in a tattered gray uniform.

She let out a gasp as she took a step back. "Can I help you?"

The uniformed man looked her over, closing the gap she had made. He grabbed her with a dirty hand, a tight grip on her arm. "You can."

Margaret wrenched her arm free of his grip with some effort. "Keep your hands off me!" she yelled, panicked.

The uniformed man had come up to her in the most secluded part of the river. It would carry away any sound she made.

He grabbed her arm once more, his grip tighter than before. Her arm started to ache with the pressure he put on it. The soldier pulled her against him, looking over her face slowly. His breath fanned over her face as he spoke. "I don't think I'll do that."

"Let me go," Margaret pleaded.

She could see the danger in his eyes—she would not come away from this unscathed. She was sure he was a Salatian rebel soldier coming with a group to raid the small town of Marbon. He would have no other reason for him to be there. Margaret was glad there were not more men with him. A raid had only happened once in Marbon since Margaret had arrived, but the skirmish had ended before it reached Aram and Elizabeth's home. She had heard of others, but they had been far more distant.

The rebel leaned in close to her, resting his cheek against hers. Margaret heard him inhale as he smelled her hair. She felt his lips move against her ear as he whispered to her. "No."

Margaret's heart raced, and tears sprang to her eyes. Her skin crawled as his hand moved up her arm to gently stroke her neck.

She tried to pull away from him. "Please, stop," Margaret begged. "Help!"

His hand was suddenly over her mouth as she was moved backward. The rebel removed her shawl with his free hand and dropped it to the ground. One of Margaret's feet dipped into a hole in the ground, and she fell backward with a gasp. Dark spots obscured her vision when her head hit the hard ground.

In a moment, he was on top of her. The soldier in the gray uniform was grabbing for her wrists as Margaret tried to push him away.

Margaret pushed against his shoulders with all her might, unable to move the heavy beast on top of her. He grabbed her wrists, thwarting her attempt to fight.

Margaret felt his lips on her neck while her hands were held above her head, both wrists fitting in his large, bruising grip. She began to scream desperately for anyone to help her when she felt his other hand trying to unlace her bodice.

The screams were replaced by a sob when the soldier slapped her; he hit her with enough force that her lip split.

"Please!" She let out another sob as his attention returned to her bodice.

The soldier kissed her down her neck to her collar bone. Margaret screamed again when he bit the skin at the base of her neck. He inhaled the perfume she had rubbed on the side of her neck that morning and gently kissed her where he had just bitten.

"Please let me go," Margaret begged as tears ran down her cheeks.

The soldier's hand moved down to her waist, pulling her up to him while he pressed himself closer.

"I like it when they beg." He kissed her with a groan, despite the blood on her lips.

Margaret bit down on his tongue when he shoved it into her mouth. She heard him yell, and he reeled back, responding with another slap.

Margaret's cheek burned under her eye, where the soldier's ring caught the tender flesh and ripped it open. Her skirts were shoved around her hips, and the soldier's hand painfully gripped her thigh. Margaret struggled to get her hands free from his grasp.

She flailed wildly under him, screaming as loud as she could manage. Her cheek stung as salt from her tears mixed with her open wound. Margaret felt pressure on her hips as the soldier positioned himself.

She let out a sob as she pleaded. "Stop!" She began to weep uncontrollably. "Please, stop!"

The soldier kissed her neck once more as he moved to take his prize.

Margaret closed her eyes and screamed.

47

It took Liam two weeks to reach Marbon, and he was glad to see the small town in a bustle. He brought Ashka to the small stable behind the Gollacks' home and rubbed him down. Smiling, he gave Duchess a pat when she nudged him. Liam went into the home and called out for Aram and Elizabeth, finding neither of them were there. He sighed and decided to go for a walk to calm his nerves. He had expected to immediately see Margaret, and his nerves were on edge.

The further down the river track he went, the more relaxed he was. He closed his eyes, sighed again, his destination the place where he had first kissed Margaret. He could still hear her joyful laugh and feel the cold river against his legs when he pulled her against him. He longed to be able to go back to that day and spend more time with her.

"Please don't do this to me!" a woman screamed loudly.

Liam opened his eyes immediately, looking around. There was an ear-piercing scream followed by a sob. He ran as fast as he could to the source of the noise. He stopped short when he saw Margaret under a Salatian soldier, his heart dropping into his stomach.

He pulled his knife from his belt as rage filled his chest. Liam grabbed the Salatian by his collar, lifting him off Margaret. He held the soldier against him, ripping the blade across his throat.

Liam didn't care about killing him face to face.

He didn't deserve face to face.

He only deserved the savagery that would send him to the depths of hell where he belonged. Liam shoved the dying man to the side, not caring where he fell.

Looking to Margaret, Liam saw she was trying to push her skirts down with her eyes still closed. He grimaced when he saw his deed had sprayed blood onto her. Liam grabbed her gently, pulling her into his arms.

"Get off of me!" Margaret yelled as she fought against him.

Of course, she had no idea who the person holding her was. He hadn't been able to tell from the ground, but her face was swollen enough it probably hurt to open her eyes. For all she knew, he could be another Salatian soldier. He gently wiped the tears from her face. "It's me, Maggie. It's Liam."

When she finally opened her eye—she could only open one, as the other was nearly swollen shut—Liam's stomach turned as he looked at Margaret's terrified expression. Her lip was swollen and bleeding, and her cheek and eye were already bruising. He brought his hand up to touch her injured cheek. He let it drop before he actually touched her, afraid he would hurt her more. There would be a visible scar there to remind her of this day for the rest of her life. He looked at her wrists and found they were also starting to bruise.

"Maggie, are you all right?" Liam asked her gently.

"He…he came out of nowhere and attacked me, wanting t-to…" Margaret erupted into sobs once more.

Liam pulled her closer to him, resting his cheek on top of her head. "Please tell me he didn't, Maggie."

Margaret shook her head under the weight of his own.

Liam felt her start to shake in his arms again. He picked her up with ease and carried her to the Gollacks' home. Margaret clung to him as sobs wracked her body. He should have been here to prevent the entire event. He should have tried harder to leave Zuev.

"Elizabeth!" Liam yelled when he came into the home. "It's Margaret!"

Elizabeth gasped when she saw Margaret in Liam's arms. "My girl!" She rushed to Liam's side as he carried her to her bedroom. "Lay her on the bed, Liam."

Liam laid her on the soft bed and cupped her unblemished cheek gently. He could hear Elizabeth calling for someone named Sarah to bring warm water and clean linens and for Aram to come to the room. Liam watched as the young woman he presumed was Sarah almost dropped the contents in her hands.

She rushed to Margaret's side. "My lady!"

Aram almost pushed Liam out of the way to get to Margaret, but Liam stopped him with his hand on his chest. Margaret shouldn't be crowded right now.

"Oh, my sweet girl! What happened to her?"

Liam was touched to see there were tears standing in Aram's eyes. "She was attacked by a rebel." He looked over Margaret sympathetically. "I was able to stop him before he defiled her."

Elizabeth touched his arm, relief evident on her face. "Thank Theotes!"

Liam wrapped his arm around Elizabeth's shoulders as he watched Margaret. The maid cleaned the rebel's blood off Margaret as quickly as possible. She was beginning to calm down, wincing when Sarah gently patted the injured cheek with damp linens.

"We'll let you rest, Maggie," Liam said.

Aram reluctantly turned to leave, his eyes filled with worry. "I'm right outside if you need me, my dear."

Margaret nodded and wiped her uninjured cheek free of the tears.

Aram waited until the door was shut before he turned to Liam. "What happened to her attacker?"

"He's dead," was Liam's short reply.

There was steel in Aram's eyes Liam had never seen before. "Good."

48

Margaret watched Liam from the comfort of her bed, Sarah attending to her. He remained silent, looking at her bruised and swollen face. Even through her swollen eyes, his guilt was evident. "Maggie…"

"No," she said firmly.

"At least stay until you've recovered," Liam tried to sway her. "It would only be a few weeks more."

"No," she said again. "I can't stay here any longer, Liam."

She couldn't stay near her attack. She would leave earlier than planned, and if there was anything that wasn't done by the time she left, she would send for it later. Margaret couldn't breathe here anymore. It wasn't safe…it wasn't home.

Sarah readied a mat for Liam to sleep on. He had insisted on spending the night outside the door to her room to be there if she had night terrors from the day's event. He waited outside while she was readied for bed, sitting in the chair next to her when she was finished. Margaret lay on her side to face him.

"Do you think you can sleep?" Liam asked quietly.

"I don't know," Margaret responded, pulling the covers up to her chin.

"I'll be right outside the door if you need me," Liam said. He left her alone, closing the door behind him.

Margaret fell asleep quicker than expected, her breath coming in a deep, easy rhythm. She found herself next to the river in her dream, an anxious feeling in her stomach. The twig snapped behind her, and she gasped as she quickly turned around, facing her attacker. She tried to move, but her feet were held firmly in place by an unknown force. Margaret heard herself converse with the man in her dream when she wanted nothing more than to run in the direction she knew Liam would be coming from.

Instead, Margaret felt herself backing up, and her stomach fluttered as she fell backward. The rebel was once again on top of her and had his hands all over the young woman. Margaret struggled with all she had, waiting for Liam to save her as he had in the actual event. Margaret began to panic when her skirts were raised and there was no Liam. She struggled even harder when she realized Liam would not be coming to her rescue this time. Margaret screamed and struggled as the rebel was able to take his prize.

Margaret gasped when she was shaken awake.

Liam stood over her, a worried look on his face. "Maggie?"

Tears slid down her cheeks that were being quickly wiped away by Liam. "A nightmare," she said, her voice thick with tears.

Liam sat next to her on the bed, pulling her into his arms, letting her cry on him. "I'm right here."

Margaret cried herself out on his shoulder, being laid down by him when she was finished. She reached out to him once he stood. "Will you hold my hand until I fall asleep?"

Liam took her hand and kissed it. "Of course."

When Margaret woke in the morning, her back was stiff from her fall, and a sizable lump formed on the back of her head. She struggled to see out of her one eye, the lid partially swollen shut. Margaret allowed Sarah to help her dress that morning, needing to take extra care to not harm herself more with the tight stays she wore.

She would face the day with courage. She would not be afraid of the rebel's return. She would not shy. She would not flinch. She would be strong.

She would not lose herself to that beast.

Margaret went to visit her little monsters to say her goodbyes. Liam refused to let her go by herself.

"Liam, I've been doing this for months," she told him as she gave him a sly look. "Besides, everyone will think you've beaten me if I show up on your arm with my face like this."

"This isn't a time for joking, Margaret." Liam crossed his arms over his chest. "And I will be accompanying you."

Her face had turned a dark purple in the night, covering her cheek and under her eye. Margaret's lip was swollen, and there was a dark line where her lip had been split. Under her eye was a puffy line that would soon be scabbing over. It was not a pretty sight to see, and neither were the looks she had received by the people of Marbon.

"I'll be fine," she said, though her stomach quivered at the thought of going on her own. She inhaled deeply, placing her hand on her stomach. She would have courage and not let the rebel steal this from her.

"Maggie, I don't want you to be by yourself." Liam looked at her seriously. "There could still be rebels around. Women are an easy target for them."

"I won't be alone, Liam," Margaret told him. "Jonathan would protect me if it came to it." She shrugged nonchalantly.

Liam's face darkened. "Who is Jonathan?"

"He's the 'father' to the children in the orphanage I started." Margaret gave him a sideways glance. "Why? Do you feel threatened by a child?" She laughed when he glared at her.

"Of course, I don't. I just don't want you to be around the wrong people."

Margaret smiled at him tenderly. "Thank you, Liam."

She linked her arm with his, letting him take her to the manor house-turned-orphanage, and walked into the house when they arrived. "Little monsters?" Margaret grinned when she heard the patter of children's feet.

The children stopped short of her kneeling form.

"What's wrong with your face, Miss Maggie?" Claira piped.

Thomas hit Claira's arm with the back of his hand. "Claira!" he whispered harshly.

"It's all right, Thomas." Margaret said. "I had a little accident, my darling." She held out her arms to the children. "Now where are my hugs?"

The children flooded into her arms. Margaret looked up to Liam, who smiled in return.

"Miss Maggie!" Jonathan's bright smile slipped from his face when he saw Margaret's. "Out, my lambs." He gave a quick glance to Liam, and his eyes went back to Margaret, looking over her slowly. "Now!" He snapped when they protested.

Margaret stood with Liam's help. "Jonathan, I'm all right."

Jonathan deliberately moved close to her, despite Liam's hard look. "What happened, Miss Maggie?" He turned an accusing look at Liam. "Did he do this to you?"

Margaret laid her hand on Jonathan's arm, squeezing it. "Liam saved me." She didn't answer his question. She did not want to upset him.

Jonathan picked up her hands, growing more upset at the sight of her blackened wrists, his thumbs running over her bruises. "What happened, Miss Maggie?"

Margaret pulled her hands from his, rubbing her wrists. She didn't want anyone touching them, especially not like that. "There were rebel soldiers by the river when I was there," Margaret said lightly, though her appearance betrayed the lightness of her voice. "The worst of it is my face."

Liam came closer to her, resting his hand on her back for support. She saw Jonathan's eyes narrow.

Jonathan nodded toward Liam. "Is this who you'll be leaving me and our babies for?"

"Don't ruin my last day with the children," she gave him a look. "I'm leaving in the morning."

Jonathan gave Liam a dark look. "Why don't you spend time with our babies, then?"

It was a tearful goodbye for Margaret when she and Liam left. She would miss her little monsters, and Jonathan too. She would write constantly to Claudette to check on the children and to tell them how she was doing. She was glad to have Liam guiding her back to Aram and Elizabeth's home, and to have his comforting presence. Margaret had seen his face soften whenever he saw her with a child in her arms. She wondered if he wanted to settle down and have children of his own someday.

"Thank you for going with me, Liam." Margaret squeezed his arm.

"You were leading that boy on, Margaret."

Margaret looked at him, shocked. "I beg your pardon?"

"All the smiles and the laughter and the gentle touches, Margaret. He thinks you love him!" Liam gave her a disapproving look. "And after months of that, it's no wonder he was jealous of me just being there and tried to keep your attention at all times."

Margaret remained silent, refusing to look at him. She wasn't aware she had been doing what he said. If Liam could pick up on it in a few hours, she must have been doing the same thing since she had gained Jonathan's trust. Perhaps she had used it unconsciously to endear the boy to her so she could help his children more easily.

"It's just the way you are," Liam continued. "You've done it to me and even charmed Aram on occasion. You need to be very careful who you manipulate, Margaret."

Margaret gave Liam a sideways glance. "Is that why you kissed me?" She gave him a sly smile when he blushed.

"When do you meet with the captain of your guard to make traveling plans?" Liam wanted to change the subject as quickly as possible.

"This afternoon when we load everything onto the wagons." Margaret sounded sad at the mention of having to leave.

After Captain Marius Vojvo arrived to oversee the loading of product onto the wagons, Margaret weaseled more information out of him. She should at least know who her head guard was aside from coming highly recommended. Vojvo had been in the service of the Lord General Robert Valar, who had control over troops from Marbon and a handful of the surrounding towns. He had gone back to his home in Marbon after being told a younger man would be taking over his duties.

Margaret sighed as the hired servants loaded the wagons with all her belongings. Her life was summed up with boxes and chests, packed tightly away.

"Take care with that!" the captain barked as one of the hired day laborers dropped a lightly loaded chest.

The girl looked frightened. "Yes, sir," she squeaked.

Margaret watched quietly as he barked at the poor girl. She had been told Captain Vojvo was the best for her interests. He took every job seriously and knew Anatalia better than any man, perhaps even better than Liam. He had white hair sprinkled with its previous dark. He was an older man, but he had stayed in fighting shape.

Margaret was amazed by his strength. He had been able to lift chests on his own that took two younger men to lift. The captain had a long scar down the side of his face from the war between Salatia and Anatalia. A soldier had attempted to cut the Captain's throat but was struck from behind by another Anatalian, and his sword fell upon Vojvo's face instead.

Margaret smiled at Liam when he came up to her.

He put his hand toward her before snatching it back to his side. "How are you feeling?"

Her smile turned wry. "As well as can be." She looked back to Captain Vojvo and started when she caught the acidic glare he was leveling at her.

"Lady Margaret, come here," Captain Vojvo ordered.

Margaret raised her eyebrows at the order. She remained where she was.

"Now!" the captain barked.

Margaret jumped and went to his side. He had bright blue eyes that stared her down intently, daring her to defy his orders. He looked over her bruised and battered face, wisely saying nothing.

"What is it?" She was not pleased he was speaking to her that way. He was supposed to be her man.

"Do you know who that man is?" He nodded in the direction of Liam.

Margaret looked back at him and watched Liam shift uncomfortably. "I do."

"We need to report him to the king," Vojvo said. "You should be lucky that I don't report you and this family."

She inhaled deeply, digging her nails into her palms to keep herself calm. "I would advise against that, Captain."

He crossed his arms over his chest. "Is that so?"

"You are currently in my employ, and you should know that would also implicate you in any wrongdoings I've committed." Margaret wetted her lips—she hoped she sounded as authoritative as she tried to be. "If you do turn him in, I will ensure that whomever you go to also knows you've helped Liam."

Vojvo inhaled deeply to respond.

Holding up her hand, Margaret said, "No. This is the way it is. Do you understand me, Captain?"

He glared. "Yes, my lady."

"Now, is there anything else?"

"With these wagons, it's going to take a month to get to the capital, if not more," he said.

"I know this, Captain," Margaret said to him. "What is your point?"

"You don't have enough guards in your possession." Vojvo glanced at the line of chests coming out of the house. "I would like to pick up more guards along the way."

"You don't think that twelve guards are enough?" Margaret was surprised. "There are three guards per wagon and still three left for my ladies and myself."

"My lady, you have forgotten a wagon to hold provisions to feed us during our travels," the Captain scolded. "I have arranged one to be loaded in the town that we will join when we leave tomorrow. Your extra groom can lead the wagon."

Margaret gave him a smile meant to charm. "This is why I hired you, Captain."

Vojvo did not return her smile but shouted out another order to her people.

Liam came up to Margaret, despite the glare that Captain Vojvo gave him. "Maggie, may I speak with you privately?"

Margaret nodded, excusing herself, glad to be away from the fierce captain. She took the proffered arm. "Yes, Liam?"

"Are you going to allow him to treat you like a child?" Liam asked her. He looked at the captain warily.

She furrowed her brow at him. There was an odd change in his demeanor she couldn't identify.

"I will let him feel like he has the control, but he will know who is in charge if he pushes me too far," Margaret said with a firm tone. Vojvo would not like being ordered around by a young woman, she knew that much from when she hired him.

"Truly acting the countess, are we?" Liam gave her a playful grin. "And you said you didn't like giving orders. Now, come. I have something for you in your bedroom."

Margaret followed him inside the Gollacks' home, her eyebrows raised. "What is it, Liam?"

"Why can't you be patient and find out?" Liam asked her as he opened her bedroom door.

On her bed was the chest filled with jewels from her home in Silvica. They barely all fit in the single chest he used. Margaret gasped when she saw them, running her fingers over the glittering mass. "Liam, when did you get these?"

"I went back to Silvica when I first left here," Liam said slowly. "I buried your father behind the house."

Margaret's shoulders slumped. "So that's what you meant when you said you took care of everything?"

Liam enveloped Margaret in his arms, rubbing a comforting hand on her upper back. "I think you already knew what I meant, Maggie."

Margaret rested her head on his chest with a sigh. "I know."

Liam tipped her chin up to make her look at him. "Are you sure you won't change your mind and come with me?"

Margaret looked at him with a soft smile and gently stroked his cheek. "Liam, you know I can't."

Liam kissed her palm. "It was worth another try."

"You can't go, Margaret," Aram protested. "I forbid it."

"You forbid it?" She laughed, her mouth twisting in a wry smile.

"Yes, I forbid it." Aram shook off the hand Elizabeth rested on his arm. "It's too dangerous for you to go. You could get hurt, you could get lost, you…you could get attacked again."

"Aram," Elizabeth gently quieted.

Aram looked at her with his mouth in a firm line. He harrumphed once and remained quiet.

Elizabeth sighed, looking at Margaret and Liam standing together, her mouth in a slight frown. "Will you send word when you arrive?"

"Of course, Elizabeth." Margaret pulled her into a tight hug. "Of course."

Aram pulled her away from Elizabeth, holding her close and resting his head on top of hers. "Be safe, my dear girl."

"I will be," she said, quietly sighing.

The goodbyes she exchanged with the Gollacks left Margaret aching; she did not truly want to leave them. There were promises of letters and visits and many hugs. Margaret wiped her eyes gingerly as they rode away, she would miss the couple and all of Marbon. Margaret felt a pang in her heart as she thought of leaving the children behind. It was necessary she leave, though it made it no easier. She sighed as she rode away, knowing that, more than likely, she would never see the couple again.

Captain Vojvo pulled Margaret aside when they took their first break. "My lady, will you not reconsider who you're keeping company with?"

Margaret furrowed her brow. She had seen the looks pass between the two of them, the captain's angry and Liam's almost shocked. She understood the captain's. It was Liam's she could not understand.

"I will not," Margaret said. "He'll be with us for the first few days of our journey and then part ways to go on his own."

"My lady, we must get rid of him now." He gave her a stern look. "He's putting us all in danger."

"He stays, or you go," Margaret said in a firm tone.

It was the first time she had to use her position of authority over him, but she was sure it would not be the last time. It would not be a pleasant journey if Margaret had to fight him at every turn.

"Yes, my lady," the captain said unpleasantly.

Margaret could see her decision to allow Liam to travel with them did not sit well with her captain. Yet, she could not bear to part from the last familiar face. While the faces of the traveling party would become familiar to her, she was still anxious to lose the familiarity Liam brought to her journey.

49

Liam chewed on his bottom lip. He waited for Captain Vojvo to part from Margaret before he made his approach. He wasn't entirely certain, but he suspected Captain Vojvo was Jorren's father.

His breath caught—Liam hadn't thought about Jorren in ages. For the first few months of his imprisonment, he'd held hope Jorren would have survived the massacre somehow, but word had come through that all of Lord General Crompton's men had been slaughtered by the end of the war.

"Captain Vojvo, may I have a word?" Liam asked quietly. "I think there's something we need to discuss."

Captain Vojvo nodded, pulling away from the caravan, moving to the back so they wouldn't be disturbed. He dismounted, and Liam did the same. "What do you want, traitor?"

"I…" Liam's chest tightened, and he rubbed the scar where he'd been wounded in the first battle of Chenalieu. The battle where Jorren disappeared. "If I'm not mistaken, you're Jorren Vojvo's father."

The captain paused, looking at Liam sharply. "I am."

Liam swallowed hard. "I served with Jorren. He…he was my best friend." He inhaled deeply, closing his eyes. "I don't know what happened to him."

"So you're that Liam." Captain Vojvo spat at Liam's feet. "My son begged me to get him in Crompton's regiment to keep an eye on you, and you got him killed for a few coin."

His stomach fell. He knew in his heart that Jorren was dead, but hearing it ripped open fresh wounds. Voice wavering, he said, "So he is dead?"

"He is." Vojvo glared at him. "And I thank Theotes daily he died before he knew his best friend was the cause of his death by being a traitor."

"I'm not a traitor," Liam said absently.

"And where's your proof?"

"Lost down the Frasisca River." Liam shuddered. "You'd have to ask Lord General Crompton for proof now."

Captain Vojvo shook his head, letting out a disgusted noise. Clearly, he didn't believe Liam.

"I promise you, I am not a traitor." When the captain scoffed, Liam said, "I promise on Jorren's grave, I would never betray Anatalia. I'd never sacrifice lives needlessly for a few coin."

"Keep my son's name out of your mouth," Vojvo seethed.

Liam sighed, looking forward. Margaret was looking back at them with her brow furrowed. "Fine, then I promise on Margaret."

"Be thankful for her—she's the only reason I haven't turned you in." The captain glared at him again, climbing onto his mount. "I think we're done here, traitor."

Liam sighed as Captain Vojvo rode to the front of the caravan with Margaret. He doubted he'd ever win Jorren's father over, especially with Jorren long gone and unable to speak on his behalf.

Liam watched Captain Vojvo closely to make sure he treated Margaret appropriately. The captain had a bothersome habit of treating her like a child, which seemed to trouble Liam more than it did Margaret. Her plan was to allow him to act as such until she had to give a firm order.

"Maggie, he's not going to listen to you if you let him do this all the time," Liam told her. "You need to enforce your authority."

Margaret sighed. "Liam, I think it will be all right. He's a military man—he knows how to take orders."

Liam gently cupped her unbruised cheek. He knew her flattery wouldn't work on the captain, but when she had an idea in her head, there was no convincing her otherwise. He would let her believe what she wanted. "If you say so."

Margaret smiled at him tenderly. "Thank you, Liam."

Vojvo cleared his throat. "No touching Her Ladyship, traitor."

Liam gave him a hard look, but dropped his hand as ordered.

Margaret pursed her lips, not looking at Vojvo. If Liam weren't so annoyed, he'd find it amusing how little he left them alone. He wondered if he hadn't had the conversation about Jorren if he'd let them be.

"We need to move," Vojvo said, a serious look on his face. "I want to get to the capital as quickly as possible."

"Captain, we don't need to get there tomorrow," Margaret retorted.

Captain Vojvo raised a single eyebrow before shouting orders to his men and commanding the ladies to mount their horses.

Margaret rolled her eyes before going to mount Duchess. "This is going to be a long journey," she muttered to her mare.

Liam would leave later in the afternoon on their fourth day of travel to make his way to Salatia. It was not his favorite place to go, but it was the only country in Aratia that the Anatalian soldiers were not welcomed. He did not want to leave Margaret, but she would be safer with him gone. His time away from her had not diminished his feelings, and he would not risk the safety of someone he cared for. He would stay in Salatia for several months until he had saved enough money to check on Margaret again.

"Do you need to leave right now?" Margaret asked, a pleading look on her face.

Liam's brow furrowed. He didn't want to leave, and she wouldn't come with him. He didn't have a choice. "I'm sorry, Maggie, I have to." He squeezed her small hand in his, lifting it to his lips. "Soon you'll be on a road where there are more frequent soldier patrols. I can't risk being seen with you."

Tears came to her eyes, and guilt welled in Liam, watching Margaret's face fall while she processed his departure. "We'll see each other again, Maggie."

"Liam," she said thickly, "before you leave, I need to tell you something."

"What's that?"

"It has to do with your mother's—"

He pressed his mouth to hers. He wouldn't have been able to quiet her otherwise. When he pulled away, he said, "I told you a long time ago that I don't want to talk about it—she's dead, and whatever delusions she had died with her."

Margaret nodded silently, her unbidden tears slipping down her cheeks. She hastily wiped them away, looking to the ground.

Liam tipped her chin up with his finger. "When you get to the capital, if you're questioned about your time with me, tell them I abducted you."

"But—"

"If you won't come with me and let you keep you safe at my side, let me keep you safe this way," he said.

Margaret's lip quivered. "Liam…"

"We will see each other again, Margaret. I promise we will." He kissed her forehead gently before mounting Ashka.

He rode away quickly, not looking back. If he did, he wouldn't have been able to leave her.

50

Margaret let out a small sob when he was out of sight. Sarah was by her side in a moment. "My lady, are you all right?"

"I will be in a moment, Sarah." Margaret sniffed, wiping her eyes. "We should head to the main road."

She could not yet bring herself to confide in her young lady's maid. Sarah would have no advice to give her, no comfort and no solace like Liam had been able to do. Now that he was gone, she had no one who could be her equal—no one to talk to without reserve. Everyone left were hired servants, paid to do as she commanded.

Margaret stared at the empty road. She wanted to curl in a ball and stay there. She started when the captain came to her side, gently touching her elbow. He escorted her to Duchess, lifting her into the saddle and settling her skirts for her. It reminded her of her first day with Liam when he'd had to guide her in everything until her senses returned.

"Would you like me to hold your reins, my lady?" The captain's eyes were soft when he looked at her, Duchess's reins held loosely in his gloved hands.

"No, Captain." Margaret said shakily. "I can handle it."

"As you wish," he said before going to his own mount. "Ride on!"

They had been traveling for a week now. Blessedly, there had been little activity on the road. Margaret had been concerned with the size of their caravan that raiders would come for them in the night.

That one would come for her in the night.

Margaret gently rubbed her cheek. It was still tender, and Sarah had told her the bruises on her face had blackened since they left. Margaret hoped they would fade by the time they reached Jalmar. The last thing she wanted was to look unpresentable for the King of Anatalia.

"My lady," Vojvo said after their camp was set up for the night, "may I ask you a question?"

She inhaled deeply, pulled away from her thoughts.

"Of course, Captain." Margaret smiled tiredly. "Anything you'd like."

"How did you ever fall in with someone like that traitor?"

Margaret tried not to bristle at the question. Not everyone believed Liam was innocent as she did. "I was at his trial, and it seemed to me, based on all the testimony, not possible for Liam to be a traitor."

The captain started to talk, but Margaret cut him off. "You don't have to agree, Captain—that is the way I view it. I didn't see him again until he knocked on my door in the midlands last year and soldiers happened to find him there."

Vojvo furrowed his brow. "Then how did you end up in Marbon and not in the capital?"

Margaret sighed, looking up at the sky. "One of the soldiers who came was someone I knew from my days in Jalmar, and we, ah...we didn't end things well." She looked back to the captain with a frown. "He especially hated my father since his illness was what broke us apart, and this soldier ended up murdering my father trying to capture Liam.

"Liam didn't know who I was at the time, so he thought in order to save me from being brought to the capital to face punishment by the other soldiers, he would bring me somewhere safe." Margaret sighed heavily, pulling at her fingers to release some of her tension. "If I weren't who I am, I would have just stayed there. But I need to ensure my title to make certain my people will be taken care of."

"But why not go to Dorcia? Do you not think going to Jalmar is a bad idea?" Vojvo shook his head. "You're going straight to the lion's den if those other soldiers saw you helping the traitor."

Margaret shrugged. "Maybe, but if I went to Dorcia, I'd only be delaying the inevitable. His Majesty would command me to the palace, and I would have to ask for permission to become the Countess of Dorcia in lieu of no male heir."

He furrowed his brows again. "Your father didn't make arrangements for that already?"

"He tried." Margaret smiled wistfully. "The king continued to deny him because my mother was young, and then my father fell too ill to ask. I am Dorcia's only hope to stay under the care my father provided them. My people come before me."

Silence settled between them, though Margaret thought the captain looked at her differently.

The company made several stops along the way to ensure they and the horses were well rested, and their food supply never ran low. It took them over a month to get just outside the city of Jalmar as the captain had predicted. He had conceded to Margaret's idea of stopping outside the city to gather themselves and air out a few dresses that would be immediately showcased in the capital.

Margaret paced back and forth as the men set up the camp. She was anxious about returning to the capital. Sarah had almost dropped the gown and gathered it in a heap to keep it from being dirtied.

"Don't wrinkle it, Sarah!" Margaret scolded.

Sarah bobbed a curtsey, "Sorry, my lady."

Captain Vojvo took Margaret into her tent when it was set up. "Lady Margaret, what's troubling you? You've gotten progressively surlier since we stopped."

"What if Lord Nicholas made it back and told everyone that I've helped a traitor?" Margaret asked him, a scared look on her face. She had told him more about Lord Nicholas having seen her helping Liam while they traveled. "What if I get seized at the gate?"

"They will not, my lady," Vojvo said with conviction. "I will not let them."

Margaret smiled at him. "Thank you, Captain, but if the king wants me imprisoned, you can't stop them. You know that I willingly helped Liam, and some of the king's soldiers saw me do it."

Captain Vojvo straightened his shoulders with a stubborn twist of his mouth. "They will not take you into custody, my lady. Not while I'm your man. On Theotes, I swear it."

He declared it with such fierce loyalty, she nearly laughed in surprise. She had threatened to implicate him when their journey first started, and he had not seemed to be growing any fonder of her on their trek. She had assumed he would leave her as soon as she paid him. "Thank you, Captain."

"Rest for now, my lady. I will make sure everything is going smoothly," the captain said as he opened her tent flap.

"Captain?"

"Yes, my lady?"

"Will you stay in my service after we reach the capital if I'm not arrested?" Margaret's stomach tightened unwillingly. He might say no—she had forced him into the job.

The captain smiled at her for the first time. "I will stay with you as long as you have a need for me, my lady."

Margaret smiled back. "Then I think you'll be with me for a very long time, Captain."

51

NOMONAT, 2281

Soldiers piled into the courtyard in front of the infirmary, setting down the single man on their makeshift stretcher. A groan came from the man once he was no longer suspended comfortably. His face was white, sweat beading on his forehead despite his shivering.

"Check the availability," the leader of the soldiers commanded, squatting next to the patient. It seemed his charge would not have long left in this world.

The soldier who left returned with Healer Orion.

"Bring him in," the healer commanded, "immediately."

Two of the soldiers in the group followed the healer carrying the stretcher, leaving their commander with the remainder of the group.

"Alert the king," the leader ordered one of the remaining men. "His Majesty needs to speak with him at his earliest convenience."

"Yes, sir." He half bowed to his commander before leaving for the palace.

Healer Orion pulled back the blood-soaked cloth on the patient's stomach, grimacing at the sight. The wound was filled with pus, red streaking away from the wound. It was beyond his ability at this point—the patient would die with or without his help.

King Sorren entered the infirmary abruptly.

Orion stood and bowed deeply. "Your Majesty."

"Can he speak?" the king demanded.

"I'm unsure, sire," the healer admitted. "I have only examined the wound. It is a fatal one."

"Leave us." Sorren waved his hand in dismissal, sitting next to the dying man.

Healer Orion bowed, leaving the king to his privacy.

"Speak of what you know," King Sorren commanded.

He struggled to open his eyes. He looked at the king weakly. "The traitor…he…" he rasped.

"Yes?" Sorren demanded impatiently.

"Lady Margaret Doremis," Nicholas Oliphant inhaled deeply, closing his eyes in pain. "Helped the traitor. She travels with him now."

The king grabbed his arm to stir him. "She travels with Liam Fulton?"

"Yes," Oliphant groaned, turning his head to the side and closing his eyes again.

Sorren stood, abruptly leaving the infirmary. He clenched his teeth, angered one of his subjects would disobey his orders of helping the escaped criminal. One who was close to him, at that.

If this was true, she would get her due soon enough.

He would make sure of it.

CONTINUE THE STORY!

THE ANATALIAN THRONE

BOOKS2READ.COM/ANATALIANTHRONE

About The Author

Rebecca Mikkelson has been writing fantasy stories since her early teens for fun and was thrilled to turn her dream into a reality when she was published for the first time in an anthology. She currently lives in Maryland with her husband and three cats.

In her free time, Rebecca likes to cross stitch to relax when her cats aren't hogging the embroidery floss. She also enjoys reading a wide variety of books, ranging from non-fiction biographies of historical figures and families to high fantasy.

As well as being an author, Rebecca works as the editor-in-chief at Authors 4 Authors Publishing, which she helped start in 2018.

Follow her online:

RebeccaMikkelson.com
TikTok: @zebookverm
Twitter: @zebookverm
Instagram/Threads: @authorRebeccaMikkelson
Facebook: @RebeccaMikkelsonAuthor

Authors 4 Authors Publishing

A publishing company for authors, run by authors, blending the best of traditional and independent publishing

We specialize in speculative fiction: science fiction, fantasy, paranormal, and romance. Get lost in another world!

Check out our collection at https://books2read.com/rl/a4a or visit Authors4AuthorsPublishing.com/books

For updates, scan the QR code or visit our website to join our semi-monthly newsletter!

Want more historical fantasy? We recommend:

One Thousand and One Days
by Renee Frey

Sutaita, daughter of the Sultan's vizier, planned on a life of quiet study. But when she learns she and her sister must be the next two brides for the bloodthirsty Sultan Shahryar al'Mamun, Sutaita decides to change their fortune. Staying alive by telling stories every night, she must buy enough time to solve the mysteries surrounding the Sultan's edict. In this retelling of the Arabian Nights frame story, can Sutaita slip past the walls around the Sultan's heart and soul? Or will she end up like so many brides before—with her head on a chopping block?

books2read.com/1001Days